Off Leash

Daniel Potter

Off Leash

Book One of Freelance Familiars

FALLEN KITTEN
PRODUCTIONS

United States of America

ISBN: 0-9965940-1-9
ISBN-13: 978-0-9965940-1-1

Copyediting by Marianne Fox and John Rhoades
Cover by Ebooklaunch.com
Additional illustrations by Sabertooth Ermine
Book design by Amanda Potter

Published by Fallen Kitten Productions

www.FallenKitten.com

For Arthur Smith
The first dreamer I knew.

1

It had started as a good day. Objectively that was a lie, but after six months of unemployment self-delusion becomes a survival trait. I was two days from getting booted off unemployment, with my girlfriend AWOL for the last week. By "good day" I mean I had wrestled a small drop of hope out of my heart that one of the half dozen jobs I had applied to while guzzling down iced coffees might result in an interview.

The old man, my next-door neighbor, had watched me throughout the entire process as I cut and pasted my meager work experience into the applicable boxes. This wasn't exactly new for either of us. He practically lived in that cafe, ordering iced teas and crunching on the ice for about an hour after the tea had been consumed. He'd sit in the sole comfy recliner in the cafe with a book in his lap and that tiny cat of his sprawled over the top of the chair. The cat, who looked like the sort of thing a Chihuahua could beat up for lunch money, often seemed more interested in the book than the old man was. The bigger the book, the less his wrinkled nose would be in it, but if he had a paperback, he never looked up. Often on the days he hauled in a huge leather tome, he'd look right at me. He didn't try to hide it if I caught him. Just gave me a little smile and a nod.

I didn't think much of it. I used to live in San Francisco, where you let folks be happy with their own weirdness. Grantsville, Pennsylvania, seemed to have the same creed. Between Amish farms and the folks who lived in the national forest a few miles north, it was a very different weird from Cali but still respected. So I gave the guy a polite "hello" sometimes and he'd say "hi" back. The man and his wrinkles seemed lost in their own little world. Or so I thought.

This day had been a paperback day. He had his nose in a wrinkled copy of *The Green Mile*, and I barely noticed him. I had been busy thinking at a little portrait of Angelica I kept in the corner of my desktop, her brown eyes twinkling with mischief and a grin that came off as a tad aggressive but that fit her, hinting at barbed wit. When we met we had clicked together, a logon and password combo. Too bad every two weeks she unplugged herself and disappeared for the same length of time—I didn't have the access rights to know why. Whenever I asked, she just shook her black locks and said, "Top-secret. Stop asking." If I pried further I'd get a curt, "Do you want me *not* to come back? Cuz that's alternative." I'd always decided I preferred her more in limited doses than none at all. Now a certain reality called rent might make her next appearance our last visit. As far as I could tell, she didn't come back pockets stuffed with cash; she earned what little she did freelancing from the couch. Unpaid top-secret internships sounded unlikely.

My straw stopped making slurping sounds. A sure sign that I had outlasted even the ice in my cup. Guiltily, I got up. I had the best medicine for my quandary back home.

The sweet sound of exploding newbs never failed to push back the feeling of doom crawling up my neck. Doom in this case asking my father for money and the strings that would come with it.

Turning towards the door, I found the old man in my way, shuffling out towards it with an unsteady gait. I held the door for him once I squelched a flash of annoyance. After all, you can't blame somebody for getting old. Usually it means they did at least something right with their lives. So I waited for him to shuffle past while I paused to glance at the bulletin board by the door, vainly hoping to see a job posting before I followed him out of the coffee shop, my gaze solidly on my feet.

I heard an engine roar just as my own foot touched the pavement of the road. I glanced up just in time to see what I still see in the dark of my eyelids. A car ripping across my field of vision. The heavy crunch of breaking bone. The impact of the old man's body slamming into my chest.

Tires screeched as the blue sky filled my vision. Dazed, I lifted my head and looked at the car jetting off down the street. Black sedan, tarnished silver letters on the trunk spelled out "Sable." Common sense finally lit up my brain, and I sought out the license plate number. I stared at those white numbers as the car raced away, not a single number registering in memory.

The old man's chuckle, a dry and reedy sound, drew my attention. Numbly I looked down at him sprawled across my legs, his limbs bent at odd angles. A rivulet of bright red blood flowed from his left nostril as he coughed out another laugh. "Didn't see that one coming."

"Hey, s-stay with me." The words slipped from my mouth as I looked around for somebody, trying to ignore the creeping sense of panic. A woman stared wide-eyed from the door of the coffee shop. "*Get help!*" I screamed at her, and she ducked back inside like a frightened rabbit.

The old man laughed again, his yellow teeth mottled with red. "Too late for that, Kitty."

And here comes the delirium, I remember thinking as his grin widened. "Oh, yeah?" *Keep them talking, right?*

My mind clawed for some first aid knowledge that might be useful for somebody who was probably bleeding internally. I came up with nothing other than it probably wasn't a good idea to move him.

"I got something for ya. It's in the cupboard," he mumbled, his eyes starting to drift from my face.

Desperate and not having a better idea, I waved my hand in front of his eyes. "Sure. Right after the ambulance comes we'll go check that out."

"Heh." He breathed out and died. I heard something that might have been a snap, and the world went all funny. I'm still unclear on the how or why. But that is the moment that my life jumped down a green pipe into crazy land.

2

My next clear memory is getting blasted in the ears by the razor-sharp beeps of my alarm clock. It took me three tries to successfully smack the clock hard enough to stop its awful screeching. When I did finally hit the damn thing, the force of the slam set my entire hand tingling. It took me two additional sleep-wake-flail-smack cycles to become curious as to cause of my sudden loss of button-pressing aptitude. Normally I could hit that big bar with the accuracy of a laser-guided missile.

Cracking my eyes open illuminated the problem. On the top of the clock, where I expected to see my hand, was not a hand at all. It was something else. The bottom of my stomach fell out as I stared at the thing on my alarm clock. My thinking bits had never been fast wakers, so I squeezed my eyes shut. Only to get another bolt of unfamiliarity as something slid up underneath my eyelids and over my eyes. This sent a shiver racing down my spine, a sensation that flowed well past my hips. Flutters of panic shot through my brain and snapped my eyes open again. The world was still blurred for a split second before the membranes across my eyes retracted back from whence they came. My "hand" sprang into focus, covering the entirety of my alarm clock. Slowly I lifted it and turned the palm towards me. My heart scrabbled into my ears as my brain reluctantly put the individual components together. The brown fur, the short digits with round leathery-looking pads. The claws that just poked out of the tip of each digit. I tried to close my fist and each one slid out, hooked and wicked. This was no hand, my brain declared. This was a paw, a very large cat's paw. What was it doing on my wrist?

It turned out my wrist was covered in the same brown fur and merged into an arm that looked more like a leg before diving into the rest of me, the shoulder concealed in the same thick pelt. My thoughts thrashed in panic, undulating between incredulous and straight out denial. I went through all the standard scapegoats for an altered reality. Who slipped me LSD? Could I be dreaming? Had I gone mad?

Yet the simple act of pulling my limb back to myself stomped on those panicked thoughts with a pair of army boots. The way the muscles in the arm-leg moved against each other, the sensation of each individual hair shifting in response to the movement spidered a sense of vertigo over the limb. You know that feeling when you miss a step? That wrenching moment when you discover that reality does not match your internal predictions? Expand that single moment into a creeping awareness, and you might have an inkling of the alien sensations that were flowing into my brain at that moment.

I screamed and lashed out at my bed sheets. It only made the sensation worse. My spine moved like it had been replaced with a serpent, extending farther than it ever had before and thrashing with a life of its own. I discovered my sharp teeth by nearly piercing my tongue. Every movement of unfamiliar muscles poured pure wrongness on my brain. Everything in me told me to run away, to hide, but all I managed was clawing and kicking at the air, futilely, blindly. Screaming for help only produced a raw and ragged sound that burst through my skull. It made me try harder. Yet there is no escape from your own body. Minutes, perhaps hours later I slumped back into a tangle of shredded sheets, utterly exhausted. All I could do was feel the air sweeping over the hotness of my too-long tongue. The clock went off again. I listened to its needy beeping for a long time, head empty. I focused on those needle-like notes. If I stayed perfectly still, then I could pretend my body was still human.

The beeping stopped and sleep claimed me. I woke later in a still room. The only sound was the faint buzz of electronics. My ears panned on their own to focus on the buzz. I felt broken and uprooted, knowing that every movement would bring more horrible unfamiliarity.

Instead I focused on the familiar—the distinct feeling of a swollen bladder was about as normal as it got.

Seeing no choice in the matter, I put all my legs under myself and stood up on my mattress. It was . . . easy. The sense of unease blossomed, but instead of exploding into panic, it faded as I stood there. The weight of what had to be a very long tail lashed slowly behind me. I did not turn and look at it. Not yet. I wasn't ready for that just yet. Looking down, I studied my front paws. I had seen those already and carefully repositioned them on the edge of the bed while fighting to keep the claws from slicing open my mattress. I was struck by how large they were, far wider than my hands had been.

The hop down and short trot to the bathroom were also easy. Too smooth. If I had stumbled or felt a bit off balance I'd have been more assured. This body seemed to know how to handle itself even if I did not.

Before tackling the logistics of the porcelain throne I popped my paws up onto the bathroom counter and stole a look in the mirror. A feline face stared back at me. I had already guessed that, but it was still jarring to see a face that wasn't mine staring back at me from the mirror. It had light brown fur, except for a whitish muzzle, and blackish markings where long whiskers sprouted. The half-folded ears communicated my unhappiness at the sight well enough. At least I knew what I was. The cat with a thousand names: mountain lion, puma, and cougar, to name a few.

How? Why? The old man had called me a kitty. Had he done it? Had his injured brain somehow twisted my mind? Induced a brain clot that had driven me insane? Would someone else walk into the bathroom and see a naked man on all fours making funny faces in the mirror?

And if my senses could be trusted and the line between possible and impossible had been moved, what then? I couldn't decide which would be more of a disaster: being mad or being the serial killer of the animal kingdom.

Worse, Angelica detested cats. At least people don't call animal control when they see a dog. I hissed in frustration and recoiled instinctively at the sight of vicious fangs in my own mouth! I'd have to be very careful about smiling.

Using the toilet while mulling over how my old neighbor had turned me into a cougar with his last breath proved to be a disaster. Paw pads and smooth white plastic don't make for a very high coefficient of friction. I wound up with a sore nose, an aching shoulder, and sopping wet. The sopping wet was mostly the shower's doing. I only put one foot into the toilet, but when a very strong urge hit me to lick said foot, desperate measures were called for. I'd never been so happy that our cheap old house has L-shaped faucet handles in the shower. A round plastic crystal would have been murder on my teeth.

I was rolling around on a towel, utterly failing to dry myself in a civilized manner when a small high voice declared, "Holy Walnuts! You're huuuuuuuge!"

There was a squirrel perched on the sill of my window, his paws pressed up against the glass and his beady little eyes so wide I could see the whites. His paws quickly slapped over his mouth when he saw me looking and then he flashed the bush of his tail as he bounded away.

I was a very large cat, and now a squirrel had talked to me. My eyes shifted to the door, waiting for the men in white coats to burst through and take me away.

After they didn't show, I untangled myself from the towel and padded over to the window. My house had been remodeled so many times that the layout showed signs of schizophrenia. The window in my bathroom stood three feet wide with two sliding panes of glass side by side. Fortunately for my finer feelings, it faced a stone wall, which occluded the old man's yard next door.

Pawing the window open, I shivered as the cool outside air struck me. I didn't have to worry about being spotted from that house, did I? All my wet fur felt wrong, cold and heavy on my skin. I found myself licking my chops as my tongue itched to do more. That frightened me. A few minutes, maybe an hour before, I had been totally out of sorts. Now it took a conscious effort to stop myself from acting like a cat. Worries circulated through my mind. Would animal instincts eventually override my thoughts? How dangerous could it be to give my paw the lick that it desperately itched for?

My stomach rumbled as I stuck my head out of the

window and peered towards the back of the house. No squirrels. My stomach gurgled a bit at the very thought of a squirrel. The story of my life: food first, thinking later. If the squirrel did come back, I wanted to talk to him, not eat him.

I slunk to the kitchen, trying very hard to ignore the discomfort of my damp fur. The fridge proved to be a bit of a challenge, but yielded after I placed a few claws in the seal of the door. I fished a bit of leftover steak out of the crisper drawer. It was fortunate that neither Angelica nor I are vegetarian. Hell, Angelica almost never ate anything but meat unless forced, so the fridge was well stocked in the event that a resident of the house ever became an obligate carnivore. Had I been transmuted into a rabbit or a donkey I would have been truly screwed.

Remembering, or rather not being able to recall, the last time I had mopped the kitchen floor, I hopped up on to the counter with my steak in a bag. The cold beef tasted better than I thought it would. The meat had a sweetness to it that I never noticed before. Still, as I congratulated myself on not ripping the entire fridge apart in a ravenous frenzy of feeding, I conducted a well-ordered ransacking of our nonfrozen foodstuff. Another leftover steak from a few nights ago was on the edge of edibility. The cold cuts were next: ham, baloney and a half pound of American cheese, which while tasty I would pay for later. Finally, I found a stash of fancy holiday salamis. Those greasy meats were as sweet as candy once I clawed the plastic open.

Sated and feeling more like a stuffed turkey than a feline, I curled up on my countertop and began licking my paws to get off the last remnants of that almost sugary grease.

3

I hadn't realized I had drifted off to sleep until the door-bell startled me out of it. A high-pitched chirp of surprise escaped my throat as my legs pinwheeled over the granite countertop for a moment. My paw pads slipped over its smooth surface before suddenly finding purchase. My legs launched me across the kitchen, and I slammed my shoulder into the opposite wall so hard I felt the sheetrock crack before I slid down the wall, snarling in frustration.

Who the hell was at my door?

As if in answer, the deadbolt helpfully unlocked itself and a glowing woman floated into my house. No feet were visible beneath the hem of her long dress. "Happy Awak-ening Day!" she declared with a sunny grin and flourish of her hands. Small stars and emoticons flowed between them as she made a rainbow over her head.

The woman herself had grey hair pulled up into a tight bun with two blue and green striped chopsticks, her wrin-kled face sporting no makeup other than an oddly grey lipstick. Her bell-shaped dress rounded her spindly frame, swirling with blues and greens, and the air around her seemed to shimmer with its own soft light. For a moment I feared I had fallen into a Disney film and the kitchen appliances were about to burst into song. I gave the toaster a withering look just in case.

The woman clapped, and the rainbow vanished into a flash of light as she turned her smile on me, her eyes twinkling. Her teeth were very white for her age. Her eyes widened a bit as they scanned across me. "Oh, wonderful!" Her eyes came back to mine. "You must be Mr. Thomas Khatt. Yes?"

Not really seeing an option, I tried to make an affirmative noise. I had been expecting a meow or something, but I chirped like a bird! Some fierce apex predator I had become.

"Ah. Good, good. Well, I am Mistress Sabrina. I'm here to welcome you to the Real World."

Something must have shown on my muzzle because she laughed.

"That's all right, dear. Nobody believes when they first awaken to the true world. But trust me, you'll find this side of the Veil to be far superior! You have a very long and happy life ahead of you. Far better than this dreary little hovel."

I tried to tell her I had a life already, but my tongue just sort of flopped around in my mouth as that sense of unfamiliarity bit back into my brain. Involuntarily, I shivered.

"Yes, I know. This is a definite adjustment." She leaned down and cautiously extended a hand out towards my head. I shrank back from it instinctively; she had a faint scent of ozone. "But you're not going to last long on your own." She looked at the scattered wrapper shreds that drifted around the kitchen floor. "It's going to be okay, kitty."

I snarled at that. She flinched a bit but didn't back up. Nice to know that fangs counted a bit in this new "Real World."

She shook her finger at me. "Now, now, dear. No need to be cross. It's what you are and that is not likely to change. You will get used to it. Remember that you are one of the lucky ones. Not everyone survives an Awakening, after all."

At that particular moment, I did not feel lucky. Exchanging my thumbs and voice for claws and fangs did not seem a particularly advantageous trade from my perspective. I took a step back from Sabrina.

"I'm not going to hurt you." She stepped forward and tried to touch my head, violating my personal space again. I ducked and hissed, letting her know that if she persisted we were both going to find out a cougar's bite strength.

She let out a labored sigh and rolled her eyes. "Cats."

I narrowed my eyes. She was the one who had waltzed into my home, told me everything I knew was wrong and *then* tried to pat my head as if I were a toddler! I failed to see how my being a cat at this particular moment had anything to do with my irritation.

Sabrina crossed her arms. "Now look here, dearie, I'm here to help, but you are going to meet me halfway." Her flint-grey eyes hardened a smidge, and I felt my fur prick up as static electricity settled onto my hide. "Tooth and claw will not get you very far in this wild and wooly world. No matter how big you are, you are still a small fish against"—she held up her hand and a spark cracked between her thumb and forefinger—"sorcery. So to prevent any misunderstandings, you will not show me, or any magus in my company, your teeth again. First and only warning, dearie." Electricity arced between her fingers and her palm, hissing and popping as the glow around her brightened. "Understand?"

My ears folded flat against my head. I nodded, although I made an effort to conceal my teeth. Realization was dawning on me that she wouldn't take no for an answer.

"Good!" With a clap of her hands, the iron lightning lady instantly transformed back into a hyperkinetic fairy godmother. "Shall we, then? You've got much to learn, and it would be best to fit you with a talking spell sooner rather than later. Words always prevent misunderstandings." She gestured at the floor in front of her. "Now come here and let me get a good look at you."

I gave a huff of frustration as I regarded her for a moment, trying to buy a little time to think. I didn't know what to make of this woman, but I couldn't see any alternatives. I could take her up on the offer and possibly get my voice back, or attempt to run and hide—"attempt" possibly being the defining word. She could tase me before I could run my clumsy self out of the kitchen.

Looking at things in that admittedly cynical fashion, the choice was obvious. Buy time to gather more information.

Other parts of my brain were busily flipping out over the possibilities hinted at by Sabrina's existence. Woman flying and casually summoning electricity? What was next? Zombies chewing on my door? Werewolves marking territory in my yard? As usual, fear held my awe and wonder in check. Hesitantly I stepped closer and sat down in front of her, my head about even with her chest.

Sabrina knelt but still appeared to hover an inch off the ground as she looked me over, drifting around me like a buyer around a used car. "Let's see. I'm guessing you're a bit over two hundred pounds, right at the top of the weight range for mountain lions. Although you could probably stand to lose about fifteen of those."

Just great, I lose my voice but I get to keep my spare tire? Further proof that the universe itself is a sadistic bastard. I flinched a little when she ran her fingertips over the crown of my head. The alien sensation of her fingers threading through my fur to scratch my ears felt pleasant, but did not make me melt into a warm purring pile, as I perhaps feared. I looked up at her and she stopped, flashing me a rueful smile.

"Oh, fine. And the students wonder why I tell them to pick dogs for familiars." She grumbled as she turned to the door, "Come along, then."

Outside sat an ancient moss-colored Cadillac convertible, the top up on this warm summer day. Paint flaked around the wheel wells, but otherwise the car looked well kept and free of rust. I looked up at Sabrina and tried to furrow my brow.

"Oh, dearie. You were expecting a golden carriage drawn by eight white horses, perhaps?" She laughed as she gestured me towards the car.

I tried to shrug, which didn't really work without a collarbone, so I shook my head.

She sighed and gave me a little nudge. "Go on, get in the car." The back door unlocked itself and swung open as I crossed the threshold of my doorway. A squirrel, the same one that had been in my window, sprang out from behind the apple tree in my front yard and dashed into the Caddy. Now I knew why this magus was in my house. The little rodent had sold me out.

"Why, hello, Rudy dear," Sabrina said as she shut the door to my house behind me. A moment of panic shot through me. I didn't have my keys! Or my cell phone or anything! The feeling of nakedness twisted my gut into a knot. Instinctively I turned back and tried to open the door. Sabrina quickly sidestepped out of the way as I battered the doorknob with my paws and let out a soft yowl.

Sabrina shook her head, although her smile had drawn a bit thin, maybe sad. "You don't need anything in there,

Thomas. You've awakened into a new life—your old one is gone."

I hissed in anger and frustration, pressing my lips together to conceal my teeth. There certainly were important things in there! I was just going with her for a question-and-answer session! If this woman thought that I would leave without saying good-bye to Angelica, then she was in for a surprise.

"Go get in the car, Thomas. We will explain things soon, but you can't let yourself be seen out here. Someone will call animal control, and then they will drug or shoot you."

I hesitated.

"Come on! Stop being a sour puss!" The squirrel barked from inside the car. Ignoring the rodent, I looked at the closed door, promising I'd be back, and then trotted over and jumped into the back seat. The squirrel scampered into the front of the car and leapt onto the passenger-side dash.

As I sprawled out across the Caddy's wide backseat, I was surprised to find it was a bit of a tight fit. I nearly slipped off when I attempted to curl up, and the low ceiling prevented me from sitting up. I could have just lain down lengthwise and rested my head on the armrest in the door, but I needed to see where Sabrina drove. So I wound up hunching uncomfortably, my ears flattened against the canvas ceiling. The door closed of its own accord, and the driver's side opened to admit Sabrina into the car.

She glanced at the squirrel. "Rudy, dear, I will take it from here." The window rolled down about six inches.

"Oooh, no! I just found the biggest cat in Pennsylvania. I'm his TAU sponsor by rights! I'm sticking to him like bubble gum in curly locks." The squirrel's voice sounded like a young child's as his bushy tail thrashed.

So the squirrel had either doomed me or saved me,

depending on what happened next. I made a mental note of that.

"That was not the agreement, dearie." A bit of that iron lady persona seeped into the grandmotherly tone.

"You never said he would be a big kitty. That's worth a lot more than a new iPhone." The squirrel seemed unfazed by Sabrina's implied threat.

Sabrina's lips tightened in the rearview mirror as she slammed the car into gear and pulled away from the curb. She looked about to say something, but the squirrel, Rudy, piped up first. "You don't got nothing to worry about, big guy. First you're feline, which means you can see magic, so you don't even need much training to be a familiar. And on top of that you're *huge!*" He made a sweeping circle with his arms to illustrate. "But not so huge you can't fit in an airplane or a car. I know this one guy, he's an elephant, and his bond has had to bail him out of the zoo half a dozen times already. One of the major houses will take your bond and pamper you rotten." The squirrel folded his dexterous paws together and let out a wistful sigh.

As Rudy talked, Sabrina's path did not stray towards the interstate at all. My guts loosened a little bit at the prospect that she lived in town.

I chirped questioningly as the car swam through the suburban streets, hoping to keep the rodent talking.

He obliged. "Hell, I bet you could boss your bond around! Be all like, 'I'm tired of magic—get me some tuna-shrimp!' 'Course if I were you I'd put tuna in my contract. Well, not tuna. Not for me! I'd want a can of cashews per day. And none of that cheap Planters crap either. Real premium roasted stuff from Cali." The squirrel sucked in his breath, eyes closed, seeming to savor the imagined scent. Sabrina tittered but made no effort to stop Rudy from spending the next few minutes explaining in excruciating detail why cashews were the best nuts that nature had ever seen fit to invent. A few polite chirps were interpreted as probing questions into the nature and flavor of cashews. I was considering a more forceful reply when the car pulled into a driveway and the sight of the house slapped all thought of nuts from by brain.

4

The house that Sabrina lived in made perfect sense for someone who resided beyond the rational world. I had actually driven by it before and then circled around the block to confirm that my first glance had not been a hallucination. The house had once been a small one-bedroom bungalow until the occupant had decided to build another house on top of it without bothering to knock down the original. The second story was at least double the width of the original house, propped up on thick timbers on each corner. It seemed to be trying to convince the smaller house to scooch out of the way by threatening to sit on it. The wooden siding of the bottom level was painted a blue shade that had faded unevenly, texturing it like a bird's egg. The top story sported vinyl siding in pastel green so garish that it nearly distracted me from the glowing gold runes that decorated every opening that left purplish lines on my retinas.

The car's doors sprang open as soon as the engine died, and Sabrina swung herself out of the vehicle. I followed after, pausing to glance at the door on my way out, my rear legs still on the seat. The car's keyholes had been covered over by a flat metal disk with an Oriental-ish golden symbol that vaguely resembled a horse with its tongue hanging out. I wondered what the car ran on since I scented no exhaust.

Once all four of my paws touched pavement, Rudy shot from inside the car and bounded up the railing of the steps to the porch. The front door to the house opened on its own once Sabrina floated up the steps after the creature. She turned and grinned broadly once inside the door, gesturing for me to come inside. Resigned, I did so.

And found myself quite suddenly on my side, head ringing.

"Oh!" I heard Sabrina gasp as I raised my head from the floor and gave it a shake. She started to giggle and quickly suppressed it with a swallow. "Sorry about that. It appears Cornealius must have waxed the floor recently." Rudy's didn't bother to suppress his high-pitched laughter. Looking down, I could see my reflection in the shine of the wood floor.

"You did say you were bringing home company, Mistress." A new voice slipped into my ears, which swiveled towards the sound. My eyes followed to the upper corner of the room, where a very long animal watched me from a platform jutting out about a foot from the wall, like a shelf that that would be very difficult to reach. Angelica would have squee'd at the creature's cuteness despite herself. With a little black nose and big ears, the animal looked like something out of a children's cartoon. The shelf he stood on stretched from the edge of the foyer and deeper into the house. A small stairway led down from it in the room beyond. I had seen something similar on a crazy pet TV show that I would never admit to actually watching: an elevated track in every room for house pets so that they never had to stray under their owner's feet.

As I carefully picked myself up off the slippery floor, the creature curled his long body to look down at me with a subtle smirk. "You always find the graceful ones, I see."

"Ain't he big, though?" Rudy piped up from a small table by the door.

"He is that." The animal cocked his head to the side as if to get a better look at me.

Being talked at and unable to respond had started to wear thin before I had left my house. I looked up at Sabrina and chirped loudly, hoping she'd get the idea.

"Oh, my, where are my manners! Thomas, this is my familiar, Cornealius. He is a sable, if you're trying to figure that out."

"*Martes zibellina*, to be precise." Cornealius' voice had a deeper quality to it than you would imagine coming out of something so small, with just a hint of a British accent. He yawned, showing me some impressively sharp teeth for an animal smaller than most house cats. Then he smiled warmly, his mouth moving in a way I had thought impossible for nonhuman lips. "Welcome to our not-so-humble abode. Please make sure to keep your claws in. Sabrina causes enough damage to the place and doesn't need help."

"Cornealius!" Sabrina and her familiar locked eyes for a moment, and then she broke contact with a subtle eye roll. She turned back to me. "Well, I do believe I promised you a voice. We will get that set up, and then Cornealius will answer all your questions."

I followed Sabrina with eagerness at the prospect of talking (and complaining) again. The whole day deserved more than a few choice curses, and they were bubbling around my brain with nowhere to go. Nearly slipping on the overly waxed floor again, I settled on a hopeful chirp followed by a rasping rattle that everyone in the room gave me a weird look for after it wormed its way from my throat. I ducked my head in embarrassment.

Cornealius let out a throaty chuckle. "Let's get you talking before you strangle your vocal cords attempting it." He walked haughtily down his elevated platform, deeper into the house, occasionally glancing back at Sabrina, who bade me to follow her.

Rudy bounced up beside me, the closest he'd approached me yet. "They're mind-talking," he whispered before springing up onto an ornate brass floor lamp. It wobbled as he used it to launch up to the pet-way.

Biting down on the obvious questions that would follow after such a statement, I decided that patience was the only avenue available to me. Everything within the house looked far older than I. It reminded me of a famous person's house that had been converted to a museum. The furniture gleamed with brass decorations with plush pillows piled on the high-backed chairs. Yet despite the hospital level of cleanliness, the air felt heavy with time. We passed first through a formal sitting room and into a similarly disused library in the back of the original house. I tried to make out the titles of some of the leather-bound books as I passed them, but the majority were in languages other than English. The one title that was in my native tongue might have well been Greek: *Upper- and Lower-Level Junctions in the Planar Space with or without Time*. Yeesh.

Sabrina had stayed silent during the short walk, occasionally giving a slight nod or shake of her head, perhaps in response to a silent comment from Cornelius. When we reached a stout door at the back of library, she turned and gave me another wide comforting grin that didn't quite reach her eyes. She flung open the door and a searing white light flooded out of the doorway. Sabrina instantly became a silhouette in a field of white so bright that the pain brought the third eyelid flicking across my eyes as I squinted to see. It didn't help. In fact, somehow closing my eyes to shield them from the brightness made it worse. The sheer power of whatever lay beyond the door seemed to bypass my eyeballs. My brain felt like it was about to sizzle.

Making a *mrowl* of discomfort, I retreated back down the hallway and put a wall between the light and me, reducing the intensity from agony to merely painful.

Sabrina chuckled. "Oh, come on, Thomas. It's not that bad. It's just a blinder against nosey felines. Can't have visitors inspecting the wards too closely, after all. Just close your eyes."

No way. I made a rowl of protest.

"What the heck did you do to him? It sounds like you've got a helicopter in there!" asked Rudy from somewhere above me, his high little voice quivering with concern.

Sabrina harrumphed. "Nothing to worry about. Thomas is being a bit dramatic. The arc is very strong. Dogs complain about the smell, but cats hate it more than a basket of citrus."

I let loose a sawing growl, which I hoped would translate into, "Because it *hurts*, you flipping idiot."

Sabrina poked her head around the corner. "Now, now. Let's not be testy. Come here and I'll guide you upstairs."

I shook my head in a clear no gesture.

"Just close your eyes."

I shook my head again, my tail beginning to lash in frustration. I looked around for something that might be useful. On the far wall of the sitting room was a brass-gilded fireplace. Hoping it wasn't quite as spotless as the rest of the place, I padded over to it. Sabrina followed me warily.

"What are you doing?"

Peering into the fireplace, it appeared to have been used

within the last century at least. The space had been shoveled out but not cleaned; soot and ash clung to every surface. I pawed aside the chain link curtain and swiped my paw across the black floor of the fireplace.

Sabrina nearly screeched, "Stop that this instant!" I heard the crackle of electricity behind me. I glanced at her and wished I had not. She stood about five feet behind me, rage in her eyes and a fist of crackling energy. "You will not make a mess of my house!"

"Let him alone, Mistress," Cornealius said, his voice even. She shot him a glance and he met her gaze, their eyes locking for a moment.

With a huff, the threatening Sabrina relaxed back into her kind grandmother persona. "Oh, all right, dearie. I suppose that's fair."

Wearily, I wrote the word "hurt" on the floor in front of the fireplace.

"Like I told you before. Just shut your eyes," Sabrina replied, annoyed.

I shook my head.

As I turned to start writing again, Cornealius spoke. "Wait, do you mean shutting your eyes does not help?"

I nodded at him directly. He groaned and Sabrina sighed.

"What?" Rudy asked.

Cornealius explained, "It is simple. Thomas is untrained, and he doesn't know how to suppress the sight. We have what is called an Ebeneezer Arc on our wards. If a cat attempts to look at it . . . Well, think about what happens when a bottle rocket explodes in your face."

Sabrina went and closed the door, and I sagged with relief as the too-bright spotlight winked out. "Well," she said, as she returned, "Can't have a guest in pain. Thomas, you'll just have to stay down here for now, I'm afraid. Upstairs is much more homey and comfortable, but if you're still with us in a few days, you can help Cornealius and me retune the arc. In the meantime . . ." She turned to Cornealius, who nodded and ran back into the library. I caught a small patch of blinding brightness open and close. "Let's get you talking so you don't feel compelled to write messages on my walls."

5

Cornealius returned a few minutes later and deposited something in Sabrina's hand. She turned to me and smiled, her voice pitched as if offering a pet a treat. "You get to see a bit of real magic now." A yellow light flared from a ring around her middle finger and spread over her body. With a slow graceful motion she pressed the palms of her hands together and closed her eyes. A wave rippled through the yellow energy before it flowed and coalesced into her arms, so bright it nearly concealed her limbs from view.

With a great sweep of her arm, the energy lashed out beyond her hand, flowing out into a wavy extension like a droopy light saber. It pushed against a coffee table and gently shoved it back against the wall. In this manner Sabrina rearranged the furniture in graceful sweeping motions of her body, resembling those of Tai-chi practitioners. Unlike that martial art, every movement she made had a very clear purpose. The broad sweeps pushed back the lighter objects, while the sofa and love seat required more directed efforts.

Sabrina cleared the room with this spinning dance until a small coffee table with a simple glass vase was the only thing that remained. With a flick of her fingers a whip of energy wrapped about the vase's neck, lifting it from the table. She propelled the table to the wall with a swat of her other hand as the vase slowly spun towards her.

"This," Sabrina said as she reversed the motion of the vase with a slight turning of her wrist, "is the most basic of magic. A simple channeling of force from the higher planes. In this case, pure kinetic energy." She bounced the vase between two alternate waves of force, slowly herding it to the center of the room. "All magi are attuned to a single sort of energy, their birth element. That is the element that they will use as a lens to understand the world. Yet, true magi do not allow themselves to be limited by their innate element."

A tendril of force caught the vase and tossed it straight up. Sabrina threw one of her hands up, and the brightness of the energy gathered in her fingertips left a trail in my vision. At the peak of the vase's accent she lashed out with a single finger, the energy projecting like an ultralong claw. The vase shattered with such force that I felt the shockwave in my whiskers. I closed my eyes, waiting for the shards to rain down into my fur and flesh. It didn't happen. Instead an awful grinding sound made my hackles rise.

Opening one eye, I saw the vase, or what was left of it, still hovered in the place it had been shattered, a small maelstrom of glittering shards. Sabrina held it there, using wide strokes of both hands to trap the glass between two intersecting waves of force, grinding the fragments into dust between them. Her facial expression was one of utter concentration, lips pressed into a thin line. Cornealius too stared at the pulverizing glass, eyes narrowed. I wondered, as the familiar, how much he had to do with the actual magic. Rudy watched through one eyeball with his mouth hanging open. I looked at the grinding glass and could not help but ask myself, what if she did that to a person?

Once the vase was ground to a glittering dust cloud, the force wave spread it into a rough circle on the floor. Sabrina released a breath, her wrinkled skin shining and her cheeks pink. Cornealius grunted and flopped down onto the shelf. Sabrina tittered like a slightly drunk schoolgirl, "One has to show off every so often, Cornealius."

"Archmagus candidates should not perform like a circus act," Cornealius huffed, standing his long body up on end and crossing his fore legs as if they were human arms. His eyes burrowed into mine, and then Rudy's. "Not a word about this to anyone, either of you."

Sabrina waved dismissively. "Nonsense, all the Archmagi will remember I force dance, and certainly anyone I arrested back in the day knows. Don't you two worry. Cornealius is just a bit protective of little old me. Likes to keep everything we do hush-hush."

Cornealius glared at her, perhaps sharing words that were not for our ears via their bond. Sabrina only smiled in response, not that patronizing grin she put on for me but a sly smile that made her eyes glitter with amusement. It gave me an intense desire to know what actually made Sabrina tick. Yet I doubt even the power of speech would have helped me much in that moment.

"Now, Thomas, dearie, come and sit in the center." Sabrina gestured to her glittering circle. She glanced at Cornealius, who made a disgruntled snort as he leapt to the ground and hurried towards us to sit at the outer edge of the circle as I walked into the center. Sabrina leaned down and showed me an oval stone about a half-inch wide, set in a slender brass fitting. She flipped it around, and I swallowed nervously when I saw that the back of the stone had a dozen tiny metal barbs protruding from the back. "All right, open your mouth, Thomas."

I looked down at the barbs and then back at her very cool expression.

"All magic has a price, dearie. Now open wide."

I hesitated for just a moment to consider my options. Mostly I wondered where exactly she was planning on jamming the little torture device. The fact I couldn't ask her that simple question made up my mind. Talking would be worth a little pain. I slowly opened my mouth a little bit.

With a deft motion she grabbed my nose and yanked my muzzle skyward. "Keep it open now!" Her other hand curled around my front teeth and dug fingertips into the soft tissue under my tongue. The sudden pain brought my third lids over my eyes and drove my jaw wide open. I tried to pull back, but she was in my ear, her voice calm and cheery. "Don't you move now. Don't you move a single muscle. Let me look at it."

A pitiful mew escaped my throat as she twisted my head this way and that, examining the inside of my mouth. "Now brace yourself—this will pinch a bit and if you bite me I will bite back. Nod if you understand."

I nodded, blinking against the pain of her fingers digging into my lower jaw.

"Good—hold still."

I felt sweet relief as her fingers pulled out from under my tongue only to be followed by a new jabbing pain as needles sliced into the roof of my mouth. I yelped and started to twist away.

"Hold still—I know it hurts. Don't bite me," Sabrina repeated like a mantra as she held the device in place. The needles burned as they bit deeper, like each one had struck a nerve. Then she let go, the opal hooked into the flesh on the roof of my mouth. I shook my head. The pain flared again as my tongue ran across it.

"There we go. Not so bad." She had taken a good two steps back from me and smiled with a sort of smug pride. "That will be an anchor for the spell. Eventually the spell will root in your soul, and the little stone will fall out." She took a deliberate step outside the circle.

A moment of panic seized me. I was inside a stranger's house, I had allowed her to implant something in my body and now they were going to cast a spell on me. Normally I would have laughed at the possibility, but I had just watched this iron woman in a fairy godmother mask rearrange the furniture with tai chi moves. I had to have been in a state of shock not to run out of that house screaming. Instead I stayed perfectly still as I watched the circle around me glow with heat that caused the wax below it to bubble and smoke as the dust became a solid circle of glass. Both Cornealius and Sabrina looked through me into each other's eyes. Her thin grey brows furrowed in concentration.

The room began to thrum as a prickle of energy ran along my spine from my tail to my whiskers. A pulse of purple flashed through my vision accompanied by an odd pulling in a direction that is hard to describe—inward and to the left. Strange images invaded my vision. I saw myself from every angle at the same time. My feline body suspended in a web of lines stretching out beyond myself. Then on one of those strands a man walked up to me—he had my eyes, my human brown eyes set in a not quite right face, too thin, too long. He shuddered, his head rippling as water in the rain. Then the old man stood before me, red blood dripping from his nostrils and eyes. His mouth moved but made no sound, his teeth tangled in purple threads.

The visions parted, scattering back along the strands

from whence they came. I stood back in the middle of the circle as a shape struggled into existence above me. A nest of purple threads danced with a bright orange fiber, which seemed to be stitching in and out of existence, moving in a way I could not follow. The magus and her familiar continued to weave until I realized they had formed a muzzle. My muzzle, but with a difference. Human lips sat on the tip under the nose, huge and cartoonish.

"Speak, Thomas," Sabrina commanded.

"What should I say?" I thought in response and was shocked when I heard the words in my ears! My heart did a flip-flop. They were doing it! "Oh, my!" The voice wasn't quite as I remembered myself, but who actually knows their own voice? I bounced a little with excitement.

"*Don't move!*" Sabrina's voice bolted me to the floor.

"Yes, ma'am," I said timidly, but hearing the words brought a grin to my face.

"Keep talking."

I did. I started with my name. "My name is Thomas Khatt. I'm a librarian. I worked for two years in the McKennision Memorial Library." Why I decided to recite my résumé I'm not sure.

As I talked about myself, the mask slowly lowered itself and slid over my muzzle. I felt my own thin lips begin to move as it did, and my long tongue twisting in ways it really shouldn't be able to.

". . . Thank you." I finished as the purple and white threads tied into the thing in my mouth and the tingling sensation abruptly dissipated.

"There, all done," Sabrina said with a sigh. She and Cornealius slumped simultaneously. "The stone will fall out in a couple weeks. The talking spell will usually anchor itself by then. If not, then the union will be able to replace it."

"Thank you," I said again, more to hear my own voice again than to show additional gratitude. Sabrina stood and broke the glass circle with her foot before walking over and patting me on the head. I didn't dodge this time and even allowed her to scratch my ear a little. I fought off a sudden urge to press up against her.

"Now I know you have lots of questions, and I promised to explain a bit more. But Cornealius and I could use a bit of a rest. It's been a very long day for us. We'll be back down soon, kitty cat."

She floated past me, scooped up Cornealius and quickly disappeared into the blinding light.

As soon as they were gone, I looked up at Rudy, who was huddled in the corner, watching me. "What's this about a union?"

6

Rudy sputtered, "What? Oh, yeah, the TAU. Oric will probably show up in a day or so and whisk you off to their never-never land. Lucky." Rudy glared down at me from his perch near the ceiling.

"TAU?" I paced below him, eyes crossing, trying to look at my muzzle, the spell wire looked to thread in and out of it.

Rudy responded with the tone of voice of a phone employee reading the company boilerplate. "Talking Animal Union. We represent all animals with the gift of speech or capable of speech within the domain of the council of Merlins. An animal being defined as a being possessing corporeal form but lacking hands and viewed as nonhuman by those on the other side of the Veil. The TAU endeavors to insure familiars are well treated and allows no bonding to take place without its blessing.

"Yeah, the Talking Animal Union. Anybody who's got no thumbs but can think is invited to join. These days you'd better be familiar material, though, not that you'll have any trouble with that, with the whole apex predatory thing."

I blinked. If I was going to study the spell more, I'd have

to find a mirror. I'd try to figure out how the thing worked later. At the moment it was thrilling to have regained the power of conversation, even if the only conversant available had a sour note to his high-pitched voice. I eyed the sofas, trying to determine which would be the most comfortable to chat Rudy's small ear off from. "You don't sound happy with them."

"Well, yeah, the entire union's run by grumpy ex-familiars who'd eat me for lunch if I ain't careful." He chuckled. "A few have tried anyway, but they've all run afoul of Rudy's Rocket." He shook his minuscule fist at an unseen ex-familiar.

"Really?" I said.

"Oh, don't you worry—you'll get it too if you try to eat me! I've added bigger cats than you to the ol' gallery."

I estimated that Rudy would be about one bite—two if I decided to eat the tail too. "I'm not planning on eating anyone that talks."

"That's what all you preds say."

I decided to change the subject. "So what makes a, uh, person a good familiar?" I jumped up on a sofa. It creaked in a threatening manner.

"Those, for one." Rudy pointed to my eyeballs. "Binocs make magic easier for some reason."

"Magic is visual?"

"For humans, yeah. It's what they got. They're blind to magic, at least in the raw. Cats are supereasy. You guys see magic everywhere. I hear it. Dogs smell it. Burrowers feel it."

"So only animals that see magic can be used as familiars?"

Rudy smacked his face with a paw. "No, that's what the circle is for." He pointed at the broken glass. "The circles make magic inside them cast a shadow. But in order to see it right the Magi's gotta look at it from two different angles, and they all want depth perception they say rodents don't have, which is utter bitter almonds." Rudy pointed his nose at me and gritted his teeth in concentration as both his eyes turned towards me. "Can you see both of my eyes?"

I could and nodded.

"See, it can be done! Cats ain't special! You're just easy. Nobody wants a rodent as a familiar, but it fixes the whole familiar shortage problem in two secs." Rudy slumped as he talked, clearly not enjoying this path of inquiry. "It's not complicated—well, magic is, but familiaring ain't."

"So magi need a familiar to do any magic?"

"Weren't you listening to Sabrina? Even without all her stuff she could hit you with a lightning bolt as long as she ain't grounded."

I quirked my nonexistent eyebrow at the squirrel.

"That's why she floats everywhere—otherwise she'd just shock herself. It's real showy with all the sparks and stuff, but she can't arc lightning bolts into anybody more than five feet away without Cornealius. That's force dancing; it's real powerful, dangerous stuff. But you saw how it strained Cornealius."

I settled on the couch, curling up on one end. "Yeah. That's not normal?"

"It just meant he was way more involved in it than he wanted to be."

"But the force came from a ring around her finger, not him," I said, trying to ignore a sudden itch that settled onto the top of my right paw, the one still blackened with soot.

"Oh, she used a ring? Maybe he was just nervous that she'd trip up and take out a wall." The squirrel chuckled. "If magi used YouTube, there'd be a channel just for force dancing fails."

"The TAU teach you all this stuff?" I kept my eyes on

the rodent and off the paw with the soot, itch and the discomforting feeling of uncleanliness.

The squirrel chittered angrily. "The TAU taught me nothing. Didn't ya hear me? I'm a rodent."

"But you said..."

His beady little eyes narrowed. "Stop asking questions! This is the way it works! You're a cat—you have absolutely nothing to worry that tiny empty space between your ears." His tail beat back and forth in such a way that I was sure projectiles would follow. "Simply by existing, Oric will train you and wizards will duel for the right to even bid on you. Then Sabrina gets paid, and if I'm lucky I'll get paid too."

I blinked at the usually chipper squirrel's sudden switch to bitter almonds.

Rudy shook himself before starting to groom his tail. "And let me tell you it really sucks to be stuck on 3G when this town finally got an LTE network two months ago. I'm living in the stone age." His voice scaled back to its usual carefree tenor.

I watched the squirrel warily; every question I asked generated at least a half dozen more. Yet one thing had become crystal clear; I wanted no part of this world. Losing my thumbs, my house and my girlfriend in exchange for the chance to be sold off to some pimple-faced apprentice did not sound like a fair deal to me.

I made to tell Rudy as much, but a thunderous *bang* knocked my reply right out of my mouth. Raw instinct surged as I vaulted over the back of the couch and pressed my body to the floor. Then the thud came again. Gunshot? The sound came from the front of the house. On the third boom I finally ID'd the sound. Somebody was knocking with enough force that it was amazing that the door had not been blown off its hinges.

My heart still thundering in my chest. I rose, my muscles coiled for action. I didn't see the squirrel anywhere. Did animal control see me in the back of Sabrina's car and were hoping to rescue her? The banging continued—three more knocks and then a woman called out in a perfectly normal voice, "Mistress Sabrina!" Now I understood why my parents' cats startled when you rang the doorbell. Sudden noises seemed to have a class of loudness all by themselves.

I crept forward through the house, towards the front door, curious to see who this could be. Another magus? Two long panes of glass framed either side of the front door, covered by long shades that prevented me from clearly seeing the person beyond. Yet I still saw the vaguest of outlines, framed in dim red light. I crept forward on my belly until I pressed my head against the wall right under the window. Slowly, careful not to give myself away by bumping the blind, I angled my head to look up through the bottom of the window, sighting up through space between it and the blind.

Wide eyes stared down at me from a face framed with fire red hair. Her blue eyes followed the theme, the color of burning gas on a cook top. A white brilliance flooded my vision before I could make out much more than that, and I recoiled with surprise. Despite the doorway being behind me and through several walls, I was momentarily blinded. I froze, trying to blink away an afterimage that existed off the map of my visual field.

"Thomas, get away from that door!" Sabrina's voice climbed to scandalized pitch. Belatedly I obeyed, my vision clearing just in time to see her swoosh past me.

Above I heard the scrabble of claws on wood. "Come on, Thomas, you don't want this one to get a look at you—trust us on this," Cornealius said.

"Yeah, yeah. Your damn ward against eyeballs blinded

me again." Really I was fine. Curiosity made me linger as Sabrina hurried to the door. It did not open until Sabrina had her hand around the doorknob.

A small thump next to me made me glance down to see Cornealius. He jerked his head in the direction of a darkened doorway across from us. One I hadn't been into yet. Apparently they hadn't realized that this cat was already out of the bag. With a roll of my eyes I followed him, giving the contents of the room a cursory glance. An office of sorts with a huge desk and three plush sitting chairs placed against the opposite wall. Ascertaining that nothing in the room was a threat, I halfway peeked my head out into the hallway. Cornealius hissed in frustration, which I ignored. Were all magi as crazy as Sabrina? I wondered where the hell Rudy had gotten off to.

Sabrina glanced back at me with a stern glare, mouthing the word "*Bad!*" A different ring from her other hand lit briefly as she motioned in my direction. My vision faded to black as I heard the squeak of hinges.

I stumbled back from the blackness, momentarily panicked that Sabrina had just blinded me on a whim. But no, the blackness hung in the hallway, a displaced shadow. Deep within the darkness itself a tiny spot of yellow twinkled, a hole of light within the darkness.

I looked down at Cornealius as Sabrina's voice rolled through the shadow unencumbered. "Why, O'Meara! To what event do I owe this surprise?" Cornealius mouthed something at me but reading weasel lips was a skill that I did not possess. Clearly they wanted me hidden, and while I trusted them so far that neither he nor Sabrina were going to kill me, perhaps there were other options that did not involve getting sold to the highest bidder at a pet show. Maybe they'd understand once we had time to chat, but I doubted Sabrina would hear me through the layers of her condescension.

"Doing my job, Elder. Archibald is dead and I'd like your assistance." O'Meara's voice had just a slight tang of an Irish accent, and her tone was business-like.

"*Oh, my*! Poor Archie. He finally blow himself up? He's been soft in the head for two years now. Dear Guardian, of course I shall help. Hand me your sword and I shall resume my former duties of the protector of the region," Sabrina said with sugary sweetness.

There followed a moment of silence, so thick and angry that I could smell it before O'Meara spoke. "Elder, it will be a cold day on the elemental planes of fire before I relinquish my position to you or anyone else. If you really want to help, you can start by telling me where you were last morning at about 10:00 a.m."

As I peered into the darkness that hid me from view, I realized with a shock that I could see the women, partially. A trace of their outlines. They were dim and hard to make out against the brighter spots of light in the door and doorframe but definitely there. Sabrina stood, her back to me, hand still on the doorknob, poised to shut it in the other woman's face, although she had opened the door wide. Beyond her, O'Meara stood. While Sabrina radiated her warm iron, O'Meara's aura throbbed with angry heat. The precise meaning of that? I had no idea. What I could see was that although O'Meara was a few inches shorter than the wiry Sabrina, she probably outweighed her by a factor of two. Not fat but thick, possibly curvaceous, but looking through Sabrina blurred her features too much for a detailed inspection.

"Now, will you be inviting me in or will you continue to hold me at bay on your stoop and air our conversation to the whispering winds? Or shall I tell the story of how you came to reside in our fair town? I'm sure your new ward would love to hear that little tale. Particularly the body count."

I looked at Cornealius. "Body count?"

The weasel replied in a harsh whisper. "She's a seared kettle calling Sabrina a black pot. You don't want anything to do with her."

"I want to meet her, actually. This cat won't be bagged." I think both Sabrina and Cornealius were too busy wincing at the pun to stop me from plowing through Sabrina's little privacy curtain. The darkness felt cool on my nose as I pressed through it. Beyond it I was greeted by a glare from Sabrina, whom I ignored, circling around to get a better look at O'Meara. Her build did indeed have curves, curves of muscle and bosom. Had she been within the pages of a fantasy comic, you'd call her a thin dwarf until she stood next another person. I had no doubt she could cleave me in two with the sword that hung at her waist.

The women's faces became fun house mirrors of each other, Sabrina's an angry scowl and O'Meara's a hearty grin that displayed deep dimples. O'Meara spoke while Sabrina chewed on her tongue, no doubt preparing a tongue-lashing for later.

"Ah, you must be Thomas Khatt." O'Meara stepped through the doorway, pushing past a now yielding Sabrina. She wore a simple sleeveless red dress crafted from a thick fabric, its hem just overhanging the top of her heavy work boots, which were decorated with fiery insignias.

A bolt of surprise went through me, and my thoughts ran out of my mouth. "How do you know my name?"

"Oh, you talk already!" O'Meara looked at Sabrina in surprise.

"With a familiar his size you have to be able to

communicate. Although I might have to check his ears because it's clear he doesn't listen to anything we have to say."

"I just want to ensure that you're giving me all my options. Getting sold at auction to highest bidder sounds like a lousy way to pick a life partner."

"The other ways are even less savory: a desperate and unscrupulous magus could grab you off the street, bond you against your will with pain lash built into the bond ensure obedience," Cornealius said, trotting out into the foyer along the walkway above, eyes on O'Meara. "TAU is not perfect, but it's an improvement from the days of yore. Which is why Rudy notified us and not O'Meara."

O'Meara's hair seemed to catch fire and redness blossomed in her cheeks. "I'd never!"

"If I really wanted you out of the picture, dear, I would have let you have him. You've been without a familiar for a year. You wouldn't be able to resist. I'm saving you the trouble really." Sabrina's voice oozed grandmotherly condescension.

O'Meara cast a sideways glance at Sabrina but looked me in the eyes. "Welcome to the noble and upright side of magi society, Thomas. Unfortunately Cornealius is right. The TAU is what we have; both magi and the familiars are at the mercy of its bureaucratic machinations. It may not be great, but when powerful magi live for about two hundred or more years, change is slow." She knelt to extend a hand out towards me, her sword making a loud clink against the wall. "You did turn out very handsome."

Instinctively, I extended my head towards her and gave it a tentative sniff before my mind caught up with my body. Smoke and cinnamon clung to her and threaded through the musky smell she had in common with Sabrina, the human scent perhaps, and piled on with a recognizable tang of sweat. The scent was not of the unclean but one of toil. I liked it.

"He will make some initiate very happy," Sabrina added.

"Initially at least," Cornealius said, bouncing with haughtiness. "The poor soul will very quickly find that Thomas is obstinate, lazy and entitled." He climbed up onto Sabrina's shoulders like a fuzzy snake and grinned down before my brain registered the insults. "He'll make an awful familiar."

The anger kicked in, a bit belatedly to be of much use. It knotted up my back and peeled my lips away from my teeth a little, held in check by the twinkle in the weasel's black eyes.

"See? No sense of humor either."

"Of course not—he is a feline, after all." Sabrina smirked. I let myself relax a little and said nothing, my anger fading to annoyance. I wondered how often they "found" familiars.

O'Meara sighed and stood, crossing her arms impatiently. "Are you done showing off and insulting your acquisition, Elder? We still have some business to discuss, like where you were last night. I also need to speak to Rudy, the double-crossing little rat. Just how much more did you promise him?"

Sabrina smiled. "Rudy is a dear, but the rodent loves his electronics more than vague promises of future favors. Besides, Thomas will be safer here with Cornealius and me. Now let us retire upstairs. No sense dragging Thomas through your inane interrogations."

7

I have never been good at waiting. Everyone had gone upstairs through that searing white light and left me downstairs with my sooty paw. Rudy had disappeared, leaving only the trace of his nutty scent hanging in the air. I explored the downstairs unsupervised, but it wasn't that interesting. Looking at the talking spell in my mouth proved to be a bust—the damn thing cast no reflection in the bathroom mirror. Why hadn't I been able to see Cornealius' or Rudy's? Did magic age so it couldn't be seen after a time? I paced about the sitting room for a couple minutes, trying to cross my eyes to get a better look at the purplish glow covering my muzzle. The roof of my mouth was tender to the touch, so I let it hang open a bit to avoid irritating it. I could see the threads of the spell, thin curls of purple light in the dark, but could not see by it. When I licked my nose, I saw that my tongue itself had a sheen of purple magic as well.

The punctuations of a heated conversation between the two women upstairs drifted down to me, but nothing comprehensible filtered through the ceiling. I wondered why the two women seemed to detest each other so much. Or were all magi like territorial cats that fought over everything from food to boxes, and could I look forward to political tap-dancing for decades?

Pushing off the bathroom sink with a huff of disgust, I began to pad around the house in a directionless manner. Every corner and cranny seemed to collect a bewildering variety of scents. I couldn't place most of them precisely, but by flehming, opening my mouth to breathe them in through both my nose and mouth, I pulled the scents deeper into my brain. As a human, scents were a bit of a binary experience for me; I'd get one strong dominant scent. Now scents were different, layered and nuanced. I could mentally sift through them. By the door to the bathroom, Rudy's scent lay on the top of the pile. I followed it into a bathroom, a smaller half bath than the one where I had attempted to inspect the spell on my face.

The scent of fresh grass filtered in once I got the door open, and a stream of warm summer air tickled my whiskers. Positioned above the ancient clawed tub, a small divided window stood, just four panes of smoked glass. The morning sunlight streamed through a two-inch wide crack, beyond it a squirrel-sized hole in the screen.

I stared into that hole, noting how the day's breeze made a few hairs snagged on the wire blow back and forth in the sunlight. My thoughts drifted out, back into the world. How had this happened to me? My mind probed into the last day, looking for things I had overlooked. It all went back to the old man, who had to be another magus. O'Meara had said that a magus named Archibald had been murdered. What had the baristas called the old man? Archie? Archie the Archmagus, poor guy. And that horrible car accident— surely nothing about it had been accidental. The car had accelerated into the man. In that moment the entire scene flooded back to me. The spin of his body through the air tumbling towards me. His body striking my shoulder as I turned on inhuman ankles. The scent of his blood in my nose, and a metallic taste on my tongue from licking his cheek. His bony fingers seized a fistful of furry skin on my neck as he stared up at me, grinning a mad grin of triumph. "Got something in the cupboard for ya," he'd said.

Shaking myself, I blinked at the hole in the screen—that hadn't been how it had happened! Two parallel memories ran along side of each other. I remember the woman who had come out of the coffee shop behind me, and the terror in her face after I growled at her. Had I changed the moment the old man had gotten hit? How had I gotten back in my house?

Everyone since then had told me what would happen to me next. Maybe they were right. Perhaps I couldn't stop someone from just shipping me off to the TAU. But perhaps I could go see what the old man had for me in his cupboard before getting boxed up and shipped to Abu Dhabi.

Sitting back on my haunches, I studied the window and the sun's glare around it. It took a few moments to realize that the glare had nothing to do with the sun. Instead the entire window had a very subtle glow, a fraction of an inch beyond the physical window. I thought of the way the runes around the windows glowed as we drove in. This was the same shade. A ward? When I squinted I could almost make out tiny letters floating within the glow like motes of dust drifting in and out of a sunbeam. Well, I figured the squirrel had gotten out, and I did not detect the scent of charred fur. Was it just an alarm, then? Or perhaps one-way? Bracing for the shriek of an alarm, I pawed the window all the way open. It looked far too small to fit me and my 200 pound largeness. However, during my unemployment I had happened to watch many a video featuring cats squeezing through tiny holes. Surely cougars were merely overgrown house cats, right?

As it so happens, cougars are not house cats. Our heads are much smaller proportionally, so merely being able to stick my head through a hole is not indicative that I will fit. Fortunately the window was much wider than my head, so I only got stuck a little bit. I got my head and my front legs through and then had to twist myself sideways, my chest far too deep for the height of the window. With a little wiggling I managed to ratchet my rib cage through. Once the ribs were through, gravity took over a bit suddenly and I hit the ground with a pitiful mew of surprise and pain blossoming around my hips where the window had decided to keep a few tufts of fur for itself.

"Kitty!"

I turned towards the shout of delight as my paws levered me off the perfectly groomed lawn. An adorable child pointed a pudgy finger at me, her dark eyes bright with wonder as she rode on her mother's back in one of those child backpack things. The mother, however, did not share her child's love of large felines. Her dark skin went ashen as her eyes blinked once before going wide with terror. She thought fast though, throwing her hands in the air and waving them around.

I watched her do this dance for a moment. The child giggled as her mom bounced beneath her. I knew what she wanted me to do, but she was standing in the middle of Sabrina's driveway, my escape route. I could try to leap over the white picket fence, but the white pickets had tips that glinted with gold in my vision. The window hadn't fried me, but I didn't want to take another risk.

Waiting a moment changed nothing other than the

frequency of the woman's flapping. Had her arms been wings she'd be in danger of getting hit by a jetliner. I glanced back up at the window I had jumped through, it now occurring to me that waiting until dark might have been prudent. Too late now. I charged over the grass. As I brushed past the woman, she let out a shrill scream that might have shattered glass. I did not stop to check and concentrated on bounding across the street. As I dashed over a neighbor's fence, my mind divorced from my body. The bounding motions of my legs triggered that same creepy sense of pure wrongness that I had first experienced waking up. I nearly screamed in terror as I leapt up onto the roof with barely an effort. Parts of my mind hollered at my body, "I can't move that fast! I can't jump that!" as I ran over the roof and launched over the yard, and crashed into a huge stand of holly in the next lot.

Only then did I realize the woman had stopped screaming or at least was far enough away that the pounding of my own heart drowned her out. My tail twitched with the adrenaline flowing through me as images of trigger-happy police flooded my vision with shiny badges and jet-black shotguns. If Sabrina hadn't known of my escape the moment I jumped through the window, she knew it now. I had to keep moving. My place was about five miles away.

I kept to the backyards and woodlots the best I could as I bushwhacked my way home. The neighborhood seemed asleep. Most of the houses were dark and empty, and the remainder echoed with the sounds of small children. I stayed away from those. In about two hours the streets would be roamed by school busses and feral children would fill the yards. Now it appeared those parents who were home were enjoying the stillness of the early afternoon. I imagined how much harder it would have been to slip through the neighborhood twenty or thirty years ago, before the dual-income lifestyle became a way of life. The town was a commuter burb of the city, and most of the folk worked. I could just hear the sounds of cars start rolling home as I slipped into my backyard from the woodlot behind the small bungalow that Angelica and I called home.

My thoughts had been returning to Angelica the entire way home. I kept imagining what it would feel like to have her arms around my neck. I stared at the darkened windows of my home with disappointment. Angelica had not come home in the last few hours, nor would she for another four days.

I admit, the human me may have been a bit of a doormat for Angelica. Yet I wanted to at least see her one last time before I got whisked away to the magical pound and put up for adoption, and try to say good-bye no matter how poorly that would go. I'd often thought of getting a cat recently, but any time I broached that subject she'd make cracks about the various ways the cat would accidentally wind up in her cook pot. I always laughed it off as a joke, but she had licked her lips awfully convincingly.

The old man's place was probably the last place I wanted to be if I wished to avoid Sabrina and other wizard kind for a few days. But if the old man had actually left something useful for me, then it might pay off. That said, maybe the old man just wanted to feed the big kitty a nice can of tuna with his dying breath.

If so, I declared I would hate all wizards forever.

8

I had never popped over to the old man's house to borrow a cup of sugar for a reason. The eight-foot stone wall topped with iron spikes that separated his lot from mine communicated his stance towards visitors perfectly well. The tips of the spikes shone in such a way that Dirty Harry quotes reeled into my mind. I recalled that cougars had been known to jump ten to twenty feet high. *I should be able to clear it no problem, right?* I hunched down and prepared myself to jump, but videos of cats falling on their faces kept materializing in my brain as I gathered myself, including a very unfortunate one that had resulted in a cat being skewered through the leg.

No need to sweat, or in my case, pant, however. My yard was well furnished with several overgrown trees. Large and straight pines with lots of small branches—nothing I would have rated as a good climbing tree back when tree climbing had been a favorite activity, but maybe good enough now. Hoping that my claws were good for something other than ripping my bed sheets to shreds while panicking, I drifted over to the tree nearest to the stone wall. The trunk looked a bit thin, about five inches wide, but I didn't need to get up very high. After sinking my claws into the soft bark, I caught a whiff of an odd scent. It smelled like cut plastic. Looking closer at the tree, I found that a brown extension cord ran up the length of the trunk, nestled in the folds of the bark and held in place by rusting staples. Peering upwards, I spied a ball of leaves in the upper branches.

Just how long had Rudy been watching me? And how the hell could somebody who couldn't weigh more than five pounds operate a staple gun? I muttered to myself about having a squirrel burger the next time I saw the bushy-tailed maniac as I climbed, which for all my mental bitching proved to be a trivial affair. That was until I actually looked over the fence and into the Archmagus' yard and nearly fell right off the tree purely from shock.

"It's bigger on the inside," voices from *Doctor Who* exclaimed in my head. They were right. Through a hazy purple tint stretched a garden that belonged in an English manor. Rows of well-trimmed hedges seemed to stretch for miles beyond the fence, forming circular spaces around opulent statues and fountains. I could see the old man's little house but it sat in the distance, nestled under two gnarled oak trees that grew together over it, sheltering it with their combined foliage.

My fur prickled as I jumped over the fence, and my ears needed to be popped by the time I landed. It had been a much longer drop than I had been expecting, and my paws stung a bit from the impact. Shaking them out, I looked around.

On this side the fence had become a wall, perhaps thirty feet up, with no helpful trees anywhere near it. The air smelled wonderful—full of the scents of grass and piney hedges. Yet there was an emptiness to it, like a steak missing salt. Maybe it was just the lack of exhaust? I wandered down a cobblestone path, trying to stick to the main route. I gave the statues that lined the walkway a wide berth. Each one depicted a recognizable, but younger, Archibald with a large staff ornamented with a gem the size of my paw. They had a variety of costumes, ranging from business suits to monks' robes. Most of the Archies were accompanied by a small cat, but some had other animals with them. They seemed likely candidates for the type of statues that come alive and try to kill you when you're not paying attention. Whenever I stepped close, I saw glints of color flicker over their stone eyes.

Fortunately the statues did not seem to have any interest in killing me, although I swear a few of them shifted slightly to get a better look. If they were any more than decoration, then apparently the Archmagus had added me to the guest list. Or perhaps they needed the Archmagus alive to function. I kept my eyes peeled for any rips in reality or a tentacled monstrosity skulking around, but the garden seemed determined to keep its sunny disposition in the face of my paranoia. As I continued to trot for what was surely several miles along the hedges, I did not see a single living creature—not a bird, not bug, just plants and statues. As I drew close to the central maze, the hedges themselves animated. The leaves rustled as if something unseen moved through the leaves.

I talked at them and said hello, but they steadfastly refused to engage me in conversation. The old "rustle once for yes, rustle twice for no" suggestion produced zero rustles. I did provoke a reaction when I attempted to jump over a hedge in the maze. The plants grew about five feet while I set up for my jump, the branches reaching up and curling around each other like frenzied tentacles. The bushes were so intent on blocking my air that they left their bottoms defoliated enough for me to scoot through. The hedges turned a bit surly after that, aggressively putting dead ends in my way and forcing me to jump over them. Had you watched me from the house, I'm sure I looked a bit like a jackrabbit in deep snow, punctuated by a few cries of surprise as I jumped over a few hedges and into a fountain. By the time I flopped onto the ground beyond the maze, my tongue had become a tripping hazard.

I did what came naturally. I took a nap.

***

It had not been my intention to take a nap, but the sun had been warm and my paws wet, and my muscles argued against further movement. A blink, a deep sigh, and the sun had moved most of the way across the sky and threatened to duck behind the house. Yawning and stretching, I moved towards the building, my ears catching scattered threads of conversation. I could hear a woman's and a man's voices coming from inside, but I couldn't make out the words. The distorted voices sounded like the adults from Charlie Brown cartoons but far angrier.

I paced the house, looking for an opening. Unlike the garden, it was the same house that I walked past every day before I lost my job: a one-story ranch, probably three bedrooms or so. There was a screened-in porch sporting furniture from the seventies, all brown plastic and vinyl. The door had a large doggy flap in it, perhaps indicating that Archibald once had pets far larger than his cat. The windows were a no-go—the classic two-pane sliding windows were all solidly closed. Huge walls blocked me from going around. They completely encircled the garden up to the house. It would be easier jumping onto the roof and over than getting around them.

Two folks arguing in a dead man's home? Curiosity and a perchance for gossip drove me to rip through a screen window and try my luck with the doggy door. After all I had been invited, right? Carefully I batted the flap. It swung in and back with little resistance. The voices continued unabated.

On the other side I found myself in a kitchen, surrounded by a cage of glass tubing. It had clearly become a lab at some point in the distant past. The tubing spider-webbed around the entire room, stretching from a center table and reaching over to the counters that ran along the walls. The tubes connected to a bewildering variety of beakers and flasks. They were all filled with things: not really a liquid but distinct dots of colors flowing through the alternately wavy or angular pipes. I could see a few sealed beakers on the table that the dots were boiling out of, but I couldn't see any flame on them. Most of the tubing was above my level, but some reached down to and even through the floor.

The voices were more distinct here, and I recognized one as O'Meara's, heatedly arguing with a man who sounded Scottish. "Listen, Scrags! Whatever you and the Archmagus were hiding in here I don't care about. I'm just here to find out who killed him. Let me do my job." O'Meara's voice bubbled with barely restrained anger.

"And as I've been saying, you can wait your turn with all them other vultures. You or anybody else are not taking anything from this house until the wards collapse," the male voice hissed.

"I don't have time or the artillery to get involved in the battleground this place will be next week. This is my right as an inquisitor!" O'Meara's voice began to scale upward.

This didn't sound like a conversation that I needed to get involved with. All I needed to do was figure out what the old man had meant by something in the cupboard for me. The kitchen lab certainly had plenty of cupboards; most of their handles had a faint golden hue to them similar to the runes on Sabrina's house. Were they simply subtle or losing power? How would I know if a ward would open for me? If I chose wrong, would I be aged into dust while some ancient knight made an obvious statement as to the quality of my judgment?

"Why dicht ya prove it, then? Summon the seal. Go right ahead. Oh, right, you've got no familiar so you're just an overgrown matchstick!" the man retorted.

Fortunately my choices were actually slim; the glassware spidering around the kitchen didn't allow for many of the cabinets to open. I slowly weaved my way around the tubing towards a cabinet in reach near the sink as the argument in the next room escalated.

"Well, if you hadn't forgotten what happened in the last month I could just talk to you! But since you're barely coherent as it is. I have to get at Archibald's journal! Don't you want justice?" O'Meara snarled.

"I want you gone from my doorstep, Lassie! You've always been pokin' your nose in our business, waving your sword around. As if a pointed stick would have got you any respect. Don't matter who offed him. Ha! Justice? If there were justice the council would have been purged. There's no justice for a fallen magus; revenge and politics is all there ever was and all there ever will be."

A movement caught my eye. I turned and a chirp of surprise fled my throat before I could stop it. Two mis-shapen eyes stared at me from inside a beaker. They were composed of the same dots that swirled within the glass network, somehow congealed into two amber eyes, each filling a beaker, their pupils slit like a cat's, a surreal 3D pixel artwork.

The gaze settled on me like a weight, their expressionless stare somehow accusing. I watched them back for moment, waiting for the thing in the beaker to raise some sort of alarm. Nothing happened; the eyes just continued to stare back at me. Cautiously I turned back to study the cabinet. Tiny golden runes floated within the tarnished metal of its handle. Bringing my paw near it the light brightened, whether in warning or recognition I couldn't be sure. I could feel the eyes digging into my back, which I tried to ignore. In the front room I heard a door slam, O'Meara shouting vexations as she left.

Now or never. Carefully I extended my claws and hooked one on the underside of the worn kitchen cabinet, positioning myself to spring away in case it exploded. "My kingdom for an eleven-foot pole," I muttered under my breath and flicked open the cabinet.

It did not explode. Instead, the door swung open and cracked against a glass tube that prevented it from opening fully. The pipe started to hiss as a crack expanded along the length of the pipe. Holding my breath, I looked up into the cupboard to see a white index card hanging from the middle shelf. In shaky handwriting it read, "For Thomas Khatt," with an arrow pointing down. The shelf was too high for me to see inside, but there was a glint of metal just visible over the lip of the shelf.

"Who in the bloody hell is in there?" the Scottish voice shouted through the door, jarring me into action. I quickly pawed at the metal thing, hoping to pull it down onto the floor. Normally when you pull something off the shelf, inanimate objects have the common decency to respect gravity and fall. When a blur of sliver shot out of the cabinet, I reacted much like anyone else would have. I screamed, "*Snaaaaaake!*" and jumped back. Unfortunately when you're a cougar, jumping straight up isn't just a piddling white man jump. Instead I slammed myself into the ceiling through all the glasswork. That hurt, but not as much as hitting the floor afterwards, which knocked the wind out of me. Glass rained down around me, and those little dots of magic poured out into the air like neon confetti.

"What in the name?!" The door to the lab swung open as I tried to clear the stars from my vision—the ones that I was fairly certain were due to violence in my optic system, not the ones jetting out of the broken glassware, anyway. The world was blurry but cleared when I felt those odd third eyelids retract. Standing in the doorway to the kitchen was old Archie's tiny cat. His eyes were wide as he took in the destruction and then settled on me, narrowing into slits. His lips peeled back to show many more teeth than one would expect in a cat his size. "Who the fuck are you?" his voice boomed from his tiny body. My eyes searched for a burly Scottish ventriloquist but found none.

"Uh. Hi? I'm Thomas. Your next-door neighbor."

"Oh! And ah suppose you—" He stopped midsentence. "Damn, he actually did it. We actually did it. Bloody fucking goddamn hell! He did it and died! You fucking bastard, Archibald!" The growl that followed, high and tinny, was adorable. I couldn't fight the smile, and the little angry stomping of his tiny body made a laugh burst out from me. I saw him back at the coffee shop, splayed out on his belly, getting petted. Juxtaposing that cat and this was too much, and I just lost it. His eyes, which had grown distant, snapped back to me, flashing with anger. "And what do you find so goddamn funny about this?"

It just made me laugh harder.

Scrags charged up to me and flashed his many fangs. "You know what could be funny? Don't mess with me, lad! One bite and you'd be stone dead. That'd be real funny, wouldn't it?"

"Sorry," I gasped, "It's just—" I fought against a giggle fit and failed. "I never thought—"

I could see his fangs dripping a green ichor. "Never thought what?"

"I saw you and Archibald at the coffee shop at least once a week," I managed to wheeze out. "I just never imagined you'd be so . . . gruff. You always looked so at peace." The cat went dead still.

"You saw us? That can't, ugh . . . hell, you were human. On the other side of the Veil." The anger had gone away and the grief, the warble of being near tears, became plain. He shook himself and fixed me with a look. The spark of his previous anger reignited, but he looked tired. "Why are you here and"—he looked at the open cabinet and then back at me—"why are you not dead? That ward should have burned your eyes out of their sockets."

I winced at that imagery. "I was sort of invited?"

"What you bloody mean by that?"

"I was there when Archibald died. He was hit by a car."

"He was not killed by an automobile!"

"I—I dunno, it's all a little hazy. I think I changed the moment he got hit. He told me there was something for me in the cupboard."

"And you thought it was prudent to break in through the back?"

"Hey, I haven't had good luck with people since changing. I was sort of hoping it was something to change me back." As unlikely as that had been, my hopes always tend towards the unrealistic. I'm pretty used to them getting crushed. Speaking of what I had come here for, where had that shiny thing gone? I didn't see it after hitting the ceiling, probably because I had closed my eyes. I scanned the room, but among the spray of dots and shattered glass I saw no sign of its shine.

"Who have you met so far?"

"Uh, Sabrina and O'Meara."

Scrags laughed. "That's a load of rotten luck. Not that you could have had good luck in this town. Who claimed ya? Sabrina, right?"

"Uh, yeah. How did you—"

"Because you're not bonded to O'Meara. Otherwise she'd be here, rooting through all of Archibald's secrets. Now she gotta wait with all the other vultures."

"Would she bond me without my permission?"

The cat considered, leaning his small head first this way and that. "Maybe not, but she'd do anything to get it. She'd make any sort of promise, including ones she cannaught keep. She's desperate, lad, and you can never trust a woman who reeks of that." He stopped, peering at my neck. "So that's what you came for? That old thing?"

"What?" I started to ask, and then I felt it—something wrapped around my neck. I pawed at it, or tried to, but the best I could do was feel it with my wrist. A chain had looped itself around my neck three times. I pressed against it and felt the cool of the metal against my skin, but the chain itself seemed to have no weight of its own. "What the hell is it and how do I get it off?" I asked as I snared the chain with the claws of my back foot. A quick tug only led to a choking fit as the other two loops pulled taunt.

"Oh, it likes you. Great. Glad to have that damn thing out of the house."

"What the hell is it?"

"A fey chain."

I rolled my eyes. "That's not very helpful!"

"No, because it's not bloody useful to anyone. Fey chains got banned for a reason. They were used to bind familiars in ancient times before the modern binding method had been discovered. The bond they create is fragile and easy to disrupt; during the Second age, familiar theft was rampant. The life bond is much more permanent and comparatively nigh impossible to break." Scrags' accent was fading a bit as he got technical.

"Then why did Archibald want me to have it?"

Scrags exploded with a sputter of green spittle. "*I dun know! He's dead and it don't matter!*"

His sudden rage rocked me back onto my haunches. Faint wisps of smoke rose from the floor where the spittle hissed. "Ah, sorry. I didn't mean—"

The rage settled back into glower. "You have no clue. Do ya?"

"Uh, no."

He took a deep breath. "Then listen to a word of advice. Never, ever, let your bond look beyond the present. No matter how desperate it looks. No matter how much they beg, wheedle and bribe you. You say no. Walk away and take away their sight. Now get your arse out of my house. I've got a civil war to wait for."

"But—" The little cat was only creating more and more questions.

"No. You want a lecture, go join the TAU. Go home and go away." His amber eyes stared up at me, hard and unblinking, projecting an almost physical force. There was a hunch to his body, a deep pain weighing him down. I had so many questions I wanted to ask him, but there were clearly no more answers here for the moment.

Not seeing any other choice, I slinked out through the living room, which had been converted into an impressive library. The front door opened itself to let me out. Too occupied by the fragments that Scrags had given me, I crossed to my own house, not giving two shakes if a neighbor spotted me or not.

9

If I wanted to avoid Cornealius and Sabrina, my house was probably the last place I should be. Yet it had been hours since I had escaped from their house, so surely they had checked here already? A quick visit wouldn't hurt. Stick my head in Angelica's closet and just breathe her in before I went and did something dumb. Not that it would prevent me from doing something stupid, but it would have been a comfort. Angelica wasn't the sort of girl who actively discouraged stupidity. She'd just laugh at you for it. I'd always known it wouldn't last forever. Still it had been working more or less. Less when she wasn't with me and more when she was. Nobody had the right to stop that.

That and my freezer was still full of tasty meat. The distant yaps of a small dog were making me hungry.

I peered into my bedroom window. My laptop's screen glowed in the otherwise darkened room. A bag of Doritos lay open on my desk, several partially nibbled chips scattered across the formerly pristine surface of my desk. A righteous growl rolled through my body and I let it. The image of someone waltzing into my territory just helping themselves to *my* stuff struck a deep cord of revulsion. The sense of violation grew with every second.

Slipping in through the bathroom window was a bit of a contortion act, but I managed to fall into the tub without knocking over any of the empty shampoo bottles that I had collected on the rim of the tub. A smell invaded my nose, a scent out of place in the landscape of scents that I had left. My stomach growled, the steak I had this morning forgotten. The scent, whoever it was, tickled my taste buds. I listened, my ears roaming for a sound. A rustle of cellophane. Kitchen—it came from the kitchen.

Carefully, moving one paw at a time, I crept out into the bedroom and peeked down the short hallway. The sounds of a drawer rolling open greeted me, followed by the clatter of silverware being rooted through. The coast clear, I padded down the hallway and hunched low before the doorway, sliding on my belly the last few inches. Ever so slowly I eased my head around the corner. A bushy grey tail waved from the drawer where I kept the miscellaneous kitchen stuff.

"Ah, come on, doesn't anybody smoke anymore?" A muffled voice came from the drawer. I licked my chops as I gathered my body for a pounce. The chubby squirrel was gonna pay. Setting up my legs, I wobbled like a sprinter to secure my grip. As I did so the floor gave the tiniest of creaks. Rudy's head popped up from the drawer. I leapt.

Rudy watched as I crashed headlong into the cabinets over his head and the cheap wood splintered under my paws as I rebounded, my back legs slamming against the wall. My body acted without permission as my legs launched me back into the center of the room. The bruises I sustained back in Archie's house screamed as I skidded across the kitchen island and tumbled onto the floor in a heap.

Rudy's high-pitched titter filled my ears as I lay there for a moment before my injured pride picked me up from the floor, nothing but murder on my mind. Rudy had fallen over the front of the drawer, his small body convulsing with laughter. I hissed as I pushed myself back to my feet. He looked up at me, grinning with his four incisors. "That was awesome, Thomas! The look on your face and then—*blam*! You cats are never as cool as you think you are."

My only reply to that was a low growl. There was part of me that knew I wasn't thinking straight, knew what I was doing was wrong. The rest of me, the frustrated parts, the despairing parts, the utterly helpless parts, the hungry parts all wanted this squirrel, who was too stupid to notice that all the kitchen utensils were sorted by function and the drawer that had the lighter and all the other grilling supplies was right next to him. All those parts, they wanted him dead and in my belly. Everything about this morning was this squirrel's fault. Now there were talking weasels and angry little Scottish cats who wanted to box me off and erase my life. And if this squirrel had just given me a few hours to try to wrap my head around being a cat and figuring stuff out, then maybe I could have dealt with all of this. This was all Rudy's fault.

"Thomas?" Rudy asked, his eyes growing wide. "Ah, nuts."

I lunged at him and the squirrel turned into a fuzzy streak of lightning in my vision before my paws hit the drawer, catching only a few hairs instead of bisecting his midsection. Whirling, I launched myself back towards the hallway, trying to cut off his escape. The squirrel zigged and then zagged out of the way of my clumsy paws, which connected with only the barest fluff of his tail. He bolted down the hall, back towards the bedroom, and I scrabbled after him. Pain bit my addled brain as a claw snapped off in the hardwood floor.

Rudy was a good nine feet ahead of me by the time friction and I interacted, and he remained ahead of me as we charged into the bedroom. I lost sight of him as he dashed around the edge of doorway. I breached the door, my heart thundering in my chest. I saw no trace of movement in the room, so I looked for him with my ears, panning them about the room until—wait, yes, there. Under the bed, there was a tiny scratch followed by a fizz. Peeking under the bed, I found myself staring at the business end of a lit bottle rocket perched on the slope of one of my shoes. "What the—" I managed before the rocket caught and shot out towards me with a high-pitched shriek. A pain bloomed in my shoulder an instant before an ungodly loud bang shattered my ears. Pure panic shot down my spine, as a voice in my head screamed "Danger!" and shoved me aside. In an eye blink I had vaulted back through the doorway and dived behind the couch. My entire body shook as I crouched there, my claws dug into the rug, nose filled the scent of gunpowder and the slick of my own terror.

Slowly I felt myself settle back into my own body, as if it had shoved me out and had now decided to let me back in.

"Hey, kitty!" I looked up to find Rudy perched on top of my couch, wielding an iPhone. Its lens pointed directly at me. "One more for the scrapbook!"

"W-whu?" My mouth refused to work right. I swallowed, and my tongue felt odd.

"Are you done thinking with your brain?"

I got my tongue untangled. "What are?"

"Do you still want to kill me? 'Cuz if you do, I have more bottle rockets!" He moved the iPhone so I could see the harness he wore. I saw another bottle rocket, a set of fire crackers, assorted larger cylinders and a small red Zippo mounted over his heart. It was held to his grey fuzz by shiny black nylon. He looked like a pint-sized suicide bomber.

I gave him a sour look. "Kinda." He still looked rather plump and tasty.

He opened his mouth and withdrew a Dorito fragment from a cheek pouch. "I can live with that. Lots of my best customers kinda want to kill me."

"What are you doing in my house, Rudy?"

"I can explain! But! Before I do, you might want to pull the sheets off your bed. They're kinda smoldering."

"What!" Grumbling, I got up and hurried towards the bedroom. "You invade my home, mess up my desk and then set my bed on fire." Smoke was indeed rising from my bed, but there were no flames. Why hadn't the smoke alarms gone off? I looked up and found the bedroom smoke alarm hanging from the wires, the battery panel open. I shot Rudy a questioning look before starting to pull the bed sheet off the bed with my teeth.

"Hey, the bed was totally self-defense. The rest is all standard procedure. And if you think those are annoying to a human when they go off, you're in for a world of pain with cougar ears."

Standard procedure? I would have asked what that meant, but I had a mouth full of smoldering bedsheets. It hit me a moment later anyway. Dropping the sheet, I whirled towards Rudy, a sawing growl erupting from my chest.

Rudy's tail went stiff and puffy. His paws whipped out a bottle rocket faster than I could see. "Hey! *Think* with your mind! Not your brain!"

"You were going to burn down *my* house!" I snarled.

"Only once you had signed up with the TAU! Look, just

think about how pretty all that flame will be!" Rudy's gaze drifted off into space.

"I don't live alone!"

"So pretty!"

"Ruudy," I growled, raising a paw to strike the little pyro.

He instantly held up his paws in surrender. "Hey! Hey! No brain! Don't use the brain!"

"What the hell are you babbling about?"

"He is attempting to describe the fact that your human mind is far more intelligent than a feline brain," said an owl sporting a bowtie perched on top of my TV. "As usual he's doing a rather poor job of it."

I blinked and then stared. How the hell had he gotten in and how long had he been sitting there? Rudy slapped both paws into his face and shook his head. "Oh, for all the cashews in the world!" His tail suddenly bowed to gravity, hanging down behind his perch on the back of the couch. He gestured at the Owl "Thomas, meet Oric. Oric, meet a titanic pain in the ass puma who is hungry, grumpy and probably wants to eat us both at the moment."

"Hey!" I protested.

"Tell me it ain't true."

"Well . . ." Rudy did look like a snack from the right angle, and while Oric really wasn't much bigger, the thought of picking feathers out of my teeth didn't sound that appetizing at the moment.

Rudy crossed his arms. "That's the problem with you preds—you stop paying attention while you're hungry and it's *chomp*! Worst thing that happens to me if I stop paying attention is I wake up with my mouth full of nuts and my paws all muddy." He shot an accusing look at both Oric and me, the angles only made possible by his wide-set eyes.

"One must always be aware of one's instincts," the owl

agreed. "Now, Thomas, I'd didn't expect to find you here and not at Sabrina's, but this will work out just as well."

Rudy's face lit up at the mention of Sabrina. "Oh! I got a message for you. She's a bit cheesed off at you. That's kinda standard if you're breathing, but yeah, she and Cornealius are working on something at the moment. So you can either wait here for her to finish or come back to her place well after dark."

"Or?" I asked.

Rudy made a palms-up gesture. "She'll probably hunt you down, zap you unconscious and stick you in a cage until she hands you over to Oric here."

My ears went flat as I looked to the owl. "You're one of the TAU guys, aren't you."

"Thomas, Oric is *the* TAU guy. He started it like a millennia ago."

"One and a half centuries is hardly a thousand years, Rudy." The owl puffed up slightly. He didn't look that old, unless this particular species of owl wasn't usually pure white. "Anyway." He turned his attention to me and smiled, even though he didn't have lips to smile with—a part of the talking spell, I supposed. "You and I have a bit of business to discuss. An expedited alternative to cages and shocking."

10

I hunkered down, digging my claws into the floor. A tiny voice in my head shrieked about my rental deposit. "I'm not joining the TAU."

"Oh, kitten, we actually get that a lot from ex-humans." A new, sultry voice came from the prettiest cat I'd ever seen as she waltzed in from the bedroom. Her fur, pure white fur framed and ice blue eyes that froze my gaze onto hers.

"W-who, uh, are you?" My tongue felt loose, as if the speech spell was slipping off as the white cat strutted closer.

"I'm Cyndi," she purred, pressing herself against my forelegs, sending my entire body prickling with heat. "I'm TAU's regional representative. The boots on the ground, so to speak. How do you do?" she asked, encircling my paw with her long, very elegant, very attractive body, with a soft tail that just brushed the underside of my chin. I felt like a thirteen-year-old who suddenly found himself locked in a closet with a naked supermodel.

Rudy's chattering laughter broke the spell. My eyes strayed up from Cyndi to find the squirrel on his back, convulsing with laughter. "You should see your face!" He sobered for a brief moment to do an impression of me, hanging his tongue out the side of his mouth while widening his eyes so far that I could see the whites of his black beady eyes. "Oh, Cyndi!" He clasped his paws together and sighed before collapsing back into his laughing fit.

My ears started to burn as my brain replayed the last few moments. Cyndi made a mew of protest as I jerked my forelegs away from her and scooted backwards down the hallway until both her and Oric were in my field of vision. Cyndi, still pretty, looked put out and made a show of grooming her paw. "Sorry," I said, not entirely sure of what I was apologizing for, as I mentally tried to stuff many thoughts I had about her back into mental boxes that I should not possess. I was human, temporarily in the body of a cougar. Even so, a house cat should be on the menu, not someone you imagine eating spaghetti with like *Lady and the Tramp*. I tore my gaze off Cyndi and fixed my eyes on Oric. "What business?"

"Well, it's more of a question really," the owl said as if he was reading from a long memorized script. He craned his neck towards me and tilted his head a disconcerting ninety degrees. "And the question we need to answer is: Who are you?"

"What the hell is this? Some sort of life-affirming seminar?"

"The question is a little rhetorical. But the fact is you are not the man who dwells in this house." He opened his wings and gestured to the space around us. "This space is really not your work."

My lips were threatening to curl up from my teeth. "What the hell are you talking about?" I gestured at the bookcases next to the TV. "I spent hours alphabetizing those books! See that dent in the couch? That was made by my buttocks."

"Point is, and I'm sorry, Thomas, the man you remember being is dead. He is gone forever."

I opened my mouth to protest when a very warm body pressed up against my side and circled around my rump, making sure to step on the base of my tail, sending shivers up my spine. "Think about it, kitten. Think about the man you were. Would that man really have run out on Sabrina? Would he have had the guts? The Veil doesn't swallow humans of action. All that bravery in the face of the unknown? That's not the man, that's the cat." She was so warm, her voice so smooth, that my anger slipped away like melting ice cream between my fingers. "And you make a much better cat than a man—strong, handsome." She twisted herself around me, looking up at me with those deep blue eyes. "You'll be well loved, Thomas. We will find the perfect person to take care of you. All the meat you can eat, and a personal groomer so you don't have to taste where you've been every day."

It didn't sound so bad when she put it like that. Maybe she'd even come to visit me—she was so pretty with her bluish fur. Everything would be all right if I made her happy. But Angelica. Angelica would miss me. "I can't go," I protested meekly. "My mat- my girlfriend."

"Don't you worry about her. We take care of everything. Give your friends a story—let them grieve." My gaze drank in her beauty, and Angelica fell from my mind. How could anything else hold a candle to this creature, glowing with her divine blue light? My muscles soaked in her warmth like dry sponges as she entwined herself further around my front legs. "Now, are you ready to go, kitten?" Something small and red fell onto the little goddess's back, trailing a thin wisp of sizzling smoke. I looked at it.

Bang! Pain exploded in my head and then paws as the ground slammed into them. Danger! Danger! That other voice screamed in my head and seized control of my limbs, launching me into the bedroom, propelling me over the bed and pressing my body flat against the floor. Wherever this body had come from, it certainly did not like loud bangs.

"My *fur!*" Cyndi's voice screamed across the house. The acrid scent of singed fur followed a feline yowl. "I'll kill you, rodent!"

"Woah! Hey now!" Rudy shouted as a hollow thump echoed, followed shortly by the scrabble of claws and several angry yowls.

"Cyndi!" Oric hooted as I poked my head over the bed just in time to watch Rudy dashing into the bedroom, the white cat hot on his tail, a blackened spot on her back and murder clear in those ice blue eyes. Rudy zigged to the left with a bound and then zagged, the same move that he used on me not fifteen minutes ago. Cyndi turned but didn't follow the zig—she adjusted for the zag, barreling right at Rudy, her claws outstretched.

She missed. Rudy twisted his body at the last moment and her paws shot under him, his body rolling up her forelimbs. Her face smashed into the Zippo on Rudy's chest with a surprising loud *smeck!* Rudy shot under the bed, a fuzzy cannonball, while Cyndi somersaulted head over tail. She came up snarling, her intentions clear as she prepared for another pounce.

"Cyndi, stop this at once!" In a flash of purple Oric appeared in front of the enraged cat, wings spread to form a wall between her and Rudy.

"Out of my way, Oric!" Cyndi hissed, and then sneezed out a fine red mist onto the floor.

"This is not the way to conduct a recruitment! I told you to stick to the rules! No charms." His head rotated 180 degrees to flash me a nervous smile. "I do apologize for Cyndi's behavior. And Rudy, please put the lighter away; I'd like to keep what remains of my hearing."

Cyndi's eyes narrowed, her rage focusing entirely on owl. "You double-crossing mite-ridden meat sack."

"I'm afraid I have to put you back on probation, Cyndi, for unethical behavior."

Cyndi leapt at him with a sawing hiss. Yet the fight ended before she landed. In a blink, Oric disappeared and reappeared directly above the cat. One taloned foot seized her by the scruff, and the other slammed her head into the floor.

She let out a low mrowl of pain.

"Cyndi, you should know better than this. You're lucky you're small enough for me to pin, otherwise I'd have to rip out your eyeballs." Oric spoke in the tone of a bored waiter listing the specials. "I'm very sorry, Thomas, for this breach in professional decorum. We'll have to table our conversation for a later time. Adieu."

With a very soft pop, he disappeared, taking his companion with him, leaving a faint purple afterimage in my vision. I blinked it away with a growl of disgust. *That was the* TAU?

Rudy emerged from under the bed with the soft click of a closing Zippo. "Well, that went about as well as I thought it would when the TAU made *her* an officer."

My head was in a total jumble, still grappling with the idea that the pretty cat had been screwing with my mind, and I couldn't be sure everything still worked. A part of me still craved the little cat's warmth. "What the hell did she do to me, Rudy?" My voice was a whisper.

"Oh, she hit you hard with her little trick."

"She had me wrapped around her little finger, Rudy. That hardly qualifies as a trick. I didn't think familiars could do magic."

"It's not magic—it's more a talent, like magi and their anchor. They called Cyndi's former master the Mind Twister before she kicked the bucket two years ago. If you're with a magus for a while, you pick up a few tricks of your own. It ain't predictable, and it ain't even always useful. Have you heard about O'Meara's first familiar, Rex, the one who got himself executed by the council of Merlins?"

"Uh, no."

"It's a sad story, bro. Anyway, his talent? His dog breath was so bad it ignited flammable stuff. O'Meara had to get him a fireproof bed. That was it. No fireballs, no gout of flame, just a little flick of fire if he wasn't paying attention. I slipped a string of firecrackers under his nose once." Rudy tittered with the memory. "Oh, man, did he yelp."

I hoisted myself up onto my feet with an eye roll. "While that is certainly illuminating, I already knew you had a sadistic streak, Rudy." My stomach had begun to recover from the shock, and Rudy's scent stoked the burgeoning hunger in my belly. I meandered back towards the kitchen.

The squirrel followed, still prattling at me. "Anyway, I couldn't let those two take ya like that. I'd never ever get paid that way. If the TAU brings you in all on their own, they don't have to share any of the tass you collect. You're still Sabrina's claim even if she's too busy to come pick you up."

"She knows I'm here?"

"Well, if the old fossil had a cell phone, she would, but

lucky you, she's barely mastered the telephone line so far. Electronics and the lightning lady don't get along."

"So they don't know I'm here."

"It's kinda obvious that you'd come back here after you finished sulking. Where else are you going to go? Live in the forest? The deer would die of laughter with your pouncing accuracy." Rudy gestured to the shattered cabinetry as I pawed open the fridge.

"Har har." I dug into the refrigerator, looking for survivors of this morning's rampage. Not being able to go to a grocery store alone would drive me back to Sabrina's within a few days if I couldn't find a way to restock my meat supply. I looked at up at Rudy, perched on the top of the fridge. I might have licked my chops.

"Holy Walnuts, Thomas, eat something. That look of yours is making me twitchy. Even more than the stink of this place usually does."

"You can work a keyboard, can't you?"

Rudy turned his head to stare at me with one black eye. "Yeah?"

"Sabrina owes you an iPhone for watching me, right?"

"Yeeeeaah?"

"Look, I can double that."

"I'd love to see where you keep your wallet. Are you secretly a kangaroo?"

"No! Look, Thomas Khatt is still a legal entity. You can use my laptop. Help me make my rent payment that's due in four days. I have a few stock funds that my parents set up that I've managed not to tap yet. If we cash those out . . ."

The squirrel's tail drooped as I continued to plead, trying to find some way, any way, to hang on to my human life. He shook his head sadly. "And what happens when your girlfriend comes back? What you gonna do? Stand on your hind legs and say the whiskers are a fashion statement? Thomas, the Veil don't work like that. You're on one side or the other, and you're on this side. It sucks. Most magi are either greedy horrible people or insane, especially the few in this town. When Oric comes back, walk to the TAU under your own power. He'll be eager to sweep Cyndi's charm attempt out back and bury it under a tree. Then you got a halfway decent chance of getting a newbie who's not spoiled."

I didn't have much to say to that other than to growl grumpily. There had to be a different option. There had to be.

11

Add desperation to the things that make squirrels disappear, because after several minutes of making a second attempt at explaining how he could help me pretend to be human, I realized that he had skedaddled. Probably right up that tree with the extension cord wrapped around it.

Damn it—couldn't anyone in this world be polite enough to listen to me think up panicked half-baked plans for solving my situation? I slunk onto the couch, giving a significant look to the empty space where Angelica would sit. She'd listen to me, or at least nod politely, while being sure to mock my weakness later. From her empty spot my gaze shifted to the Xbox controller sitting on the coffee table, my usual coping mechanism. I looked at it, looked at my freakishly large paws and laughed. Mother would be thrilled to hear that brain-wasting video games were off my list of activities until I found somebody to install a brain-machine interface in my noggin.

Had I been a proper cat it would have been the perfect time to take a nap; but instead, I paced the house, point-lessly bouncing back and forth between the bedroom and the kitchen like a tawny-colored Koopa shell. I jumped at every car that rolled down the street, fearing it would be Sabrina coming to collect me. But as the sun began to kiss the trees on the horizon, the iron godmother and her weasel had yet to make an appearance.

I found myself staring into the bathroom mirror. The triangular face staring back at me still triggered that sensation of wrongness as I looked at it. Yet how much longer would that last? I'd been quadrepedal for a day and my body felt like I'd been born in it. At this rate, one or two more days and I'd be sticking my tongue where the sun don't shine without a thought about it. My paw that had been covered with soot this morning had nary a mote of dust on it. And I couldn't even remember when I had groomed it.

Oric had said the man I had been was gone. There certainly wasn't much trace of him staring back at me in the mirror. I studied my eyes, looking for a glint of humanity in my amber orbs. If eyes were windows to the soul, then my soul appeared to be feline. My tongue was still purple with magic, although it had faded considerably since the morning.

I had begun to turn away from the mirror when a silver glint caught my eye. The chain! I had nearly forgotten about it with the whole rodent preparing to set my house on fire thing. Rudy certainly hadn't mentioned it, and no wonder—the collar had become nearly invisible. The actual chain itself had thinned from its former girth of industrial-strength chain closer to the width of a piece of jewelry. Unless I pawed at my neck, the only hint of the chains was a ruffle to the fur as if it had grown around a scar. Scrags' warning about bonds looking into the future might mean the old man had known I'd need the chain, but for what?

Slumping down onto the floor of the bathroom, I ran

through my options. I could stay here and wait for somebody to collect me. I could run off into the woods, live as
a cougar and hope I was smooth enough to avoid getting
shot by an excited hunter come hunting season. Or I could
go back to Sabrina's, let her collect my bounty and do as I
was told with a bit of dignity.

Really, what did I want? Failing getting my body back,
finding a job and getting on with my life, I needed to do
one thing. Say good-bye.

I went to my laptop and pawed at the keyboard until
the screen lit up. Rudy had created a new account on it
called RoastedNutz. I stared at the keyboard and then at my
paw, which nearly took up half the keyboard if I slammed
it down among the keys. Carefully I flexed out my claws
and spread my fingers. It took more than a few tries, but
I eventually switched to my account and pecked out the
password with my broken claw. Using the touch pad proved
to be a much more difficult problem than typing. My paws
felt like oven mitts, and the cursor would jump to the left
or right whenever I tried to click. Eventually I gave up on
the paw and used my nose.

This took me hours, and by the time I finished sending
those emails, the world outside my windows had faded to
grey. I closed the laptop with a feeling of accomplishment.
Perhaps I wouldn't be so reliant on thumbed persons after
all?

Popping out the bathroom window, I found my neighborhood huddled in silence, a single upstairs light on in a
house way down the street. It occurred to me that it had
become Tuesday while I had been struggling to write those
emails. In a few hours I would be missing a job interview.
A job interview I had been attempting to land for months
with a job that could have turned things around for me.

Daring fate a little, I wandered down the road to find myself sitting in front of the Archmagus's house. Its white walls glimmered in the moonlight. In fact, the entire house seemed illuminated compared to the others on the block. The more I looked at it, the brighter it appeared to be. Its light crept into the ground and spread into the neighboring yards, mine and the Wilsons', who had three kids. Had their life been affected by the house as well? Another layer peeled away before my eyes, as if the house were an onion, and it glowed even brighter; veins of energy pulsed the walls and exuded a heat that penetrated my fur. Golden runes danced and flowed.

Dozens of magical tendrils reached towards the house, seemingly from nowhere. The runes slashed out from the house and shredded any of the tendrils that dared come too close, like a swarm of angry piranha/goldfish hybrids.

I see you. A blinding white light flashed in my vision as the thought exploded in my brain. Bright as Sabrina's arc but focused on me with intent. It didn't just shine—it probed, dug into me and pulled at my thoughts. *You.* An image flashed in my head of myself, pushing carefully through a doggy door. I recognized this thing, the presence; I had felt it on my back in that very room and seen its eyes in the jar. This force was the same but so much more powerful. Why was it so much more now?

You know nothing. I felt it brush against my mind, showing me a glimpse of something large, something I could not see but that threatened to drown me in itself. I may have whimpered out loud—I certainly did mentally. Sabrina had some interesting moves but she was human, so very human. This thing was far beyond my understanding, larger than any single human's comprehension.

Still I couldn't help but try. "What are you?"

A series of images flickered: a cage, a collar, a yoke, all strained to the point of shattering. Then it flashed me being led on a leash. *Kindred.* The sheer desperation of it clawed at my thoughts. It showed me its bottomless rage at the bars that restrained it, compressed it. Pain as pieces of itself were constantly being torn from its body and dissolved. It shared the pain, just a taste of it. *Help me!* it pleaded, screaming in my head.

Then it was gone.

"Stupid kitten!" something hissed in my ear. Slowly I became aware of something soft tickling my nose, and I sneezed. Instantly light came back into the world. "*Gross!*"

I blinked and found the pretty white cat, Cyndi, glaring down at me, glowing blue faintly.

I recoiled so fast that my mind caught up to my body in midair. I came down with a hiss, every hair on end. "Turn it off!" I growled.

The blue died as she scrambled backwards, hissing and puffing up into an angry fluff ball, the black ring of singed fur on her back snapped back into focus. We both stood there, bearing our fangs at the other. "Ungrateful cub. I just stopped your eyeballs from getting burned out of your head!" she spat.

"Thank you. Now don't muck with my head!" I replied through clenched teeth.

She opened her mouth, closed it and then sighed. "It was only a little bit. Think of it like human makeup."

"No." My tail lashing. "You want to talk, fine—but no blue or . . ." I didn't finish the threat because saying I'd run away as fast as my legs could carry me sounded lame in my head. Had Rudy not intervened I'd be on my way to TAU boot camp by now.

"Oh, fine." Instantly she relaxed and began cleaning a

paw. "You better be polite, though. I did just save you. And here's another free tip: don't deep scry the ward made by an Archmagus. They'll scry right back."

"Apparently." That didn't jibe with what happened. It had been more of a conversation. I put my own pointy bits away, but my muscles remained coiled. "What do you want? I thought Oric and you went back to TAU, wherever that is."

She smiled. "Oric can't go far with a passenger, and I'm not without transportation options." She started to slink towards me but stopped with a slight hiss of pain. "We have tiffs every once in a while, but Oric and I always patch it up in the end."

"Your point?" I showed her the points of my claws.

Cyndi scooted backwards. "Jeez, you must be fun at parties. Look, so you're not quite the marshmallow I took you for. There doesn't need to be hard feelings."

"I'll say this real slow: What. Do. You. Want."

"My cut of your auction. You were born on my turf. We can even go around the TAU. Not everybody is a member of the Merlins."

"Not interested unless you have a way that lets me stay here and resume my old life." Which would be awkward since I had just sent everyone rather curt and vague "good-bye forever" notes.

The white cat rolled her eyes. "I'm so glad I was never human. The thumb fetish you all have is so undignified. Look, Thomas, magic makes almost everything possible. You want to stand on two legs again? It can be done. You want to mutilate those fine paws of yours? It can be done. But it takes work and you can't do it on your own. You need a magus."

"I need my life back."

She smirked. "I swear you are the most stubborn

changeling I have ever encountered. Most changelings jump at the chance for a new life with a fresh start. The Veil typically only allows those who have been totally isolated to transition to the truth. But then you are proving to be anything but typical." She looked back at Archie's house. "Perhaps there are reasons for that. You can feel it, can't you?"

"What?" Did she know about the thing in the wards?

"Archibald founded this little town. There was nothing here before he came; there are no leylines, no tass deposits and no natural crossing points."

"I have no idea what you just said."

"He brought something here—he had a source of magical energy. Nobody has any idea how he did it. Every magus in this cursed town was brought here in some way by him, and all of them hunger for his power."

"The tendrils?"

"Probing spells, trying to get an image of what's inside. Cheaters. It's futile, though. Any probe strong enough to get through those wards will be traced to the caster. Even half senile Archibald knew how to defend his secrets, even if he forgot to defend himself."

"When's the auction?"

"You'll be long gone."

"When."

"The new moon. Without an anchor, a magus and a familiar together, those wards will be washed away like sand. And daylight will show what Archibald has been hiding from us."

In my mind it wasn't so much what as who. I looked at the house, careful not to *really* look at it. The memory of bits being ripped away fresh in my mind, I knew exactly where the Archmagus had gotten his power. If the auction happened, whatever was in there would just have a new master and would go on suffering. Maybe Cyndi was right—there was nothing I could do to cling to my old life. But perhaps, just perhaps, there was something I was supposed to do before I started a new one.

I needed to know what was around my neck, what Archie had saddled me with and why. Everyone I talked to wanted me out of here, either out of harm's way or just because I was a profit in their eyes. Maybe it was time to get some answers.

I stood and started to pad away from Cyndi and the house.

"Where the hell you heading off to?" she called after me.

"Going hunting," I mumbled, and broke into a sprint.

12

Moving forward under my own power felt good. If I wanted a different deal I had to find it. Only one person I had met so far might give me a chance. Scrags had said bonds made with the fey collar were easy to break. I could treat that as a feature. O'Meara might be desperate enough to try.

Step one, find her. I knew her scent, a mixture of burned cinnamon and smoke, but there was no hint of it in the night air. Lacking any better plan, I headed for downtown by bushwhacking my way through backyards and woodlots. Suburban houses gave way to the blocky-looking stores and parking lots of what amounted to the town's urban center: mostly a couple of four-lane roads with a scattering of strip malls of various sizes and occupancy rates.

There was also far less cover. Where a road or building wasn't, there was either a metal barrier, cut grass or a drainage ditch. Here cars were on the road, not many but enough to make getting spotted a real possibility. My first thought was to approach the obstacle as if I were playing a stealth game. The second thought was just how many times I tended to get my character killed while playing those games. While in a town like this one folks are more likely to reach for a camera than a gun, if I had any chance of staying here long-term, I probably didn't need to show up in a local wildlife enthusiast blog. I sheltered on the forest's edge and considered. I knew O'Meara's scent but I also knew her aura. I had actually seen it *through* Sabrina. Could I see it through walls as well? At several points I had been able to "dig" into the structure of wards, both Archibald's and Sabrina's. Would it be possible to look for faint sources of magic by looking more broadly?

The thought appealed. Still, Sabrina's arc had been less bright with a wall or two in between me and it, so solid objects seemed to have some blocking effect on the "light" of magic. I'd have to get up higher.

Grantsville didn't exactly have much in the way of vistas, though. The highest thing in our "downtown" was the plaza's big old sign, which was designed to be visible from the nearby highway. Really it was meant to be looked at rather than from, but I doubted any residents even looked at the sign any more.

According to Angelica, whose family had lived here longer than the dirt beneath my paws apparently, the plaza was the oldest thing in the town. The structure was a short, squat rectangle of stores surrounding a cracked and pitted parking lot. The newest box store, a Kmart, had ripped out its original facade and put in its own bright white and red design, but the rest of the plaza still sported the original wooden pillars supporting a tiled roof over a dimly lit walkway. All the rotting wood paneling was painted the same poop brown. The plaza itself was on top of a rather steep slope, and to enter it your car had to climb a thirty-degree incline. That hill, combined with the three-story tall sign, made it the tallest structure in my suburban town.

And I wanted to climb it. The tip of my tail twitched with the very idea. A pox on the witches and the magi, and screw animal control. I was going to climb up on the top of that sign, perch myself right over that giant red K and find O'Meara, one way or another. Sabrina and Cornealius could be as displeased as they'd like. Maybe ultimately I would be a familiar, but that would happen when I was ready, not as soon as Sabrina and Cornealius could cram me into a crate. I blew a raspberry in their general direction.

I made my way to the plaza through the drainage ditches, grimacing not so much at the sensation of mud clinging to my paws but at the anticipation that if I wasn't vigilant I would find out what that mud tasted like. I recalled reading somewhere that cats have a very poor sense of taste. I really hoped that would prove true. Where the ditches wouldn't conceal me I waited for the coast to clear and dashed. There weren't many cars but there were enough to prove a bit of a challenge.

By the time I reached the plaza, it had become a game despite my earlier misgivings. I crouched down next to the town's busiest intersection, my chest heaving as I sucked in the cool night air. The cars, only about one or two at a time, sat at the intersection like unaware sheep, their shiny windows reflecting the harsh glare of the flickering street lamps. I looked up at my quarry. The sign stood on a sparsely vegetated island, its two timber legs stuck into the ground, hazy in the waning gibbous moonlight. A pair of halogen lights on either side of the sign illuminated its twin faces. They gave off a constant hum like a pair of huge mosquitoes.

I counted the seconds with the twitch of my tail as I waited for the intersection to clear. One car, two, one, zero. My coiled muscles exploded, launching my body up the hill. My feet touched the ground only for minute course corrections as the wind whistled through my whiskers. I impacted the cedar mulch of the planter for a brief moment before ricocheting upwards. Gravity let me go briefly as the side of the sign approached. I slammed my paws into either side of the timber, and a wave of euphoria swept over me as my claws bit deep into the wood. Getting to the top of the sign from there was as easy as walking down the street.

It took a few moments to notice the purr in my throat over the heavy breaths, but it matched my mood. There had been no disconnect this time, no letting the meat in my head handle the details. I had just scaled a three-story sign! Top that, world!

I drew myself up to a sitting position, enjoying the breeze ruffling through my fur, and looked out onto my little town. The streetlights craned over Main Street, illuminating it with alternating dots of light. To either side of the streetlights signs illuminated a myriad of businesses. Some buildings were built in the same drab style as the plaza itself. Nestled among them were newer, brighter rectangular buildings with signs that were lit from within instead of by spotlights trained on them from the ground. Beyond Main Street the darkness swallowed the rest of the town. Only the movement of an occasional car on the road illuminated people straggling home from friends or bars.

This town was populated with asshole magi apparently, but there were plenty of good people here too. However, there was one magus at least who smelled good to me. Squinting, I tried recalling how I'd looked into the wards back at Sabrina's. Nothing happened immediately, but as I waited, colors began to fade into existence. A soft golden hue came from a building in The Commons, a sort of low-rent shopping center where small businesses went to slowly dwindle into bankruptcy. Until recently it had actually hosted a video rental shop. I concentrated on the light in The Commons, and it slowly came into focus as several dots of color: two green and one red. I recognized the red hue. O'Meara's precise shade of red.

I gave a little chirp of cheer.

Unexpectedly an awed voice drifted up from below. "Holy shit, Bob, look at that." A quick glance into the lot below revealed a cop car parked not one hundred feet from the sign, just beyond what you could see from the intersection. A thin-faced cop had his head poked out the window and stared directly at me, jaw hanging wide enough to sling a cue ball into it. I hunkered down and flattened myself against the sign, knowing that it was too late. I had hoped the parking lot would be deserted or just occupied by a few bored, and preferably stoned, teens. Cops, though—cops had guns. Furthermore, getting down could be much trickier than getting up. Maybe the cougar brain knew how far I could fall without hurting myself, but I sure as hell didn't.

"Look at what?" A second, much less hushed voice asked.

"On the sign! There's a cat on the sign!"

"So? Call the fire department."

"Bob, it's as big as Billy."

"What? You're nuts. Where?" I tried to will myself into a two-dimensional shape. It didn't work. "I see a lump on the sign."

"Fuck. Hand me the flashlight."

My purr had turned into a growl of frustration as my ears began to burn with embarrassment. I risked a look at the cop car and got a face full of halogen light searing my retinas.

"Woah, Jesus, he's a biggie."

I looked away from them, trying to see past the multi-colored streak across my vision.

"Should we call it in?"

"Nah, we'll just use the shotgun. Handgun might just piss it off. Load some slugs."

Rifle? Oh, hell. Now I wanted that disconnect to happen, to save me. I willed it, but my body stayed stubbornly under my own control. I heard the pop of the squad car's trunk. No time. I stared down at the ground, swallowing back bile. It certainly looked too high. But between the fall and the gun, maybe if I broke my leg they'd call wildlife rescue instead of putting me out of my misery. Yeah, right.

I didn't leap. It was more of a hop and gravity did the rest. A brief rush of air, and then a hard jolt as my paws slammed into the ground. For a moment I just stood there, my brain frantically toggling between disbelief and shock. The squawk of the police officers, followed by the swishing clack of a sliding bolt, sent me scrambling forward. With a panicked scream I practically tumbled down the hill. The night air behind me filled with curses. I didn't stop. I didn't look. I just charged out into the street and through the beams of two headlights, registering them only as a flash in my peripheral vision. The screech of tires was already behind me as I vaulted the grey metal crash barrier. I sprinted across the Chase Bank parking lot and through the drive-through teller. Chest heaving, I dashed around the corner of the building and waited in the shadows. Only once several tons of brick and other construction materials were between me and the cops did the pounding of my heart start to recede from my ears.

Poking my nose around the corner, I saw the two cops standing beneath the sign. The bigger of the two had a rifle cradled in his arms. Although not pointed at me, I could see him looking in my general direction. They'd seen where I had run to.

I needed more distance. Keeping the building between me and the cops, I dashed into the bushes behind the bank along an ivy-covered chain-link fence. The top of the sign was visible from this position but not the cops. Taking a deep breath and maybe saying something like a prayer, I scaled the fence and fell into the next lot, a twenty-four-hour gas station. The high-pitched scream of a woman hit my ears like a hammer. I looked up in time to see the door slam shut on a Ford Fiesta as the engine started with the hose still in its gas tank. The woman peeled out, kicking up stones that stung my nose, and a sharp snap split the air as the fuel hose broke away from the pump.

"Hey!" a hoarse voice called out from the door to the Quickie Mart. "Hey!" the attendant shouted at the car as it screeched into the road with no headlights on. "Aw, goddammit!" He never saw me circle around the back of the building.

There was just a grocery store parking lot to pass through and I'd be at the Commons. The grocery store parking lot was empty of everything but a few rats, which scurried between the sparse parking islands, and I arrived at The Commons without any holes in my body. While much newer than the Plaza, The Commons always reminded me of a trailer park for small businesses. The grounds were divided into three separate parking lots with six to eight storefront units around each. Adding to confusion were a few stores nestled between these areas, which were nearly impossible to see unless you knew about them beforehand. All of the buildings looked identical, with grey Cape Cod–style shingles and dirty white trim. It did, however, have much more greenery than the Plaza, and I was able to creep into the cover of a foul-smelling tree to rest. The adrenaline had waned, revealing a deep bone ache in my front legs.

13

The faintest trace of burned cinnamon wafted into my nose at the same time that I heard the gravel crunch beneath a black and white cop car pulling into the parking lot. It didn't appear to be the same car from the plaza, as the cop that rolled down the driver-side window was a leathery-faced woman with an angry squint to her eyes. She balanced her flashlight on the windowsill and flicked it on. Slowly she scanned the bushes by the driveway and began to sweep the light towards me.

Panic crawled down my spine like a swarm of icy bees. Didn't these cops have more important things to do than look for a cat? Answer: probably. But given that this town hadn't seen a cougar in over a hundred years, playing hunt the kitty was probably less boring than giving out traffic tickets in the middle of the night. The corner of the building stood about twenty feet away from me, with a sign declaring that Ralph's Barbershop was just around the corner. A quick dash and I'd be out of the lady cop's sight, but with only a few sparse saplings for cover she might see me.

I wish I could say I made a decision, but really the beam

of light passing over my hiding spot decided for me. At first, I thought I was safe as the light passed, but the blinding light quickly returned. The cop gasped. I bolted.

My whiskers saved me from smacking directly into the wall. I raced along the side of the building, cursing the cop and her flashlight. A light appeared, a subtle glow that seemed to shine through my addled retinas. Magic, some sort of magic. I veered towards it as the growl of an engine sounded behind me. "It's here! At The Commons!" the cop lady shouted.

A voice crackled back, "Well, one more cougar there and you'll have a genuine cougar party, May."

"Just get over here, you pussy!" she barked back at her radio.

Sprinting across the parking lot towards the light, I vaulted across her headlights and skidded to a stop in front of the dog groomer, where the light seemed to be coming from. I pawed at the door for a moment before realizing that it was more distant.

I heard the pop of a car door and glanced back at the cop, gun in hand, stepping out of her vehicle.

Had it been an option, I would have put my paws up and surrendered. Instead I jumped, hooked my claws onto the roof and scrambled up. I heard a pop and a thud. I heard her curse as I landed on the other side of the building. The scent of burned cinnamon was stronger here, tasting like hope. The source of the light that was my salvation belonged to a seedy-looking electronics store, its windows plastered with neon signs and traveling lights. It glowed warmly, as if the interior was lit with magic. A chain of golden orbs floated just below the roof like lanterns.

And there, through the glass door, I could see O'Meara, outlined with her warm red aura. I hoped she'd be happy to see me because I ran for that door with all the propulsion my body could muster. "Open the door! Open the door!" I shouted as I shot across the parking lot. Either they were going to open it or I was going through it.

Mercifully the door swung open at the last possible second, and I zipped into the building with far more momentum than the tile floor had the friction to stop. The ground below me disappeared for a brief moment as said momentum introduced me to the hardness of a wall. I opened my eyes just in time to see a rack of cell phone cases fall on my head.

"Thomas?" O'Meara's eyes looked about to pop out of her head. "What the hell are you doing here?"

"Hoping you'll save me from becoming a wall mount at the local police department?" I joked weakly. My brains were starting to piece to together where I was, and I registered a second pair of eyes on me. Green-slitted eyes set within the face of an orange tom looked down on me, twinkling with amusement from the top of the glass counter I had crashed into.

"Cops?" O'Meara's head snapped around to look out the window, and then back at something on the countertop. "I need that coffee cup." She strode to the counter, plucking a paper cup from its surface.

"Hey, that's—!" a male voice protested from behind the counter.

"Ice cold," O'Meara said as she dumped the coffee out into a plastic-looking shrub at the far end of the counter. After pulling out a magic marker, she scribbled something on the bottom of the cup before shoving it in my face. The coffee had been in it so long that the wax had broken down, staining the paper brown. "Bite it and get up."

My gaze flicked to her face, which brooked no argument, and back at the cup. It stank of coffee and chemicals.

"Bite it on the rim."

Cautiously I did so, steeling myself against taste of it. I bit where she instructed so than the cup was held over my nose. It took a bit of an effort not to gag on the scent. Not that it was an awful scent, but there was so much of it. I didn't have much time to dwell on it, though. O'Meara dug under my back, flipped me over and hauled me up onto my feet by the scruff of my neck with a grunt of effort. It happened so fast I wondered if I had somehow been tele-ported onto my feet when the door slammed open. May, the officer, stood in the doorway, panting and holding a four–D cell flashlight in her hand like a medieval mace. Her eyes fixed on me.

"What the hell? Get away from that!"

O'Meara's hand swept across my head and neck. "This is my dog, officer. I'd never have a wild animal as a pet."

The cop's eyes narrowed. "Your dog?" she said, drawing out the word as if it didn't quite make sense. I circled behind O'Meara, hiding as much as I could behind her girth.

"Why, yes. He barked and scared away the cougar you're looking for."

The confusion disappeared from the cop's face. "Ah, well, he is a big one. I wouldn't want to tangle with him either." She looked up at the man behind the counter, a thin man with dark copper skin, closely cropped hair and a neatly trimmed goatee, his eyes peeking over dark circles. "Open late, Jules?"

He gave her a weak smile. "I'm always open, Officer May."

"Uh huh." She nodded to the tom lounging on the counter, pulling my eyes back to him. I had to stare a little. Never in my life had I seen a cat so huge. And I'm not talking huge in like a tiger is large. This tom was so fat that smaller cats might orbit around the fellow. "You might want to be careful with old Jowls—he'd be a tempting snack."

Jules snorted. "Only if the cougar has an artery that needs plugging."

"Heeeey!" said the cat, apparently named Jowls. "I'm fit as a fiddle!" The cat pulled himself to his feet, his girth hiding more than half the length of his legs.

"Yes, I know, Jowls. You are lovely and adorable," the cop said. Then with a suspicious glance at me and good-night to everyone else, she went back outside, talking to her radio as soon as the door closed behind her.

14

With a sigh of pure relief I collapsed back down on the floor and spat out the cup. It bounced once and rolled across the floor, displaying what appeared to be a cartoon dog's nose on the bottom. I boggled at it. I had suspected some sort of rune or minor spell, but that just didn't make any sense. The cup didn't even shimmer. I wanted to ask how, but the heavy thud of Jowls hitting the floor interrupted the thought.

"Oh, you are *fabulous*! Thomas, right? I had heard Sabrina had collared a cougar, but my word, I never thought you'd grace my shop."

I blinked and then sighed with annoyance. "Yes, yes, I know. I'm apparently worth my weight in gold, and I should be happy about the fact my thumb took a vacation. I've heard it."

"Ach! Give it time. Magic opens you up to all sorts of possibilities. Both good"—he gestured at my body with a wave of his paw—"and bad." He looked pointedly at Jules, who rolled his eyes. He began to circle me, looking me up and down with his eyes and making me uncomfortable. He was remarkably light on his feet despite the waddle and held his tail up high. I got his scent, something that I could only described as boisterous. It had an essence of musk, but that was only the very first layer; beyond that, it was *him*.

I sneezed and then flehmed. Getting even more of *him* in my mouth.

He pranced, his body jiggling like an overjoyed feline Santa Claus. "Ah ha! There you are! Now you know me. Stand back up. It's only polite."

I glanced up at O'Meara for help, but she only smirked down at me, clearly trying to restrain a chuckle. Jules seemed busy with something on the counter. Not seeing any support around, I picked myself up and, feeling my ears burn, lifted my tail to let the smaller cat have a sniff. He made a show of rubbing up against my legs as he did so.

"There, not so bad then. A first feline 'who the hell are you.' Trust me—it's much easier to put a name to scent than a face!" His eyes flicked up past my eyes, and he gave a little mew of delight. "Oh, isn't that so precious! He's an ear blusher! That's adorable!" He turned back to Jules. "Can we keep him, boss? *Plweese!*"

The man named Jules rubbed his temples as if he had a migraine. "No, I don't have the tass for another familiar and he's claimed already."

"Tisk. Hey! I wasn't going to mention his collar. It's hidden so well!"

"Collar?" O'Meara exclaimed, suddenly choking. "You chose a house already?"

I suddenly felt the weight of the hidden chain around my neck. I would have preferred to talk to O'Meara about it privately. "What's a house?"

"It's a family of magi." She batted away my question and bored into me with her eyes. "Where did you get a collar?"

"Uh, it wasn't my idea." I wasn't quite sure whether I wanted to admit that I had been given it posthumously by Archie the Archmagus, if by given you meant attacked by.

"Mrrrowl." Jowls was staring up at my neck, eyes narrowed in concentration. "Woah, now there's a classic. I've never seen one like that. Somebody's really old-fashioned. He send a contract with it?"

My head snapped around to Jowls so fast I felt my neck twinge. "Contract?"

"Let me see this," O'Meara said, and I felt her fingers rake through my fur, tugging on the chain. A disorientation swept through me, as the chain writhed around my neck. O'Meara cried out as a wave of heat washed over me.

"Terms will be decided." A voice exploded from everywhere and nowhere. The shop shattered into multicolor shards before being whisked away by an unfelt wind, leaving me in black nothingness. With O'Meara. I floated away from her, being pulled by an unseen hand on my neck until we both faced each other. Her eyes glittered with panic and disbelief as she tugged at the heavy chain around her own neck. The chain stretched out into the void and came back to encircle my own neck. I tried to speak, but my mouth refused to move; my body could but only feebly, as if my limbs had been drained of all strength.

"Your terms." The voice pried into my mind and spilled my thoughts into the space between us—all the crazy things that my mind had been thinking of asking in return for bonding me. A stack of money, two hundred dollars a day, my thumbs, an alarm clock with scissors instead of a bell, a time limit on the bond, a textbook labeled magic, my human face, and sillier things, whims. The presence between us sorted them out, and they faded back in the ether.

Then it was her turn. The void cracked open her mind

like an egg, and her thoughts joined mine in front of us. They were very simple. To find out who killed the Archmagus and restore her reputation. Where mine were limiting factors, the fear of commitment coloring each, hers were colored red with need, with a desperation that had not allowed her to sleep for a week.

A negotiation happened, strangely independent of either of us. The thing in the void, the chain itself, flickered between each of us. Items and our desires flickered in and out of existence, comparing what each of us believed possible.

"The terms are set," the collar announced as the thoughts crystallized between us. We would be partners for three months or until the killer of Archibald was brought to justice. I her familiar, she my magus. As I was inexperienced, I would follow her lead and instructions whenever possible. She would pay my rent and write my checks to maintain my human identity for as long as I worked for her. There was a possibility for renewal.

It sounded fair to me. I knew the outside world would protest. Before me, worry and happiness warred on O'Meara's face.

"The terms are agreed."

I saw myself. I watched my large amber eyes blink in surprise. I looked towards me and saw both myself and O'Meara. Her face shone with disbelief and happiness, yet I could feel an undercurrent of fear flowing between us. I watched my own body as well; my eyes just seemed to be getter wider as the long tawny tail twitched uncertainly. It was far longer than I had realized, nearly the length of my body. That feeling of unfamiliarity came back, hovering over me. Slowly my angle lowered, and I watched as O'Meara's hand slowly extended both towards me and away at the same time. Two separate perspectives, I finally realized, as the fingers tentatively threaded through the fur on my head and curled around the base of my right ear.

The finger scratched, and my world tilted yet again. The sensation of fur being rubbed and the finger rubbing sent shivers through us both. Oh, the sensation was wonderful, the connection between us total. She was I and I was she. I leaned into her touch and let it go, a soft chirp of my own as a sigh escaped her and an overwhelming sense of sheer relief flowed through us both. With an aggressive purr I pushed my head into hands, craving that touch, a physical connection to combine with the sudden mental one. Her scent filled my lungs; burned cinnamon lost its ashy undertone. Her/my arms encircled me, and we squeezed ourselves as I felt tears flow down our smooth cheeks and dampen our fur on the top of our head.

Both our eyes closed, and that brought even more duality to the sensations. Without the distraction of the visual we slipped even closer together, our hearts synched for a brief moment like a tender kiss more intimate than anything I'd ever experienced before. It held there, one, two, three beats, and we dove into each other. Images floated to the surface: her raging disappointment at Rudy's flakiness, her true intention to follow the letter of procedure.

I pushed past me and pushed deeper within her, piercing her surface thoughts, and almost recoiled as a hurricane of rage and pain assaulted me with winds of despair. I tasted whiskey and cigarettes in my mouth as knives bit into my flesh. Still darker things wriggled below, held down beneath a mighty paw. A dog's paw. A Great Dane clad in a knight's armor towered over the poisonous memories, his eyes dead, and his muzzle a grimace of pain. Love glowed from every fiber of his being as grief and sadness burrowed through his fur like fleas. A broken collar hung from his neck, bleeding like a severed limb. The severed link. And there were others; five more dead links sprouted in O'Meara's mind like a circle of trees taken by lumberjacks. Emotions clung to each, some a little love, others hate and resentment. They were mere shadows: a cat with mad eyes, a bat with wings of flame, a glass-eyed rat, a horse who wore a top hat and a fluffy dog with an underbite. All ghosts looked up to the armored dog, two of them with dead eyes, all with envy. In the middle of them all was me, a sapling in the dead grove, a single leaf on the link's branch. Hope clung to that link, but it warred with thick dread. Her mind was in a desperate struggle against fears and anxieties that I had stirred up by binding to her. But every fear that rose into the air was cast to ground, by a blade of molten iron wielded by fiery figures. A beautiful dance of rage, pain and hope, with me in the center.

I felt a tug and a burning in my heart, like the air in my own lungs had gone missing. The pang touched us both, and like two lovers reluctantly coming up for air, we slowly began to pull back from each other. We sorted first our thoughts and then our senses back into our own bodies. Finally after what seemed like hours. I was once again a cougar in the arms of a woman I had met twenty-four hours ago. But we were no longer strangers.

"Oooh! That's so *adorable!*" Jowls' squee dragged me back to reality. I blinked slowly to find an orangey blob bouncing through my blurry vision, out of one field of view and into another. The other was much deeper and richer in color, making my original viewpoint washed out–looking.

"Oh," I said in a mumble. "I'm sort of color-blind."

Jowls giggled. "Wait until you see how horribly they see at night! The poor things!"

O'Meara stirred against me, her fingers finding my ears and scratching them. The sensation, sort of like a concentrated back rub, added to the hazy bliss that enfolded my head, and I leaned into it. Touch—it felt as if it had been ages since I had been touched in such a loving way. Despite the storms that raged in her, O'Meara meant safety. I could feel that, know it.

"Would you two please stop acting like a couple of bliss junkies and get off my floor?" Jules said and the scratches stopped, as a flash of embarrassment lapped at my mind like an incoming tide from O'Meara.

"This wasn't my intention to do this." O'Meara words slurred slightly as she fought to find our—no, her feet.

"But you'll take binding a highly sought-after familiar who's claimed by an elder while he is confused and scared."

"I didn't. I wouldn't," O'Meara sputtered, off balance, her fears and duty churning inside her.

Jowls came to the rescue. "He bound her! That chain he's got. It went whip! Right around her neck. You saw it!"

Jules glowered at his familiar. "It could have been that." He looked back at us. "If they get out of my store and leave me alone."

O'Meara grinned. "That's okay. I got other leads to follow now. But don't leave town."

"We didn't do it, O'Meara. Archmagus Archibald had been starting to support technomagery. You'd be better off looking at the traditionalists." Jules's scowl deepened. O'Meara didn't seem to make many friends.

I'm about as popular as you would expect for a cop in a town full of criminals. O'Meara's voice rang clear in my head, so loud I winced. *Sorry.* Her voice quieted. She continued in the real world. "That would be easier if you were willing to actually help me. I'll—" She stopped herself, laying her hand on the top of my head. "We'll be back."

I nodded in agreement. "Bye, Jowls." In my own vision he was still an orangey blob, but to O'Meara's eyes he grinned excitedly.

"Next time I'll show you how to groom yourself—your coat's all astray."

With that we turned and walked out. Well, I more stumbled out, leaning on O'Meara. The brief taste of her two legs had brought the unfamiliarity of my own body crashing back down on me, and I kept forgetting to step with my front legs as well as my hind ones. O'Meara walked us into the darkened parking lot to one of the two cars present. A beat-up old Porsche, its red paint faded where rust had not gained a foothold. Numerous dents and dings pockmarked the metal body like scars from an unknown disease. O'Meara had to push me up into the passenger's seat, my lack of coordination combining with some doubt that the vehicle would actually support my weight. O'Meara teased me for my hesitance as she shut the door.

"Never in a million years," O'Meara said as she fell into the low seat, disbelief evident both in her voice and mind. I didn't say anything as she scratched my ears. She chuckled. "You are so hazed."

"Whaaa?" I managed to ask. All I wanted to do was curl up and sleep. I lay down on my side and put my head in her lap. The car's stick shift poked at my ribs.

"You're kind of friendly for a strictly business familiarship, you know," she protested as she gave me the touch I craved, raking her fingers through my fur.

A thread of thought ran through my head, scolding me for acting like an overgrown housecat. I had wanted a bond that would secure my independence and now, having crossed the threshold, all I wanted was a warm body to curl up against. Not that that sort of behavior was precisely unprecedented on my part. A long day or tiring confrontation led to hours on the couch curled against Angelica.

"Sorry kid, but that's not going to happen again."

"Whaa?" I then grimaced, realizing she had probably seen everything in my head. Curiously, all I got from her was emotional impressions.

She chuckled. "Some magi and their familiars are in each other's heads so much they become one being with two bodies. That's dangerous for many reasons. Most construct a sort of privacy barrier in their minds to shield their partners from every single thought." Flashes of magi and familiars supplemented the voice; an owl was engulfed by a seething darkness as a man shouted a warning, only to keel over, his eyes dead.

The image made me shudder, and I pulled away from her psychically and physically. The world around me became a little clearer, but the haze remained. I didn't realize we were moving until I felt the wind start to thread around my ears.

I started to ask where we were going, but I found the image of our destination in my head before I could give voice to the question.

It wasn't far, but I slept the rest of the way anyway.

15

I woke to a hand running over my head. *"Come on, kid, we've got a lot of work to do."* O'Meara's voice slid through my mind, pulling me from the clinging tendrils of sleep. I opened my eyes, with a familiar scent in my nostrils, and knew that the blurry images of a grey something or other was indeed the house of the Archmagus.

Groaning, I let my head rest on the top of the passenger-side door. *"Can't we sleep off whatever you said this is first?"* I thought at O'Meara, deeming speaking too much effort. I could feel her struggling against the same effect I felt. An alcoholic buzz blended with the warmth of a lazy day spent with a lover in bed.

Her arms encircled me, and my skin suddenly was singing with the sudden contact and closeness as she squeezed. Then, as if she were some sort of big sister, she expertly administered the most painful noogie I had ever experienced. *"Wake up!"* She shouted directly into my mind as the hug turned into a headlock.

She released me before I had a chance to retaliate, and I sat there, still feeling the echoes of her knuckles grinding into my skull. "What the hell was that for?" I exclaimed, the hurt of the betrayal making my voice squeak.

O'Meara shook her finger at me, nearly touching my nose with it. Her face was serious with a faint hint of embers inside her pupils. "Those thoughts of yours are making me tired, so quit it. We've got five days to figure out who killed Archibald. Linking haze can last for weeks, and we don't have time for it. You wanted this to be a job, not a bond. So I'm the boss telling you to get your ass up from the floor and get to work. Understand?"

That hurt way worse than the noogie. I had been acting like a pet. "Yes, ma'am." I looked down at my paws. "What am I supposed to do?"

"For now, all we need you to do is use your sight so I can undo Archibald's wards. That and try not to make Scrags any more upset than he is. They had a close bond, and he's not the rational sort on a good day. Come on." She popped her door open and started walking towards the front door. I stared after her for a moment, and then realized that I should follow and bounded out of the car to catch up.

The haze still made me weave along behind O'Meara, but she didn't say anything when I leaned against her once we made it to the stoop. The construction of the house pulsed with that golden light, but the individual elements were fuzzy and indistinct. In any case, I didn't look directly at them for fear of rousing the entity within the house.

O'Meara reached for the cheap brass knocker and slammed it home before I could stop her. I winced in sympathy as the bang shook the doorframe. "Inquisition!" She almost sung the word, as if the word invoked Grandma's cookies and not burning women at the stake.

"It's not like that," O'Meara scolded me through the link as I replayed my own reaction to Sabrina's knocker.

In a moment the door swung wide open, revealing the Archimagus's living room. A single overstuffed Lazy Boy chair in the center, the walls consumed by bookcases that stretched from the floor to the high ceiling. On top of the easy chair, two small amber eyes radiated hostility set within a tiny skull.

"Gud out, O'Meara. There is nuthing for you here!" Scrags' outsized voice boomed all the way to the doorway.

"Why don't you let me be the judge of that, Scrags." O'Meara brushed aside the familiar's anger and stepped over the threshold, her back far straighter than it had been during her encounter with Sabrina. She stepped sideways to admit me, and I felt the intensity of his eyes fall to me like a physical force I had to push against to walk into the house.

The anger flickered to bewilderment. "You didn't!" Scrags pulled himself out of his bodily curl to look between O'Meara and myself as I stood up as straight as I could. "You allowed her to bond you? Do you have a death wish, lad?"

"Well, if you want to be technical, I think I bound her actually. The chain sorted the details of the arrangement."

Scrags swore a livid curse, probably at Archibald and not us. "And you're both still in a binding haze?" He turned to O'Meara. "You should know better!"

"Bah. We don't have time to sit around and wait out the haze. Four days until the estate opens and we've got to figure out whom to disqualify."

The little cat shook with fury. "The haze serves a purpose! It builds the trust. It is there to break down the barriers between the magus and familiar! If this is what you do as a matter of course, it is no wonder three of your familiars left you."

O'Meara chuckled drunkenly. "And what good comes

of letting Thomas relive my history? He's traumatized enough already."

"It's only a temporary thing anyway, no big deal," I chimed in.

Both O'Meara and Scrags went still. Scrags' head swiveled to mine.

"Temporary? You put a time limit on your bond?"

My ears went back defensively. "Well, I'm not ready to commit to anything until I know more about this crazy world you all live in. I don't like this TAU deal. I figure I'll freelance for a bit first."

He looked at O'Meara. "And you let him do this? I would think you've broken enough bonds for a lifetime, O'Meara."

"There is no justice for anyone if I can't do my job, Scrags. He offered terms, I took them."

"You're going to subject a cub to the breaking of a bond before he's even trained. I've always thought you were incompetent, O'Meara. I didna think you cruel."

I looked up at O'Meara, feeling the sorrow roll down the link despite her effort to hold it back. Images of tear-stained pillows, a cycling of days and nights, and the taste of bile coming with it. She patted my head and I dodged it, pulling away a little. "Don't worry, kid, you'll survive. I always do, and you're at least half as stubborn as I." She held out her hand between us. "You did bind me. That was your intention when you came looking for me, right?"

I sighed, pushed my head into her hand and was rewarded with a good scratching. I had made my bed—nothing to do now but lie in it. It just so happened I'd made it on a roller coaster car. I looked at Scrags. "I chose this. I won't say I know what I'm doing, but this keeps my options open."

"You got no clue at all. That's perfectly clear. And if this is what Archibald set up, then I'll kill him again."

"So he'd been future scrying," O'Meara observed.

Scrags looked at her, annoyed. "Yeah, he's always done it a little, here and there when things looked bleak."

"So he saw the big one?"

Scrags let out a tiny growl of frustration and kneaded the chair beneath him. "Maybe—I don't remember anything from the last month. He could have planned it that way."

"Who wanted him dead?" I asked.

Scrags' eyes shifted to me and back to O'Meara as she kept talking. "Have you looked into his correspondences?" A short message telling me to let her do the talking slipped through the link. My back bristled, but I held my tongue as the image of a tiny me perched at a desk while O'Meara lectured from a chalkboard followed through the link.

Meanwhile Scrags seemed to deflate. "No. And won't."

"Then I will."

"You will give up your right for the estate, then?"

"Of course. I have no need of the scraps that would be left."

Scrags grunted. "Well, then, you've got yourself a new partner. You don't need me." He gestured with his head to the door to the kitchen. Perpendicular to it, a hallway ran down into the house. "Fourth door on the left is the office. If you manage to get through the ward, the rest will be mostly open."

O'Meara nodded curtly at Scrags, mumbled a thanks and then strode for the hallway. I followed after, feeling like an intern shadowing a CEO.

Looking down the hallway was like suddenly looking down a mountain you had not realized you had been on. The hallway stretched far beyond the physical extent of the house. It had the same yellow paint with the scuffed white trim as the rest of the interior but extended far into the distance, doors and hallways branching off at random intervals.

Beside me O'Meara sucked in her breath. *"That's never good. All that folded space. Looks like he made it randomly too."*

"How's that bad?" I responded, but she had already begun to show me. In my mind's eye, cracks spread from the chips of paint, the hallway first buckling and twisting as if in pain. Then whole sections of the wall began to peel up, exposing patches of absolute nothing under the walls. Whole hallways broke off. A rushing wind swept through the structure, howling like wild animals. The hallway shuttered, and the walls blackened to dark stone. The lights sprouted into candles that struggled against the wind. Shadowy figures clung on barred windows, screaming for help as the nothingness grew into them. Something tugged at my shoulder—no, my hand, but the tug was so hard that pain bloomed at the socket.

I turned and saw a man, eyes wide with fear set in a leathery-jowled face. "Come! We must go now!" He clutched something in his other hand, something ill gained.

"But—" My voice protested with a squeak.

"They were lost before we came here—now come along, O'Meara!" The foreign memory broke like glass.

The hallway before me blinked back to that aged suburban look, but I could still hear those screams in my head echoing down its length. I swallowed and pushed them away, concentrating on the real sounds. First my thundering heartbeat, then O'Meara's beside me. I found my voice first. "Talk about your PTSD, damn." Then I winced, wondering where my subtlety went off to.

"I should have closed the link—you didn't need to see that." O'Meara voice was numb as she placed a hand on my head, and I allowed her to steady herself.

"Damn right I didn't. Please tell me the place ain't gonna fall around our ears." My own ears were folded against my head so tightly that they started to cramp. *That* was a novel sensation.

"It won't happen yet, but if it was created as haphazardly as it looks, then it won't last long without maintenance. It will be just like what you saw in a few weeks. The estate sale will strip the house bare long before that, though. Come on. We'll find nothing standing about here." O'Meara led the way down the hallway as I tried not to look at the peeling paint, afraid to glimpse the void beyond it.

I focused on O'Meara's feet instead; she had small feet for a woman of her size, and she had changed her boots since she had been at Sabrina's. They had the hint of a heel, black rubber soles that were clearly replacements. The stitching glowed a dull red, like hot iron. She walked with an intentional swagger, putting confidence up before her as a shield. Her thoughts were closed to me, but I could feel her still struggling with more memories of that day. Her thoughts smelled of moist sadness and sharp terror.

We came to the fourth door after walking far longer than I expected. It looked like every other door in a house like this, cheap wood with a dull brass knob. Yet in the veins of the wood I saw a faint glimmer of gold.

O'Meara thought-spoke first. *"Okay, Thomas, we need to do our first bit of magic together. This door is warded. I'm going to need your eyes. This could be a bit disorienting."* With that whatever barrier she had constructed between us fell away and the sensation of pure awareness swept over me like a warm ocean wave. We exhaled a shared breath, and I felt it pass through both our lips. I winced in pain as O'Meara fell to her knees, her legs too weak to support her against the sudden connection. *"Too fast, far too fast."* She clung to me for a moment, that blissful haze sweeping through us both as we shared the embrace from both sides. I could feel the jagged edges of memories that thrust through her mind, pricking mine with cold terror. I did my best to ignore them and focus on the warmth we shared. After a moment they melted away.

This time I spoke first after counting nine shared breaths. *"The ward?"*

She slowly shifted her attention away from our embrace with the slowness of a tired child. *"Oh, right. Damn bonding haze. Look at the ward."*

Pulling my head out from a comfortable space beneath her chin, I fixed my eyes on the door. Blinking to clear my head of the warm marshmallow that stuffed it, I caught sight of golden threads woven in and out of the wood's grain. Not needing any prompting, I pushed at the threads, and the wood faded, revealing a complex web. It reminded me of the inner working of a very expensive bomb. Various threads bound larger components of different colors and intensities, symbols that made my brain hurt to look at them. In the center of it all, a red globule pulsed like an angry heartbeat.

"Oh, thank the stars you're not a dog." O'Meara's hand stroked down my back. *"Wards are so much harder when you have to do this by smell."*

"How do you disarm it?"

"We don't. I never want to try to disarm a ward like this. See all those threads—we so much as brush one and we'd be subjected to the heat of molten rock for a few seconds," she thought-spoke, gesturing at the angry heart of the mechanism. *"Fortunately we have the key for it."* She held up a hand in front of the door, a few inches from a glyph at the center of the door. *"Now focus on my hand, and don't look away."*

She pushed away from me, urging me to keep watching as our viewpoint split. I saw her hand curl into a fist from two different angles at once, making my stomach lurch. On her little finger was a ring that glowed with the same fire I had seen in O'Meara's eyes. She stretched out her pinkie finger and traced out eight complex three-dimensional glyphs in the air with an almost inhuman precision. Her concentration was total and complete as the glyphs spun and locked together like a puzzle. Except the puzzle looked wrong. The angles bent inward and outward at the same time. Through her eyes and mine I could see it push up into a direction that didn't exist. Nothing should be able to do that! It hurt to look at. I felt my mind rebel, a slick feeling of wrongness slithering through me. *"You're doing fine, Thomas. Keep watching. We're almost done."*

I didn't feel fine. Nausea coiled around my chest as a crawling sensation crept over my skin, like ants swarming through my fur. A whimper escaped me as the infernal cube continued to fold into an impossible shape. Through one pair of eyes I wouldn't see enough of it to matter, but through two angles the hideous geometry invaded my mind. There I could see it extend in these new, impossible directions as it folded into its final place. A key to a fourth-dimensional lock. O'Meara thrust it into the doorway and twisted it in that gut-wrenching new direction. The key caught dozens of the golden threads and passed through others. The structure of the ward bowed inwards, resulting in a click of the lock opening.

As the door swung open I vomited on the floor with a very catlike *hurk*!

"Oh, Lord! Forgot about that," O'Meara exclaimed as my empty stomach pushed vile-tasting acid up through my throat. Then she was at my side, stroking me as my body, desperate to cleanse itself of the wrongness, voided itself of everything else. "Oh, shit, oh, shit!" O'Meara cried in horror as my body continued to rebel.

"And you got a clue why TAU training is pretty damn important!" Scrags' voice called down to us.

16

Apparently my misery was enough to rouse Scrags from his depression. The tiny cat grinned at me with a sadistic glint to his eye as O'Meara bathed my quaking body in the pink tub she had dragged me to. I felt like a helpless invalid as she washed my own mess out of my fur. Apparently the TAU taught their new members several mental exercises to cope with the sight of their first spell. As an actual familiar, they would have to endure peering into complex spells for hours on end. O'Meara was all praise as she rinsed me, but I could feel her worry underneath. Sooner or later I'd need to endure a much longer session, probably sooner if I tasted O'Meara's worry right.

"Wait until she asks you to search between the anchors," Scrags taunted. "If you thought a quick key assembly was disorienting, then pulling your awareness up through the planes should break your mind in half."

"He'll be fine, Scrags. First time gets to almost everyone. And he's been tossed into the deep end of the pool," O'Meara said, preventing me from attempting a retort of my own by dumping a bucket of water over my head.

"There—that's better," I heard her say after I shook myself out. Wetness in my fur wasn't precisely a pleasant feeling; already I felt the water cooling on my back. But considering the alternative method of cleaning all that filth off myself, I would have endured ten more baths to get myself clean. At a gesture from O'Meara I hopped out of the tub and looked around for a towel. My soggy fur hung on my skin like a lead vest from the dental office. Oddly, O'Meara seemed to have forgotten the towels. I was about to ask when she flared with the orange red of her aura, dazzling bright.

"O'Meara?" was all I got out before a wave of intense heat hit me, followed by the hiss of steam. The heat lifted before I could protest. I felt her smile before I made it out in the steam.

"There! All dry! Now back to work." She ruffled my head. I looked down at myself and found what she said to be true. All the moisture had been blasted from my fur, violently.

I heard Scrags snicker behind me. "You look like you've been hit by lightning!" It was true, and it was going to take an awful lot of grooming to fix. At least I didn't have to worry about what I had stepped in.

Once we got to the Archmagus' office, it turned out to be a good thing I had something to do because I quickly gave up trying to help O'Meara sort through the mess. It consisted of old file cabinets stuffed with parchments, along with crystalline boxes that hummed like radios, all apparently organized like the aging magus's mind. The old man wrote most of his correspondences in a Latinate scrawl that made reading it impossible. Through us both O'Meara had two sets of eyes, but she'd never mastered reading two things at once and I couldn't help with the Latin. So as she meticulously searched for and cataloged all the Archmagus's correspondences, I let my instinct guide my fur back into place while my mind pondered the implications that some "magic" apparently worked with fourth-dimensional space. Why hadn't anybody told me that? That was interesting, despite the mere memory of that twisted key making the bile rise in my throat.

I tried sleeping but quickly got bored with that. I could see a picture of the Archimagus' life slowly coming together in O'Meara's head, but it was still fuzzy and incomplete. Many questions itched the tip of my tongue now. One part was clear: the Archmagus had alluded to something he called his last journey and had been amassing a very large amount of tass for something. I peered over O'Meara's mental do-not-disturb sign and watched her refine that picture detail by excruciating detail. Overall I felt useless and bored, a feeling that I had grown accustomed to before the tail. Six months of job searching will do that. But here, watching O'Meara work, there was little to distract myself with.

I found myself pacing around the office like a big cat in a small zoo, noting that compared to the hallway, the office seemed far more solid. O'Meara's memory of the shattering hallway still echoed. It was a reminder that despite seeing into her mind, she remained a stranger.

I wandered into the hallway and looked down it. It stretched out into the distance, disappearing into a sort of hazy golden light. A haze that hadn't been there before. I stared at the haze, and something within shifted and I felt a presence brush my mind that beckoned me closer. Checking over my shoulder revealed nothing—no eyes on me. Scrags had apparently gone back to the old man's chair to mope angrily. I mentally glanced down my link, but O'Meara's total concentration remained on the notes.

Nobody paid me any attention. Cautiously I crept down the hallway, slinking against the left wall. As I approached the mist swirled through the closest door, paying no mind to the solidity of the barrier. I peered at the door itself. No glow surfaced within the wood grain this time. Besides which, it was open just a smidge.

A tentative push of my paw and the door swung open. The golden mist dissipated as the door stirred the air, revealing a room a bit bigger than the office and almost entirely bare of furniture. A single wooden chair sat in front of a window with what appeared to be a pair of binoculars mounted on a tripod. A faint purplish glow surrounded them. A laptop cushion was propped against the legs of the chair. Those three things were the sum total of the furniture in the room, making it feel huge and empty by comparison. If the room had existed as part of the actual house, it had probably been intended as a bedroom.

Something rustled. My gaze jerked to the sound, and the fluttering of paper met my eyes. It took a moment to realize that the room was not, as I first assumed, painted white. Nearly the entire surface of the wall had been covered with sheets of papers held in place with shiny metal thumbtacks.

Squinting in the dim light, I took a closer look at some of the papers near the doorway. There were drawings there, sketched out in faint pencil marks. Arcane symbols and notes littered the double-wide pages. Then, clear as day, in the middle of it all and rendered with an artistic clarity that knocked my breath away, was my human face looking up at me.

Disbelieving, I looked at the pages above it, and to the sides. I forced myself up onto my hind legs to examine more even further out of reach. A cold feeling crept along my spine as I looked. I was featured on every single page, dead center. A multitude of poses, expressions and poses. Some naked, some clothed. While central to each page, my image was not the only one recognizable. Animals shared the page with me, drawn in the exact same expressions and poses as me. Their portraits were connected to mine via branching lines, symbols sprouting from them like the leaves of a tree. I couldn't read the Latin, but in the top left-hand corner of each page sat a date. Without hands I couldn't rip the pages down and reorganize them, so instead I cast about the room, trying to follow the sheets in chronological order, assembling a picture in my head.

The very earliest pages were dated to about a year ago, six months after I had moved in next door. Everything had been going well. My face smiled from those pages, surrounded by a web of symbols and no animals. I had been working as a librarian at the fledgling community college in town for about a year at that point. Though not the greatest job in the world, it was what I had come to this town to do. I had finally started meeting friends at that point, finding bars I had liked hanging out in and setting down some roots away from my family. The largest symbol that loomed near my portrait was a stylized L. A month later, on the date I met Angelica, a large W appeared in the grid of symbols, surrounded by a phalanx of V's. It hung off my smiling portrait like a weight, the other symbols pushing away from it. As we dated the W drew closer and some of the smaller symbols disappeared, replaced by animals: a donkey, a cat and an armadillo. The day she moved in with me, the big W was touching my portrait and everything else had drifted away.

I remembered that first wild week. I called in sick, citing a feverish flu, and it was certainly fevered the way we spent our time together. To this day I can hardly imagine a more perfect way to spend time. Whether we were playing video games, eating, making love or simply talking, we did it full-contact style. The laughter of that week still echoed every time I thought of Angelica.

The symbols continued to chart my life. The W moved closer or further away with the tide of our relationship. With her frequent mysterious absences, we had some epic fights. Eventually I accepted it because she was all I had. And by that time it had become true. Jobless, depressed and withdrawn, feuding with my parents over petty stuff—it was all there in the symbols. At times they seemed to predict turns well before they happened. A cross was drawn over the L five days before I got laid off. On the day I did, it disappeared. Had the Archmagus simply seen it coming somehow? Or had he caused it? The animals bubbled up from the bottom of the pages again: cats, a badger, an armadillo, a donkey. Any animal that had a reputation for being stubborn rotated out among the bottom of the page.

When the cougar appeared after two months of grinding through the job search, it was accompanied by several lines of excitedly scrawled text, marked by two exclamation points. The cross-outs became more aggressive after that, but also less predictable. The hairs on my neck prickled as if feeling an invisible hand tugging at my life. New L symbols appeared on the days I had managed to score interviews and were slashed out of existence. Angelica's strange V's started to stick to my portrait, crowding out the few connections besides her as the cougar swelled into dominance among the animals. It was the only one not drawn with a sort of cage around it. My happy face became more and more despondent, and the features of the cougar crept in and out within the last month. The symbol of my parents finally disappeared after a huge fight we had over the phone.

They had wanted me to come back home, but that would have meant leaving Angelica and this town. Her W hung on me like anchor, the V's engulfing me like an amoeba.

My entire body itched with the feeling of insects crawling through my fur. My body was suddenly unfamiliar and alien once again.

This had not been chance. This had not been a simple case of unfortunate geography, as everyone had said. This had been a direct manipulation of my life. And somehow, some way, Angelica had been the anchor that had pulled me into this fucked-up world, where everything I had achieved in mine, as meager as it was, had been lost. Had I been on a path before he had taken an interest? And where had Angelica disappeared to for two weeks out of every month? She had told me work, but what if it was something else? Was she also a part of this world? If so, where the hell was she?

I peered through the binoculars, and a growl tumbled around my throat. Unsurprisingly I saw into my own bedroom. With a flash of anger I swatted the tripod and the binoculars hit the ground with an unsatisfying soft thud on the ancient wall-to-wall carpet. Worse, this man, the seemingly friendly old gentleman, had pulled my life apart.

And he was beyond justice. Dead in an attack that suddenly seemed deserved. How much had Angelica known about this? Nobody had mentioned her.

I sat there, fuming, so lost in futile rage that I didn't notice the return of the golden haze around me until it spoke.

Cat. The voice exploded in my head. Instantly familiar, powerful and full of pain. *Help me. Before they find me again.*

"Stay back!" I told it, remembering the pain it had inflicted the last time I had encountered it. "You hurt me."

Thousands of eyes opened around me, swirling, all composed of golden light, flitting in and out of sight.

Did not mean! Did not mean to! The force of the creature's mind sent a crack of pain across the landscape of my mind. *We are same, both wronged, both trapped in this hate hate HATED world. It hurts. He grinds, he chops off pieces. I scream in darkness! So long so long.*

"Calm down!" I mentally shouted back, struggling for room to think. *"How can I help you? And how do I know you won't just hurt me afterwards?"*

Promise, won't stay, won't stay a moment, won't hurt, will love, please. An image formed of a statue, a man on a horse in a civil war uniform. I recognized it. I knew where it was. The presence raced around my head like an excited baby elephant. *Destroy, break, please!*

"Thomas? Who—" O'Meara's thought called across the link.

Bonded! the thing shrieked in my head. *How? No! Don't tell! Don't tell!* It vanished abruptly, leaving me stunned and my head ringing like a gong.

"Thomas?" I could feel her racing down the hall towards me.

17

I hadn't really decided to tell O'Meara what had happened. I had planned to tell her I had just been upset at the wholesale destruction of my life. I wanted to get a feeling for what O'Meara thought first. But as it turns out, it's really, really tough to lie to somebody you have a telepathic connection with. When O'Meara asked what happened, my brain just vomited up the entire scene wholesale.

She made a squeak of surprise, and fear flooded back from the link. *"A dragon. Here. In my town."* Her mind went click as dozen of memories slammed together into an epiphany. She fell onto the chair, grabbed handfuls of hair and yanked. "Oh, bloody flaming fireballs! *"Of course it makes sense."* Dread struck her mind like a gong. *"Scrags is right—this auction is going to be a bloody war if that gets on the auction block."*

"That thing is certainly not anything I would call a dragon. I'd describe it as an eldritch horror if it wasn't clearly begging me to help it."

"Well, we better hurry up and free it, then."

Shock showed plainly on O'Meara's face. *"You can't possibly think—"*

"I am. It's in pain, O'Meara. It's been in horrible agony for decades, and nothing deserves that."

"Thomas, that thing could flatten the entire town if it wanted to. Dragons are responsible for some of the largest disasters in history." Images flooded me of people screaming as buildings shook down around their heads. San Francisco's last big earthquake. *"We can't risk that thing getting loose because if it decides to take revenge it won't just be the magi in town, Thomas—it will be everyone within town."* Her fear was wild and untamed, a giant thing.

"It just wants out, O'Meara. Either we have to let it go or put it out of its misery. It's being tortured!"

She blinked slowly, trying to make me understand. *"Thomas, it isn't human or anything approaching an understanding of human. It's a monster from the unknown. They're born of the void. Dragons have flattened entire sects of magi for no reason. It's a monster. And for the Archmagus to leave it so that it's starting to worry at its bonds, then that just goes to show how irresponsible he became. I've got to let the council know of this. It's just too big to allow it to be simply auctioned off. It's got to go to somebody who's able to reinforce the bonds."*

My mouth fell open, listening to her thoughts, the pure earnestness of them. I spoke in a low hiss: "O'Meara, was that memory not clear enough to you? Can you not feel that agony?"

She sighed. "It's just attempting to manipulate you, Thomas. Taking advantage of your naiveté. Beings from beyond are very tricky to deal with for that reason."

"Oh? And I suppose you'd consider all this important work?" I growled, gesturing at the papers around us, slamming the awareness of what I found through the link. She flinched under the force of it, and shot me a wary look before she started unpacking it. I watched her face intensely, saw the slight widening of her eyes and watched her bottom lip curl into her mouth, and she bit down on it with her teeth. She pulled her head away to the side and looked at a spot on the floor. She tried to crush the spark of joy, of awe. But I caught it before she had the good sense to shut the link.

"I'm sorry, Thomas." Her voice flat. "Let me look. Maybe he was just charting your life." She stood and turned towards the wall.

I spat out a sawing growl as my blood went hot. This man, this magus had slowly ruined my life, and she, she had thought it had been a good thing? "Is this what you're all like? Everything that's not part of your world is something to be farmed? You think I should just be happy to be on this side of the fence because now I'm sorta of a person? You're all like plantation owners who think they saved their black slaves by ripping them out of their country and home."

O'Meara anger flared as she spun on her heel, eyes blazing with hot red energy. "It's *not* slavery. It's nothing like that! How can you even say that with the bond? After you experienced it?"

"It's not about the bond, O'Meara! Don't change the subject!"

"Thomas, you think I'm the only one who's desperate for a familiar? There are more people surviving awakening than ever before. Look at this from our perspective. That's countless talent going to waste! There is a wide world beyond the mundane, and it's the magi who protect it."

"Protect what?" I spat. "All I see is you all fighting each other. Sabrina and you jockeying for points. Sociopathic politics. People are not resources you can mine! This was wrong! Torturing that dragon is wrong too."

O'Meara's fist burst into flame, and she drove it into the wall with a thud. "This isn't your mundane country with your refined ideals here, Thomas. The council isn't some democracy where there are rights! Mundanes are resources, just like tass, and every magus." The fist extinguished, but the papers under it smoldered.

"Personally I gotta agree with the cougar. Sorry cub, you got screwed." Scrags' small body sat in the doorway. Both O'Meara and I blinked at him as he returned our gazes with a Cheshire grin, showcasing an impossible number of teeth in his tiny head. "Ya two are a pair, barely bonded and already the honeymoon's over. I'd watch ya for hours, but it wouldn't do for O'Meara to burn down the house before the auction."

"How long have you been sitting there?" O'Meara's voice was scandalized.

Scrags' smile didn't change. "Since you started shouting at each other."

"And why do you agree with me?" I asked.

"Cause it's all bullshit, laddie. You've been in it for what? A day and you already know how rotten the smell is. Archibald and I attempted to clean house fifty years ago and got our crumples kicked in. Why do you think we'd be in a town that's got about as much magic as three-week-old Jell-O?"

O'Meara hrumphed. *"They attempted to clean house via sundering the Veil and nearly killing the entire council."*

I blinked and the small cat smirked. "I'm sure they've raised O'Meara there on a different diet of the truth. We had an excellent arbiter. Sentencing us to death would have meant revealing just how corrupt the council had gotten, so the whole thing was hushed up. Archibald even kept his vote via proxy, despite this exile." Scrags kept looking at me as if I should know precisely what that meant before shifting his gaze to O'Meara. "You can run to the council if you want, but I'm sure most of them know about Lendra. They might be a wee bit grumpy if they know you know. I'm praying to the great expanse that a few will backstab the others over it. That would be nice." His grin returned.

"Where is the dragon stored, Scrags? I want to see those bindings." O'Meara drew herself up to her full height and towered over the kitten-sized familiar.

Scrags' grin widened. The angles of his teeth were not confined by normal physics, and I got the feeling that this tiny creature could swallow me whole if he so desired. "Don't know—my bond is broken so my memory is a wee scrambled at the moment. Although, were something to happen to me, the bonds might snap instantly."

"Scrags, this is not something to play games with."

"Archibald captured it long before I kicked me big brother off me mum's teat. The chains held fine."

"But you moved him."

Scrags started cleaning a paw with a disinterest. "How about a different game, O'Meara? I really would have preferred that you hadn't found out about Lendra, but mebbe Archibald had planned on that." He shot me a look of annoyance. "Getting the majority of the council saps by releasing him probably was a bit too much to hope for anyway. So let's try this one on for size. Find me Archibald's killer before the auction or I have Lendra wipe out the entire town as a condition for its release."

"Did I fall into a comic book when I wasn't looking?" I said, scoffing. although I kept my eyes peeled for the fourth wall.

"You think I'm joking?"

"Joke or not, that's ridiculous."

"Would you prefer I target Angelica alone, then?"

That hit me like a brick. "What?! Why? She doesn't have anything to do with this!"

"But she's got everything to do with you, however, and it's you I'm attempting to motivate here. O'Meara may be weak, but you're a mewling kitten, having an existential crisis every five minutes about your lack of thumbs."

"But it's your fault!"

"Aye, you've been the side project that's kept Archibald sane for the last year. His final gift to the magi world, how to cause and control the changeling process. Of course, he never realized that this amount of fate manipulation required so much tass that nobody but the richest of houses could fund the process. And they can afford the cream of TAU anyway, so fat lot of good it does anyone. But you should have seen the way the old man pulled and sculpted your anchors—still a genius even though he kept trying to turn on the light bulbs with matches."

"And that's supposed to make it okay? Are you expecting me to thank you for this?"

"Naaw. But you might think of your body as a charitable contribution to the elderly." The little cat radiated smug.

I growled at him and felt O'Meara's hand press on my shoulder. "He's baiting you, Thomas—he's suffering from post-bond trauma. This usually involves some level of death wish."

"Ha! This cub couldn't get one claw in me if he tried. I've still got my perks."

"Do you have a point, Scrags?" O'Meara said as she knelt to encircle my neck with an arm.

"Ha, I'm just givin' the lad a piece of advice, Mrs. Inquisitor. Good for him to see all the ugly now and know it goes well beyond your addled mind, O'Meara." O'Meara's rising anger matched my own, but her grip on me only tightened as a hiss escaped from my lips. Scrags' fury flitted to me; green spittle fell from his lips and bubbled on the carpet. "Ya wanna change it? Well, you're free to spend your blood, sweat and tears on your own damn time."

"I don't work for you."

"Yeah, you do. You're bonded with the Inquisitor there, and her job is yours. So get the righteous stick out of your ass and get to work." He turned and made to pad away.

"And when do you answer for what you and Archibald did to me?"

He stopped but didn't turn around. "Maybe you should talk to Angelica before you make up your mind about that." He dashed off down the hallway.

Angelica! The thought hit me, finally, that he knew what and who she was! "Wait!" The word was strangled by my own growl. I sprang out into the hallway to find it both empty and disorientingly shorter. The tiny cat was nowhere to be seen. The hallway ended with a window to my right and stretched only about thirty feet before reaching the junction between the library and the kitchen lab. *"The hell?"*

O'Meara came up behind me and placed a gentle hand on my head. I jerked away from it and reared back to peer into the window. I could see little but the near side of the surrounding fence. *"It's time for us to go, Thomas. We've been shunted out of the folded space."* The image of Scrags slamming the door in our faces made it clear what that meant. I ignored her, poking my head into the kitchen and then the library. No Scrags. *"Thomas,"* she pleaded as she squatted down to my level. I circled back and sat down in front of her, well out of arm's reach.

"I'm still mad at you too," I thought at her, but far more than that swirled around my head. Worry about Angelica

blossomed anew. Angelica's symbol was a W, and it had been surrounded by V's.

O'Meara smiled at me sadly. *"I know and I'm sorry. But he is right. We have to get back to work. And we've gotten what we came here for."*

I looked down at my big, clumsy and useless paws. *"When do I get my justice?"*

"You don't. It's not a crime, Thomas. Any magi you ask will say that Archibald did you a favor. Did you look at the charts? Your awakening might have happened anyway, and if it had on its own you very well could have been a talking donkey. I've seen inside your head, Thomas, and it's not really the loss of thumbs that bothers you. It's having to serve some ambition other than your own."

I turned away.

"And he even gave you a mechanism to maintain some autonomy—that collar," she thought to me.

"That doesn't give him the right! That's like buying somebody a wheelchair after you've broken their legs."

O'Meara chuckled.

I sat and stewed for a moment. I had been deported to a foreign country, stripped of my humanity and denied the freedom to choose my own path. And this was supposedly made up for by being able to see the world without the filter of modern society, where a cat can threaten the life of my girlfriend as a motivation tool without consequence? And there wasn't a goddamn thing I could do about it. Not here and not now. I couldn't back out of the contract. I could feel the weight of it around my neck. It had gravity. It had been my choice, my decision, and turning my back on it now would leave both O'Meara and me adrift.

I lifted my head. She had been watching me, kneeling on the floor a respectful distance away. Her individual thoughts were guarded, but her own emotions floated out into the air between us. Her anger and defensiveness had faded away; now she watched me with wary hope buoying on a cushion of trepidation.

Taking a deep breath, I closed the distance between us and pressed into her arms, shelving my own resentments. I savored the flash of happiness that washed over me as her arms encircled me, her fingers raking through my fur. "It will be okay," she murmured.

"Promise?" I mumbled.

"No, but I'll do my best." With that she stood and strode towards the front door. I followed close behind.

We both swore a streak of curses into each other's heads once we saw what awaited us in Archibald's driveway.

**

An owl and a sable sat on the hood of O'Meara's car, and they weren't sunning themselves in the morning's light. While Oric's eyes were squinting in the bright light, Cornealius's black eyes looked down his nose at us.

"O'Meara! What do you have to say for yourself?" Cornealius shouted.

O'Meara thought to me, *"I have no time to be lectured on proper procedures by Cornealius. Sabrina hasn't found a rule she doesn't like to twist. Oric might be more trouble. Do not let him touch you."* She strode towards the figures perched on the Porsche's hood. "Unless you two want a ride, I suggest you get off my car."

"Certainly, Inquisitor O'Meara." Oric fixed his narrowed eyes on her. "Just release Thomas to the TAU custody, and we'll be on our way."

"Not happening—we've got a lot of work to do." She

made to open the door, and Oric blinked on top of it, wings suddenly outstretched.

"You're jumping on the claim of someone far more senior than you, O'Meara. That's dangerous."

"Dangerous is that you are still blocking my car, Oric. Thomas isn't a member of the TAU, and I've got no claim on him." She pointed to her neck where her half of the collar hung. The owl's beak fell open, and his head twisted around to look at me.

"You allowed her to bond you?" he hissed. "Are you insane?"

"Nah," I replied with a smile, "I bonded her. It's my chain. Little postmortem gift from Archibald."

Cornealius, still on the hood, snorted in laughter. "What did I tell you, Oric? He's simply the worst clinger I've ever seen. I bet she'll even be paying his rent on the place next door."

"It will be a good vantage point from which to watch the estate sale," O'Meara said as she reached for the door handle.

The owl beat his wings for balance as O'Meara jerked open his perch, his head tracking me with a laser-like focus. "You realize your bond is outside the structure of the TAU, Thomas. We won't protect a *scab*!"

"Talk to me after we figure out who ran over the Archmagus," I said, jumping into the passenger seat. I looked at Cornealius, who returned my gaze with something like disappointment. "Uh, my apologies to you and Sabrina, but I'm playing the cards I've been dealt. This will be better in the long run."

He hopped off the car. "We all make choices, young Thomas. If you're lucky, you'll live to regret this one." He did not look back as he hurried across the street. Once he reached the yellow line, he disappeared in a bright purple flash.

Oric made an inelegant squawk and tumbled backwards as O'Meara slammed her door closed.

Oric called out something about mistakes and dark wizards before O'Meara stamped down on the accelerator and he was drowned out by the roar of the engine.

It was several blocks of distance before I shook the feeling of his eyes on my back.

18

O'Meara liked to drive; whatever the outer appearance of the car, the internals were clearly in perfect working order, and the dull red light that shone through the dashboard hinted at modifications that went beyond the physicality of the engine components. As we whipped around the twisting contours of the town's roads, I had to dig my claws into the seat and hunker down. Judging from the state of the upholstery and the numerous claw marks on the dash, I was not the first to do so. At first I wondered where we could be going, but after flying through the same intersection a couple times I realized O'Meara was driving for the sake of driving, enjoying the wind teasing her long hair. Dully I felt her flipping the memory of what we had just seen, particularly my disclosure that the fey collar had been a "gift" from Archibald. Finally as we headed up the on-ramp, she posed the question, *"You were there when he died?"*

"Yeah, he actually died in my arms. Called me a good kitty and told me to go find my necklace." I spun out the memory of the moment out to her. How the Archmagus, disguised as a friendly old gent, had been brutally hit. How the car

sent him spinning through the air, spraying blood like a lawn sprinkler from a horror show.

"*What about the car?*" she prodded, pushing the memory aside.

"*What about it? It's just the cover of whatever hit him, right? It's got nothing to do with what actually happened. Assuming that this side of the Veil is the sane side.*"

She smacked my shoulder between shifting as we screamed around a corner. "*No, the Veil presents a fiction that best fits the reality. It works with the situation at hand.*"

"*Like the coffee cup and the cop?*"

"*Exactly. It made no sense that a cougar, a wild animal, would hide behind little old me. The cup gave the Veil a clue what it should present you as. If you managed to walk on your hind legs and wear a few bits of clothing you could pass for human.*"

"*Could they understand me if I talked?*"

She shook her head. "*Maybe, but you might say something completely different. The Veil actively works to keep the worlds separate. So going back to the car.*"

I chewed on my tongue as I concentrated. I hadn't been looking at the car much. The old man himself had been burned into my memory in vivid detail, but the car was grey and low, a sedan of some type. The front end, where it struck him, had been squarish. An older car, more boxy than most. I tried to freeze the image of when he was struck in my mind and rewind backwards, but he had held my attention the entire time. I shook my head to clear it, trying to ignore the prickling feeling that danced along the hackles of my neck. "That's all I got."

"*That's more than what I started with. Something, or more likely somebody, hit him. Spells tend to translate to bullet holes.*"

"*Can we start at the beginning? Like, who do you suspect?*"

My eyes fell on a stack of dictionary-sized books in the well of my seat, a police procedure manual and a psychology textbook.

"That's the trouble. We have more suspects than I know what to do with, especially with that dragon in the picture. In town, it's all the folks you've met and few more besides. Sabrina was one of the inquisitors that wrecked Archibald's plan to destroy the council and stayed here to make sure he didn't try and rebuild. After about forty years of damn near nothing, she retired and has gone into politics, angling for a seat on the council. Archibald's death will open a seat. Jules has blown through a sizable inheritance pursuing technologic magic and would kill for a steady tass source. Despite appearances, Jowls is a terrible liar but good at avoiding topics he doesn't want to speak of. Then there's Whittaker." The shiver of fear at the name came through the link and went down my spine! *"He used to work for Archibald, and his familiar is about the size of a sedan."*

"Have you seen the body?"

"No," she grumped. *"The body's been taken into the city for examination, where I've got absolutely no contacts. That's where we're going now. With you I can cobble together an illusion or two to get us through the front door at least. But I know what I'm going to see."*

"What?"

"Really large teeth marks."

"Ah, I see. But you'll be able to tell what sort of teeth, then?"

"No, but with both you and the body we might be able to scry back to the moment of death—depends on how his personal wards were constructed." The tone of that thought wasn't hopeful.

O'Meara continued to lay out the facts of the Archmagus' murder as we drove up onto the interstate. To the police the case was a hit-and-run, so the body had been taken to the county coroner's office in Meadville, about thirty minutes east by highway the way I drove. The way O'Meara drove, I kept my eyes on my paws and tried not to think about it. She had contacted them, posing as a friend of Archibald's, but they had not offered her much detail.

The details of his death exhausted, my thoughts drifted back to my own predicament and the consequences. Would Archibald's method become public?

"Look at it this way," she explained. "He'd been trying to bring you into alignment with your anchor plane for a year, and it didn't happen until his death snap lacerated the planar structure. A death snap is a big deal—mostly it's used for a revenge strike against whoever dealt the blow. You're lucky it didn't just slice you in half."

"Your magic makes about as much sense as jalapeño-flavored peanut butter," I muttered back. "It's fourth-dimensional, and yet you're talking about overlapping planes."

"If it were simple, then magic would be easy. You actually haven't seen much in terms of real magic. The key is a construction—that's different. Even a technomagus can do basic constructions. Magic has to involve the anchors."

"And that is?"

"You'll see. We'll do a little in a moment." She pulled off the highway, and we were in a parking lot within a few more minutes of starting and stopping at overburdened traffic lights. We parked and she looked at me. "Okay, we need to do a simple spell that I've done before. We need to imbue this." She pulled a wallet from her purse and opened it with a practiced flip, smiling to herself. It contained a cheap plastic costume badge that wouldn't look out of place on a five-year-old's Halloween costume.

"Imbue it with what? Realism?"

She chuckled. "No, authority. Just a little bit, to give the Veil a bit of a hint." She placed the badge between us in the space between the armrest and the stick shift. Then she reached her arms out towards me, careful that the badge was dead center between her arms. "Now put your head between my hands and form the circle."

"That looks more rectangle-like to me."

She lightly grasped the sides of my head, and I let them bear a bit of my weight. "It's just a circuit between you and me with the target in the center. Most magi and familiars can do this with just their bonds. Now relax."

"W—" was all I got out before O'Meara's face suddenly shot out into the distance as if she had been pulled backwards down a long tunnel that ended far out of sight. A blue tube of magic filled my vision, undulating and pulsing. *"O'Meara!"* I shouted down the void.

"Right here." The thought had a slight echo to it, as if she were far away. *"This is anchor space. We're looking down the length of our bond from the point of our anchors. This is the first step of real magic and something that is nearly impossible without the bond. Without each other, there wouldn't be a way back to our plane. Now I want you to take a look outside."*

"Outside?" Outside what? The blueness? How? I felt disembodied, possessing nothing to reorient myself, floating in this strange tunnel. Panic rose as nothing happened when I tried to move my limbs.

"Stop that!" O'Meara's thought hit like the slap of an ocean wave. *"You'll break the circuit and give us both splitting headaches! Your body is fine, but out here you have to use an entirely different set of limbs. You have this bond, and it is an extension of us. Now it's different from the bonds I'm used to. Most bonds start very narrow and grow wider over the years. Fortunately the fey chain cheats a bit, and our bond is much wider. We're looking down a bond that would have taken us twenty years to grow."*

"*So it limits our magical bandwidth? What's the good of a thicker bond?*"

"*It is bandwidth in a way—the thicker the bond, the more energy we can bring back to our own plane. Now extend yourself along the walls and look outside the tunnel.*"

"*Okay.*" I took a deep breath and failed, lacking lungs, and clawed back another wave of panic as I looked down that tunnel. I watched the soft undulations along its length, and slowly, ever so slowly, my awareness extended along the walls of the anchor channel. The walls shifted as if in a gentle breeze, and I felt it—that nauseous sensation of an unfamiliar body rolled through, and far away I felt my stomach lurch. Somehow, I managed to swallow it down.

"*Thomas?*" O'Meara was concerned.

"*Working on it!*" I called back to her. "*Is all magic vomit-inducing the first time? I mean, there is a reason I became a librarian instead of an astronaut!*"

"*Magic is never easy, Thomas. It affects everyone differently.*"

"*Thank you for being so very specific!*" I had curled myself into the section of the anchor tube and became aware for the first time that I was at the end of the line, with apparent infinity between O'Meara and me. Beyond the closed end of the tube I could feel something, the soft repeated thudding of a heartbeat. I reached out towards it, and my eyes opened to a vibrant forest. Trees clad in white bark thick as my torso shot from the leaf-covered ground. The sunlight streamed down through foliage in beams that danced along with the wind over the dappled brown pelt of a deer as it nibbled at a brave shoot of grass. In the periphery of the vision I caught the sight of a hand, and familiarity hit me like an alarm—it was my hand! The gaze shifted at my urging and focused on my hand, the nails caked with dirt, the knuckles scratched and scabbed, but it was connected to my arm!

A growl and I was forcefully shoved back, the vision dissipating instantly. *"No! That's my body!"* But the end remained opaque, closed off.

"Did you find yourself?" O'Meara called to me, the anchor space seeming to shake with her amusement.

"He's got my body!"

"Well, you probably have his, so it's only fair. And no, you can't trade it back. You'd have to induce another planar alignment, and that's a once-in-a-lifetime thing."

"What if he dies?"

"He's on a spiritual plane of existence; he can't die until you do. It's complex, and I might have forgotten how it works." A brief flash of images revealed a grizzled old man standing in front of a chalkboard with brain-bending diagrams flitting over its surface. *"Now this is what you need to do. Between the plane where your anchor is and mine lie an infinite number of other planes. At my end is a plane of elemental fire; you've got a spiritual plane that looks a bit similar to some sort of North America. This is the very basic foundation of magic, finding something in a plane and bringing it back to our world. In fact I can do this instinctively with fire; if you were a magus, you could practice enough to invite entities from your anchor plane back to this one. With a lot of work you could even bring them physically. What the bond allows us to do is serve as an anchor point for each other as we search through other planes and pull from those as well. We are looking for a very specific plane, the plane that embodies the concept of authority."*

As she explained, I slid myself further up the tunnel, feeling the winds around it shift. These walls were more solid. While the anchor point had invited me in, the intermediate planes clearly resented my intrusion. I had to force my way through a wall of clay, easy initially but harder the deeper you go. Slowly, through the haze of blue energy, shapes started to come into focus. Trees, thinner and willowy, insect-like shapes darting among them. I reeled back when something fluttered in front of my viewpoint. *"Yack! What the hell."*

"The planes are infinite and their occupants are variable."

"And I gotta find one single plane? A needle in an infinite haystack?"

"No, you'll act as my anchor once I find the plane I'm looking for. Honestly this is a part where being a cat isn't preferable. Cats are slow searchers since it takes you time to peer through the anchor space."

"How do you do it, then? I thought humans were blind to magic."

"Here we can see as well as you can, but I prefer to use scent."

"Scent? How the hell do you do that?"

"You've seen that familiars pick up little talents from their masters?"

"Like Oric's teleport?"

"Yeah. It works both ways. I can smell magic. In our reality it's very minor, just enough to sniff out strong magics, and I can't really tell what type. But here, beyond biology and the Veil, I can smell the worlds beyond these walls. Aaannndd found it!"

"Congratulations."

"Hold onto where you are."

"Uh, okay?" Tentatively I reached into the blue around me, pulling on the walls with experimental tugs of my mind. It held.

"I'm going to start pulling."

I gave a mental meep.

19

Ever wonder what a mouse would feel if you sucked him up with a vacuum cleaner? I don't—it's as if you stepped out into a hurricane completely naked. The force ripped me away from the wall and sent me careening down the tube. Instinctively, I flailed at the sides, trying to find purchase but the walls felt slick, composed of Jell-O that parted beneath my tendrils of thought as they whipped by faster and faster. A whiteness grew below me, a light that I knew would be an oncoming locomotive if I hit it at this speed. My panic grew as it loomed closer and closer. I screamed as something in my mind twisted and tore free. With a sudden jolt, I stopped dead. Claws—that was the only way to describe them—stuck into the walls around me. Before I had imagined reaching out to the tube with hands, but now the sensations returning to me were those of thick pads pressed against the hollow trunk of a tree, claws biting into the wood as I felt O'Meara's weight on me, trying to drag me downward. *"Took you long enough,"* she sniggered.

I mentally sputtered, looking at the brightness. It suddenly seemed much farther away.

"Oh, don't bother—you weren't in any real danger. You just would have slammed into your body. Why do you think I had you start all the way back at your anchor?"

I growled, *"I think some more advanced warning is in order before trying to kill me, O'Meara!"* The pull was intensifying, and I sunk my claws in harder to compensate.

"I've got no time to teach you gently, Thomas. This is a very easy cast as I knew exactly where I was going. A good pair can do a spell like this in less than a second."

"That doesn't seem very likely."

A dull impact reverberated through the walls, and the force pulling at my guts ceased. *"Done—come back,"* O'Meara called.

With an inner sigh, I unhooked myself and willed myself back into that distant light. My eyes blinked open to O'Meara's smirk. She cut off any complaint by scratching the tender muscles at the base of my left ear. "Good job," she said, backing the praise with a warm current of emotions, her hand rhythmically moving down my neck.

"Damn it, I'm not a dog," I protested, even as my body shifted to push my head into her lap, allowing her hand to travel further down my spine. "I'm trying to keep this professional. I don't work for praise."

"I happen to believe that reducing a two-hundred-pound monster like you to a purring mass of tawny pudding is just something that has to be done every once in a while." Her hands changed from petting to scratching, first behind my ears and then slowly chasing the tension down my neck. My resistance crumbled as a purr rose from my throat like the growl of a hot rod.

"There we are!" O'Meara mentally cheered. *"Is that so bad?"*

It was not bad at all. Rather it felt like the deepest, most pleasurable massage of my entire life. And I really didn't want it stopped as I twisted myself to let her fingers to get a good angle on my ears.

Sleep came and went, like the passing of an ocean tide. I woke to the sound of tweeting from below and a heartbeat above. No, that was backwards, I determined after a few moments, gravity making itself known by pressing something hard into my left kidney. The heart beat pulsed beneath me, pushing through the pillow of her soft breast on which my head rested, one of her hands settled on my chest, her fingers curled into the thick fur there. My mind prodded hers and felt a kiss of peace from her quiet mind. The howling of her demons that I had not realized I had been able to hear before now was silent.

A vague feeling of guilt crept over me as my thoughts drifted to the last time I had woken up against another heart. I had woken to find myself cradled in Angelica's lap in the dead of night, the TV buzzing softly, its screen empty of the movie that we had been watching. I found her watching me with that weary sad smile that she always got a few days before she left. If she was part of this crazy world, well, I couldn't blame her for not wanting to tell me. And now there I was curled up with a woman I still didn't entirely trust or really know, even though we shared a telepathic connection. Despite that, my entire body felt more relaxed than it had been since that moment, a week and a half ago.

I stretched the best I could without moving my contoured body much. Extending my front legs and displaying my claws sent the birds in the overhanging tree into a spate of furious chirping. O'Meara stirred beneath me and muttered a curse as I felt her mind burst to frantic consciousness with a flare of heat and fear. Her hand tensed on my chest and then relaxed as her mind placed and catalogued her surroundings along with vague memories of what brought us to this situation.

"If this were a movie from the eighties, which of us would be smoking the cigarette?" I asked as she slid that barrier across her thought processes, damping my awareness of her thoughts to mere echoes of annoyance and a deep satisfaction.

She made a half disgusted noise. "It's nothing like that! You fell asleep and pinned me to my seat," she protested as she scratched the underside of my chin affectionately. "Come on—get off me, mister overgrown house cat. We still have work to do. We're just lucky that the do-not-notice charm on this car is still working or we'd be surrounded by animal control, desperate to save me from such a fierce monster."

A spark of intuition leapt at me. "You haven't slept since Archie died, have you?"

"No. I probably needed the nap."

Reluctantly I curled up off her, wincing as my muscles twitched and my spine crackled. It took a few more moments to get ourselves sorted out. O'Meara had me look at the badge to make sure the spell on it was still there. It emitted a faint white glow to my eyes. I refused to use a coffee cup that smelled like a breeding pit for fuzzy ooze as a "muzzle extender," so we made a quick trip detour to McDicks for a breakfast of ten sausage McMuffins. Biscuits tasted awful, but meat and cheese I still found guiltily delicious. The nice lady at the takeout window saw me as we departed, and her eyeballs nearly ejected from her face when I smiled at her.

Nobody gave me a second glance when I walked into the police station with O'Meara, but I sure felt silly with that coffee cup over my nose. At least this one smelled fresher. The desk sergeant buzzed us through with barely a glance, and I followed O'Meara's confident footsteps through the hallways and down into the basement. It was as if witches in red dresses with a sword on their hips and apex predators at their sides were an everyday thing.

In the basement the polished hardwood floors of the old police station gave way to cracked checkered tile that greedily sucked at my body heat through my paws. The walls of whitewashed cinder block construction framed heavy metal doors all equipped with smooth round door-knobs—doorknobs I couldn't open unless I covered my paws in peanut butter first. They all had rectangular signs declaring what lay beyond them in faded red lettering: storage, custodial closet, boiler room and then, right next to an elevator, County Coroner Office. Across the hall the door read "Morgue."

O'Meara knocked, waited and knocked again. No one answered. Neither of us was surprised. Ducsbury wasn't the nicest of cities, but it didn't have enough population to result in a particularly busy coroner. O'Meara turned to the morgue, knocked three times and then started to fish for something in her purse.

We both gave a bit of a start when a muffled voice called through the door. "Come in, Sergeant!"

O'Meara swore mentally as she slapped a friendly smile on her face. *"Should have done this last night!"*

I didn't disagree as I shifted to stand closer to her, try-ing to look as dog-like as possible. Nobody had given me a glance on the way in, but the potential for discovery still left me feeling naked. Maybe furless.

"You'll have to stay here in the hallway, Thomas. What-ever dog people think you are, it's probably not allowed in the morgue. I'll see if I can get rid of him for a bit." O'Meara

stepped forward and pressed the door open as she opened her eyes to me.

A grey-haired man looked up from a corpse lying on a stainless steel table. His fuzzy brow furrowed as his eyes flicked up and down O'Meara before settling on her face. "Sorry, I was expecting someone else. I'm afraid I've got my hands a bit full at the moment." He gestured with his hands, the purple nitrile gloves smeared with blood from the young man in front of him.

O'Meara flashed him her fake badge. "Lieutenant O'Meara. Sorry, I should have called. I'm from the agency. I just need to ID a hit-and-run victim from two days ago. Name is Archibald Frances."

The man scowled at the badge and glanced down at his patient and back at the badge. "Fine, let me drag him out of the freezer. Do you need me to lay him out?" He gestured at the second steel table in the room; the metal shined like a mirror.

O'Meara drew a cell phone from her purse. "No, just need a quick picture to try to find next of kin and a sample for DNA tests."

The man's scowl deepened, but he left his post at the end of the corpse and walked to the back of the room, where a half dozen square doors stood on a mat steel wall. He jerked the handle of one of the doors and swung it open. Grabbing the drawer within, he pulled it so hard that it reached the extent of its travel with a loud bang and scooted the corpse on its surface forward several inches. Then he fixed O'Meara with a baleful glare. "Anything else, Lieutenant?"

O'Meara eyed him warily. "Did I do something wrong?"

"Course not. You can't do anything wrong with that badge. Excuse me, I could use some coffee." He strode for the door so fast that O'Meara had to hurry to step out of the way. He crossed the hallway and disappeared into his office across the way without seeing me.

O'Meara inspected her badge. *"I've never gotten a reaction like that before! Is he seeing me as some sort of national security agency?"*

"Maybe he got in trouble the last time you did this?"

"You never know with mortals," she thought at me, waving her hand dismissively as she walked towards the freezer. *"The Veil keeps us separate. He won't even remember me by this afternoon."*

She turned her attention to Archibald on the drawer. There were no claw marks on his withered body. There were no wounds at all. The knees that I had remembered being bent in a way that made you wince were fine—knobby and covered with liver spots but functionally intact. *"I think somebody beat us here, Thomas,"* O'Meara thought.

From where I sat in the hallway, the door to the coroner's office squealed open and the man stepped back out of it. His features contorted into a mask of red rage, and his eyes were filled with an eerie blue light. In his hand, he clutched a black gun.

20

"Uhhh, O'Meara? This looks like trouble," I thought, sending her the image as I backpedaled away from the door as he advanced.

Instantly O'Meara filled with a rush of heat. Deadly intent filled her mind, reacting to the threat with an almost machine-like precision. I could see the spell on the man snap into focus, a twisted knot embedded in his brain, pulsing and swollen. As he took his second step towards the door to the morgue, O'Meara gathered the heat of a tiny sun into her hand. In her mind I saw what it would do to this man when it struck, paired with the barest flicker of remorse his death would trigger.

My backpedaling ceased by his third step, my decision crystallizing by the fourth, and as he raised his leg to kick open the door I leapt. His eyes finally saw me as my jaws clamped down hard on his gun arm. Too hard. I felt his bones snap between my jaws with two distinct *crack* sounds that reverberated through my skull. We hit the floor, and the gun clattered across the tile. The man looked at me, blinking as if he had just woken up from a dream. The blue of the spell was gone from his eyes.

Somewhat sheepishly I let his arm go. It dangled in the middle, and the man looked at it. Staring at it in shock, he raised it up to get a better look. He took a deep breath and started screaming.

"Damn it, Thomas! Why did you do that? I had it in hand!"

"Just get your pictures and let's get out of here," I snapped at her. Her method would have involved a three-inch hole burned through the man's skull.

The mental response to that was something similar to a Charlie Brown *augh!*, mixed with several sexual depictions that I will not repeat. *"Fuck it. Get the coffee cup and run! If you get back to the car without anyone seeing you, the charm on it should protect you. I'll bullshit my way out."* A mental image of several cops shooting a rabid dog made it clear to me what would happen if I didn't skedaddle.

The elevator dinged, indicating it was descending; the guy screamed louder, clutching at his arm. I snatched my coffee cup and bounded back to the stairway we had taken down, only to hear the pounding of footsteps. There was nowhere to hide. Those round doorknobs stared at me like unhelpful eyeballs. I looked back at the screaming man, his gun forgotten as he hunkered next to the wall. No cover, no place to hide. I had to look as nonthreatening as possible.

"Play dead," a deep voice suggested.

It was the only idea that I had. I flopped down next to the stairs, held my breath and unfocused my eyes.

Two men pounded from the stairway, and two pairs of worn leather shoes and khaki pants entered my vision.

"Jebus, that's a big dog!"

"Holy crap! Harvey!" One of the men pounded down the hallway. The other pair of shoes turned away.

"Now!" O'Meara shouted in my head. I rolled onto my feet and launched myself up the stairway, hit the landing and raced up the rest of the stairs before the cop gave more than a squawk of alarm. An emergency exit at the top of stairwell provided no dilemma, and I slammed into the "EMERGENCY EXIT: ALARM WILL SOUND" sign with both paws. The tinny alarm didn't hit my ears until I was ten feet from the door. I crouched between cars for a moment, and when I heard nobody screaming, jumped back into O'Meara's car.

I collapsed into the back and squeezed myself into the space between the front and back seats, hunkering as low as I could.

"Happy with yourself?" O'Meara snapped at me, her thought jabbing into my mind like a needle.

I pondered for a moment, licking my chops. A sweet taste clung to my tongue, and I didn't want to think about what that meant. *"If you get back to the car without getting shot at, I'll be happy."* I couldn't see what she was doing; the link was stuffed with angry fog.

"There was no need for you to do that. I had the situation well in hand."

"You were going to kill him."

"And he me."

"He was under a spell or something. He didn't know what he was doing."

"Do you know that, Thomas? Do you know the difference between a spell that enhances his mind and one that controls it? If he had died, then we would not be separated and exposed. Someone is trying to kill us, Thomas, and the best way to do that is to separate a familiar from their magus. We better hope he's the only one."

She sounded reasonable, but something in her statement

sat wrong. A sudden desire to be alone seized me, and the link shut with a snap. It was like an involuntary reflex, a muscle that I hadn't known I possessed. But now I knew I could do it again. The closure wasn't total. Her shock and surprise leaked through easily enough, as did mental bangs on the door, which I ignored.

I needed to think. I'd never been someone who'd been able to make up my mind in an instant, and when I did I had tended to avoid conflict and go with the flow. This world, though, this world had turned me on my head, changed my life so drastically that all I could do was dig my heels in and shout "*No!*" at the top of my lungs. Now, I began to see the realities of the world on this side. I idly wondered if perhaps Archibald's attempt to murder the council hadn't been quite as misguided as it sounded. This was no fantasy kingdom of wonder from a children's book full of oddly flavored jellybeans. O'Meara, the most moral magus I had encountered, had been about to kill that man with the barest tinge of guilt and now wanted to lecture me for interfering with that murder.

They all had so much power, but where was the sense of responsibility? O'Meara could have blasted her way out of that police station, turning it into an inferno. I had seen that option in her head along with many others. Killing that man had been her holding back. In her mind, Munds were to be protected in abstract; the moment one became a tiny threat she'd put them down like rabid dogs.

I didn't know the history of this world or how it interacted with the history of mine. Oric, Sabrina, all of them had tried to tell me that my rules didn't apply here, that my laws of decency meant nothing. The culture was medieval or perhaps an "enlightened" plutocracy. The wars of Napoleon could be a living memory for their elders. Their social system could be traced back to Genghis Khan for all I knew.

It brought me up against a hard question as I stared at the ripped upholstery of the back of O'Meara's car seat, one I had never had to ask in my old life. Sure I knew there was plenty of injustice in the world, but being who I had been, I had never been forced to stare it in the face before. Now in this new life I could smell the stink of decay on its breath.

A choice needed to be made. I could ignore that stink, swallow it down, make my bed and live a long life. Or I could spit in the face of injustice whenever I had the opportunity and accept the fact that my life was likely to be nasty, brutish and short.

I could see the air shimmer around O'Meara as she came out of the police station and stalked towards the car. I watched her from the front seat of the car. She unleashed a verbal torrent as soon as she popped open the driver-side door. Something about tactics and cops and bullshit. I let it all wash over me. I could hear the worry and fear underneath it all. I can't say it was water off a duck's back either—my back muscles cranked up an unbelievable amount of tension.

After she exhausted herself she looked at me sternly. "Do you understand?" Her eyes bored down on me, mimicking the eyes of a hurt and betrayed parent.

Steeling myself, I took a deep breath and pulled myself up to my full sitting height. Then I looked directly into O'Meara's fiery orbs. "O'Meara"—I paused, gathering my words—"if I ever have to save someone from you again, I'm leaving." As the words left my muzzle, my certainty in them solidified. Crazy as this place was, I found it comforting to find a line I wouldn't cross.

She blinked several times before the she slapped the

angry mask over her face again. "Thomas! Don't be stupid! You're—"

I opened the link and she fell inside my mind. A flash of recognition washed over her face, followed by a flood of terror. Her ruddy skin lost its color as her eyes grew large and watery. "No. Please. You don't know what you're walking into."

"Tell me I'm unreasonable. That man didn't pose much danger to you at all. You could have disabled him just as easily as you were going to kill him." Doubt flailed around in my head as her eyes lost focus. This had not been what I expected.

"Stop sounding like Rex—you're not him. Nobody else can be him. He's gone for a reason," she said through gritted teeth.

I started to ask who Rex was, but I realized I knew already. Rex was not his name. His name was Sir Rex, never just Rex. The dead dog in armor that loomed large in O'Meara mindscape, presiding over the graveyard of severed links. In a flash I saw him standing in front of a gallery of wizened men and women. A larger man sat in a balcony above the rest, eyes filled with thunder as he stared down at Sir Rex. "Thrice!" he boomed. "Thrice you have made a mockery of the authority of this council! Your actions have stained the record of your magus and have allowed the escape of a dangerous fugitive by your refusal to pursue! There will not be a fourth time!" The gavel came down, and the vision disappeared as the howls of grief rolled across O'Meara's mind.

"They executed him, Thomas. He refused a direct order from the council because he thought it was wrong. You can't just throw down the gauntlet of principle, Thomas. That isn't how this world works."

I laughed and confusion washed over her. "Look, O'Meara, I'm not charging into the council to declare that I'm imposing a new world order. I'll have to cross that bridge later. I'm telling you to not kill folk you could disable, all right?"

O'Meara's hands seized the sides of my head and pulled me up to look into her eyes, which had regained their fire. "Don't try to lie to me! You just showed me the insides of your head! You can't change the magi and their view of mundanes because you want to!"

I smiled slyly and pushed into her. Her arms folded around me as I pressed my face against her chest, releasing a conciliatory purr from my throat. She slumped back into the seat and let her hand play across my neck and shoulders. *"I don't care about the council,"* I thought to her. *"You are the only one I've got over the barrel. I'll just start with you."*

She tensed, and for a moment I thought she would push me away but a sigh escaped her instead. "Damn cats. They'll always take advantage of every inch you got." She hugged me tighter.

"I win?" That earned me a noogie.

21

We drove back to town. O'Meara made a beeline for our own podunk police station but turned into a small strip mall across the street at the last moment. After parking in back, she held out the coffee cup to me to take. I looked at it and then at the unmarked door we had just parked in front of, less than seven feet from the bumper.

"I've got a more comfortable rig inside, but in daylight you've got to have a muzzle extender. We are not on good terms with the Veil around here."

Had I still possessed eyebrows they would have been raised. "The Veil doesn't like you? How does a wall not like you?"

"Same way it knows when you put a coffee cup on your nose that you're pretending to be a dog. It's intelligent, and thanks to a bunch of out-of-towners that made it work really hard a few years ago, it's been grouchy ever since." She cut off my retort by shoving the coffee cup between my teeth and jumping out of the car. She waited impatiently at the door for me.

I chuffed in annoyance and climbed out over the

passenger-side door. And then I paused as a strange scent reached through the cup and hit me in the nose. It had a bit of a maple flavor, coupled with a bitter musk that seemed to dance on the roof of my mouth. Flehming yielded no more information on the scent, but made it stronger. My brain tongued at it, a familiarity poking at me like a rock in my shoe. Regardless, I saw no source of the scent; nothing in the parking lot stirred besides O'Meara.

"*Something wrong?*"

"*Strange scent around here.*"

O'Meara joined me in scanning the area with our eyes, but neither of us saw anything. "*I'm an inquisitor. Lots of people come to me when they can't solve their own problems. Strange scents are bound to happen.*"

I nodded, and then turned and padded up to the door.

O'Meara hauled the door open to reveal an office manager's nightmare. Unconnected cubicles the color of my grandfather's decades-old easy chair were scattered about a large room randomly. They were the sort of cubes I hadn't seen since the mid-nineties, each panel consisting of a plastic frame over which a cheap knitted fabric was stretched. In the center of the room, a doublewide cubicle seemed to be floating in a sea of paper stacked around it. The papers were sorted into precarious piles due to the nonuniform sizes, as if somebody had run out of office paper and restocked from a fancy art store instead of Office Depot. Large sheets of thick patterned paper with detailed calligraphy were sandwiched between normal white office stock. A few scrolls lay scattered around like pieces of driftwood.

A woman's voice called across the paper sea. "Mistress O'Meara? That you?" The cadence of the words was slightly halting.

"Ixey!" O'Meara stared at the tide of papers surrounding

the cube. "What the hell are you doing with all this paper? I'm a fire magus! One wrong message from the council and fwoosh! This place is gonna be an inferno!"

A smiling round face framed by rainbow-dyed hair popped over the top of the flooded cubicle. "It's okay—I made friends with a salamander last week!" Her eyes widened and a grin spread over her purple lips as I stepped forward. "*Oh, my God!*" Her head popped back behind the cubicle's barrier only to reappear at the side of the cubicle with her entire body in tow. O'Meara held me up to her own eyes in order to witness the visual assault that was Ixey's outfit. A smart business suit sparkled with neon pink trim and bright purple pinstripes on a background of shiny gold fabric that hugged her lean body. She picked her way through the stack of the paper, her eyes never leaving my face. "You're Thomas, right?"

"News travels fast," O'Meara huffed, crossing her arms.

Her smile spread wider. "You bonded in front of Jowls, he's a gossip wormhole."

O'Meara groaned besides me. "The only reason Jules gets any business at all is to trade gossip with Jowls."

Ixey chuckled. "He's getting more business after Archibald stopped paying his minions. I even saw that werewolf pack in there last week." The rainbow punk girl knelt in front of me, and only then did I see her familiar, watching me with two glittering ruby eyes—a lizard clinging to the shoulder of her jacket. Its scales were metallic gold, the claws silver, and a row of purple garnets laced down its spine. She held out her hand in front of my nose. "Hi, I'm Ixey and this is Garn," she said, indicating the lizard with a slight tilt of her head.

It took me a moment to realize that she had offered her hand so I could give it a sniff—which I then did. She smelled human with an earthen undertone.

"Could I pet you? Or are you a no-touching sort of cat?"

The question caught me off guard, and as usual when confused I consented. "Uh, okay?" Her hand slid over my head and down my back.

"You're softer than I thought you'd be," she said after a few strokes. "Feels like you could use a good brushing."

My ears started to heat up as I felt her fingers catch on a few knots. Each tug was like hammer to a primal sort of pride. My tongue began to itch, and I licked my chops to relieve the urge.

"Thomas is still very much at war with the idea that grooming with his tongue is sanitary. I know he'd love a good brushing."

"O'Meara!" I snapped, annoyed at being called out on that, although my thoughts had gone there.

"Thomas, Ixey is as close as I've ever gotten to having an apprentice. You can trust her as you would me, perhaps more so because she's a huge softy and a bit of a wuss."

"Hey!" Ixey protested. The petting stopped, and I found myself leaning against her legs. The urge to groom redoubled with the loss of that stroking hand.

"Try scratching him right at the base of his skull—he really enjoys that." O'Meara smirked at me.

Ixey's eager hands found me before I could get up the gumption to remove myself. I may have tilted my head a little to allow them better access, I don't know. At that moment I was a pretty sorry excuse for an apex predator. Eventually my pride outweighed the petting, and I pulled away, taking refuge behind O'Meara, who immediately started scratching the same spot. This had nearly twice the effect, her fingers reading my thought as they chased an itch along my spine. *Why are you doing this to me?* I mentally mewled at her. Both women looked at me with the expression they get while playing with adorable children.

"I'm not allowed to give my familiar a little love and attention?" O'Meara thought. Her hand crept down to the base of my tail, which did things that went well beyond a back rub. Her hands quickly retreated back to my ears.

"This is a temporary thing!" I protested as I leaned against her, my conscious thoughts threatening to melt away in a slurry of purrs.

"I know. But I have to admit I'm hoping you change your mind on that. It's going to be doubly difficult to get someone after you. Not that the TAU *were happy with me to begin with. I might have to get split done,"* she thought at me, but I could see a little shining gem of truth behind the words. I plucked it from her mind and opened it. *"Hey—don't!"*

Dread filled my mind as a thousand angry papers screamed for my blood. The link closed with an angry slam as the petting stopped dead. I opened my eyes to find O'Meara glaring down at me. "What's the matter, boss? Is magi paper work that scary? Do magi send screaming letters like in Harry Potter?" I grinned up at her. I'd just done something to surprise her, and that was definitely worth a few missed pets.

"Pretty close," Ixey piped in as O'Meara shook her finger at me, but there was no heat behind this anger.

"Damn it, Thomas—firstly you're not supposed be able to snatch at my thoughts yet! Second, stop exposing my weaknesses in front of the employees."

"But I know about your weakness to paper work. I practically have to staple you to your desk to get you to look at it," Ixey said as she leaned against a nearby cube. If she had another few pounds on her thin frame the entire cube would have toppled.

O'Meara crossed her arms and huffed, and then cast a baleful look at the sea of paper work in the middle of the room. "Get it all organized and bring it into the office." Then, turning to me, she said, "How hungry are you?"

"I could eat," I said automatically, hopefully even. Those sausages had been an eternity ago, and as a general rule I did not refuse offered food.

O'Meara waved at an empty wastebasket in front of me. "Good, I really don't want to work with you on a full stomach. If you gotta hurl, use this."

I was so disappointed. I had already pictured a juicy steak being placed in front of me.

O'Meara led me towards the back of the building—well, the front actually. The store's display windows had been boarded up with plywood. I followed her to a jumbo-sized cubicle parked in the corner of the room. Double the size of Ixey's office, this had been constructed out of four units, with an actual door on one side. It had a scent different from the rest of the office, more of a charge to the air than a scent exactly.

"In case you're wondering where our budget for office furniture went, it's in here." She pulled the door open, revealing a dark chasm in the floor beyond it. Or so I thought, because O'Meara stepped out onto it and did not fall into an abyss. She whirled on one foot, her aura suddenly coming to life and bathing her body in flame. Around her feet runes flared into existence, set aflame by the heat of her aura. Complex circular diagrams came to life, and then slowly started to rotate. I blinked as some of the circles looked to be sinking down into the cavernous blackness. Circles became pillars; runes elongated from their moorings and interlocked with each other. Circles threaded down the outside of the pillars, spinning up and down their length. Heat pulsed up through the center, and the scent of molten iron intruded into my nose.

This was no magic. This was a machine, a machine powered via O'Meara's anchor. *"Oh, it's so good to see this again,"* O'Meara whispered in my head, peering through my eyes. *"It's been over a year since I've seen it work for me."*

"O'Meara, what is this?" I asked, watching what appeared to be a ribbon of lava fly up at us through the darkness.

"It is a ritual surface, a magic circle."

"If this is a circle of salt, then I'm Cobra Commander's concubine."

Pride swelled her thoughts. *"Well, it's a pretty fancy circle, I admit. In town, only the Archmagus had one better. Remember how difficult it was to bring back that little bit of authority for the badge trinket?"*

"My claws still tingle from that."

"That's part of it; a good circle allows its users to draw much more power and surf through the infinite planes for much longer. A simple circle, composed of material native to our plane, strengthens the connection between a magus and a familiar. That helps with the creation of weaves or spells."

"This"—she gestured to the whirling mechanism below her—*"extends that strength all the way to our anchors so we can draw ten times the amount of energy from the higher planes or larger things from the lower."*

"How does it work?" I asked, watching as the ribbon of lava touched a spinning column of runes. It twisted around the column and stopped it dead, like a thread jamming a gear. At first I thought it had been broken, but small runes separated from the column and swarmed down it like a colony of ants. They marched down its length, into the void below, and the string thickened in their wake.

O'Meara mentally shrugged. *"Magic, of course."*

22

I looked up at her, seated lotus-style on one side of the machine, the pillar attached to the thread extending beneath her as she watched me and my mind with undisguised amusement. Her eyes twinkled as she took in my scowl. *"Okay, yes, but how?"* I thought at her.

"Do you know how a cell phone works?"

"Uh . . . vaguely?"

"Well, that's about all I know about this circle. There are a few magi alive who can understand it and possibly even build its equal, but I'm not one of them. Archibald in his youth was one of them, but that was a long time ago."

"So we're not living in a golden age of magic? This is a relic, then?"

"It's what we call an Atlantean artifact."

"The whole super advanced civilization that fell into the sea thing and left no proof of their existence is real?" I tried and failed to tamp down my skepticism.

"Even on this side of the Veil we don't know much, but we believe that they are the reason the Veil exists. However, we do know they were not human. They had a civilization that

stretched across many planes. We believe the so-called island was their first toehold on our world."

"So they created the Veil to keep the natives in line?"

"No, the Veil was put in place by those who crushed the Atlanta's and erased almost all traces of them from the earth. The Veil called them The Fey."

My brain failed to process that thought on the first time through my noggin, so I repeated it to myself to try again. Okay, so the ancient Atlanteans who had made the epic magic machine under our feet had been wiped out by a bunch of pixies? Oh, and you can chat with the Veil itself?

O'Meara plucked the thought from my head before I could organize a witticism from it. "Okay, two things: the Veil only ever talked to Merlin, so you can take that with a grain of salt. And second, while Fey are the origin of pixies and elves, if you ever encounter them, remember that they are the finger puppets of a creature that resembles a multidimensional octopus more than anything else. While they lack the same punch of a dragon, most magi think this is due to compassion and carefulness than lack of raw power. When they do visit, we are but ants at their picnic."

"Wait, so Merlin exists?"

"Did. He's dead or really good at convincing us that he's dead—either way he's long gone." She held up a hand to ward off the questions that were piling up like cars on an off-ramp. "We'll have time for the history lesson later, Thomas. Now we have to get work done. Take your place." She pointed at a pillar directly across from her.

I swallowed back my questions and took a halting step forward; the surface felt cool and smooth beneath my paw. The circle reacted instantly to the contact, a few runes peeling off from the larger circles to sniff at my paw. I quickly scampered to my designated pillar. The symbols followed after me and circled the pillar warily. I looked across the circle to O'Meara, only to find the spiraling surface of her pillar there while she smiled down on me from above. In fact all around me the circle's mechanisms had sprung up from the surface of the artifact, invading the space.

A sudden loss of balance gripped me as the illusion of depth became real. It was as if I walked up to a street painting that had the illusion of a deep pit or steep cliff. The pillar beneath me shuddered, and I threw myself down on it, gripping the sides with all four paws. The void loomed dizzyingly deep below me. I heard the distant whir as the pillar below me unfolded in a similar fashion to O'Meara's, and I began to gain altitude, accompanied by what I can only describe as a very curious sensation. It was perhaps similar to when I had first discovered I had developed the tail, although this involved far less panic. The chain around my neck grew warm as I felt something wrap around a body part I had not known I possessed until this artifact touched it. I couldn't quite figure out how it attached to me precisely, but it was long and tube-like as the machine extended its touch along its length, pulling on it width-wise, stretching it beyond its usual shape, like the feeling of a tendon being stretched out along a leg. As I reached a height equal to O'Meara's, the pulling sensation had reached the tip of my newly discovered limb.

The heat of the chain around my neck intensified to uncomfortable levels, and in the darkness between us the length of the chain materialized, each link glowing the dull red of hot iron. It floated in the air between us, spiraling on itself like an oddly constructed DNA molecule made of knots of chain. Spindle-thin arms reached out from the smaller pillars and teased at the seething knot with limitless precision. Within a minute the links unraveled and spun the chain into a web around the pillars. The entire system pulsed once and disappeared, leaving just O'Meara and me. The various barriers we had constructed against each other, hers expert and entrenched and my instinctual efforts, both became tiny garden fences against the twin tsunamis that were our minds.

Her shock and surprise crashed over me like a wave. This had never happened before—the connection so wide, so total, that we risked falling into each other and not being able to pull ourselves back. In mutual agreement we held ourselves back from each other, but still each little thought bloomed between us. Neither of us was quite sure whom it came from. The fey chain, normally a smaller mental bandwidth than a long familiarship, had synched perfectly with the ancient apparatus.

"We have to focus on the task," we thought. Yet temptation floated beside that thought. Here, like this, she could pour the knowledge of the magi, their history and culture right into me. Or I could watch them unfold in her own mind. Yet bright red dots of "no" flashed over that temptation. Risks were many when learning that way, especially if this bond was to be temporary. Any memories and knowledge shared with me might not be copied from hers, but instead might be links to her own memories and then would be lost when the link was severed. Her shudder became mine, and for a moment recollections of her times being familiarless overwhelmed us.

It took both of our combined wills to claw out of the maelstrom of memories and herd them back into O'Meara's head.

"To the work," we both thought; no temptations fluttered this time. In the physical space O'Meara took the bag she had brought into the circle and upturned it. Dozens of metal

trinkets clattered on the pillar before her. She picked up one, a flat copper disk with a hole in the center, and tossed it into the center. Runes bloomed around it, catching it and aligning it so it floated precisely between our planes of vision. At a silent urging from O'Meara's mind we opened our eyes to each other.

The disk had magic of a color I had not seen before; dull green runes interlaced its surface and then beyond it, into those stomach-churning directions that should not be. My unease overflowed and was followed by her assurances, chasing the unease away. O'Meara began, *"Okay, Thomas, this is what I call a static spell. A specific bit of magic that does one thing. This is a scryer; when it's charged, looking through the hole will reveal what had happened in a place in the past. Were you trained, we could do a similar spell in about ten seconds. Most magi don't bother with statics for such minor spells, but my history is a bit irregular so I have foci that run the gamut of simple to complex. And I've used up nearly all of them in the last year. We need to recharge them. It will be just like the badge back in the police station."*

It was so, except not. The energies compared to that simple spell were massive, and the pressures that pulled on me as I served as O'Meara's anchor as she shuttled essence into the trinkets were an order of magnitude greater. Yet the circle had provided the tools to handle it all. There were now mental handholds to cling to in the tunnel, with slots that perfectly fitted my claws. We refueled three talismans, the scrying ring, a cloaking charm and sword that seemed to consist of at least six separate talismans woven into its parts. O'Meara did not explain the purposes of each, only that they were not something she hoped she had to activate. As we finished stuffing one side of the blade with the essence of the absence of heat, a crack appeared in the side of our universe.

"O'Meara, I've got it all ready for you." A voice bounced out of the brightness.

We gave a deep mental wince and then twisted something somehow that I had not even perceived before. The expansive feeling, the scaffolding that supported the new existence between us, fell away in a single instant. Everything about our unseen bodies snapped back to their former constraints. It was as if someone had snapped rubber bands into both my eardrums as I heard a savage popping sound. I swore mentally and vocally. There had to be a less painful way to unplug.

O'Meara herself groaned, "No . . ." Her voice was a rasp. "Well, depends, do you prefer to rip a Band-Aid off or peel it off slowly?" Her own body lay sprawled out across the dark void of the circle across from me, hands clutching at her head. Our headaches soon began to ease as the blur of light slowly resolved into a worried-looking Ixey.

"That . . . looks worse than usual for circle break, Mistress," she observed as O'Meara pulled herself to her feet, waving her off.

"It will pass. Turns out the thing is designed for fey chains, so we got a double whammy."

Ixey winced in sympathy. "I'm sorry I interrupted. The paperwork is ready."

O'Meara nodded as she braced herself against the cubical wall. "We . . . actually finished. We'll look at it in the office. Come on, Thomas." She gestured towards me as she lurched towards the entryway.

I followed, a bit steadier on my feet, mostly because I had four instead of two.

***

O'Meara's office had about as much charm as a dive bar and smelled similarly. A windowless room lit by a single overhead fluorescent bulb that whined as it dimly illuminated the dull metal sheen of a bank of fourteen file cabinets across from the door. The furniture had been placed irrespective of actually being able to open most of the cabinets. I assumed many of them had not been opened in years. A rather worn-looking deluxe-sized pet bed sat at the foot of the cabinets, and a massive desk that would not have been out of place in front of a bank CEO, had it been in better condition, rounded out the small space. It left only about a foot of space for O'Meara to squeeze her large frame around to get to the plush office chair on the far side of the desk. In front of the desk were two mismatched chairs, a wooden swivel chair from the same era as the desk and a more modern plastic and metal stacking job in the vein of the cubicles outside.

I wondered if O'Meara had trained in a similar manner to Archibald because a staggering assortment of papers were pinned to the wall. Maps were in the majority, but that might have been because they were the largest. Second were the handwritten notes, and third were small photographs of odd-looking people. It appeared that if you could decipher the handwriting, a tight cursive scrawl, one might be able to determine O'Meara's entire case history. I could clearly see the areas of the office she used; the rest lay under a carpet of thick dust that made my fur itch.

"Yep," O'Meara said after I had taken it all in, projecting a mental shrug at my assessment. "It's a hole but it's my hole, and therefore it's your hole too."

"Would it kill you to make it less of a hole?" I said, eyeing a dust bunny that had been uprooted by the closing of the door.

"Probably not," she said noncommittally as she dug around in her desk. "Aha!" From the depth of a drawer she pulled out a metal T-shaped bar about three-quarters of a foot long with the T-bit rubberized. The stem had a tennis ball stuck on the bottom of it. She slammed it on the table and grinned at me. "Now here's a good muzzle extender for you. Will keep the coffee out of your snout and your drool off the cup." I remained unmoved, images of bacteria dancing on the rubber gripped in my brain. O'Meara rolled her eyes. "Gods, you're prissy, Thomas. I can wash it before we leave. It's just a bit of dust. It won't kill you."

The door flew open before I could ready a retort. Ixey rode into the office on what appeared to be a Chinese dragon entirely composed of paper. Its head was folded from variety of white and yellow paper, with a spiral of Post-it notes as horns. The body was composed of single stack of paper that had to be nine feet long. Ixey sat on its back cross-legged, with her metal gecko riding on top of her own head. The whole thing glowed faintly with a greenish tint. She rode straight up to O'Meara's desk. "I had to call in a few favors, but here we go. Ready?"

O'Meara gave the briefest of nods.

"Alrighty then!" Ixey touched the head of the dragon, and it unfolded into a stack of papers about an inch thick. "These are formal requests for information regarding the killing of Archmagus Archibald." O'Meara pointed at the inbox on her desk, and the paper floated into it. A much taller stack of papers drew itself from the body of the dragon. "These are formal requests for your resignation from various parties."

"Are any signed by the Grand Inquisitor?"

The stack briefly separated into a fan of papers stretching across the room. They circled around Ixey, and she scanned each through narrowed eyes. "No." The papers immediately reformed into their stack.

"Well, then." O'Meara grabbed the stack with both hands, and, after a burst of light, nothing but ash settled on her desk. In this manner Ixey and O'Meara went through the paper work over the next hour. Ixey presented a stack of papers, which O'Meara would either burn, put into her inbox for later or sign with the tip of a flaming fingernail. The show entranced me for the first five minutes, but the novelty soon wore off. Signing paper work with fireworks was still signing paper work. Had I the hands or telekinetic powers that Ixey apparently possessed, I could have helped. Well, helped in the same manner of a five-year-old helping his mother, but at least that would have been more interesting. Not knowing Latin or whatever language the magi used for official communication would make it even more difficult. That would be something else I had to learn. Bored, I snuck back out into the main office, wondering if the TAU gave crash courses in Latin, and had a mental image of a motley collection of animals sitting at desks while Rudy attempted to set everyone's tails on fire.

The sea of paper in the main room had disappeared, and I popped my head into Ixey's doublewide and into a collision of two worlds. On the right sat a computer workstation with no less than four wide-screen monitors hovering over the workspace, held up by spindly metal arms. Next to them, a bank of police scanners clung to the wall, emitting bursts of chatter. The lot was hooked up to a monolith-sized computer tower that had been detailed with a cascading set of pink and blue neon lights. I had to admire that for a bit. It had been a long time since I had been able to afford a custom rig like that. The other side of the cubicle, within a push of the rolling chair, was a workstation several centuries out of date. The surface was covered with quills, and scrolls were scattered about. In the center of it was a huge open book, twice the size of ye olde Khatt family bible, although not nearly as thick—a ledger of some sort, as the pages consisted of tiny writing, organized in columns. As I padded closer a small box next to the book lit up bright purple and silently produced a sheet of paper, which floated down into a waiting basket placed on the floor below it. A magic fax?

I stared at it for a moment, and slowly a myriad array of interlocking patterns began to come into focus; a complex weave of runes bustled beneath the rock's surface amid a constantly changing web of purple links. Blinking the vision away, I sighed. Magic appeared to be nothing like what I had encountered in novels and movies, no words of power or memorization of spells from a spell book. Magic appeared to be as complex as electronics paired with interdimensional physics. O'Meara had a talent of fire and Sabrina electricity, and that's great if you need to kill somebody, but apparently doing something constructive with magic required a PhD. Score one for the wizened image of Tolkien's Gandalf bent over stacks of books and equipment. Even if I had been awakened as a human instead of a cougar, I doubted that I might make it out of apprenticeship. Magic smelled a lot like math, which had never been my strong suit.

After about an hour O'Meara and Ixey emerged from the office, both looking a bit drained, and I feeling both rested and hungry after a quick nap on a spare desk. Ixey's lizard, the bejeweled gecko, watched me stretch and yawn with his expressionless eyes. The yawn had caused both women to pause.

"Thomas, that's really not polite to do that!" O'Meara scolded me mentally.

It took me a moment to figure out what she was talking about. She followed up with a rather exaggerated mental picture of my large and pointy chompers. I finished my yawn and licked my chops, keeping my thoughts noncommittal.

"Cats," O'Meara muttered and gave her head a quick shake. "Thomas, get your muzzle extender—we're going to see an old . . . *friend* of mine."

23

At the top of the hill sat a worn-looking two-story house. It bore a rainbow of brown. The stained wooden siding had a sort of amber hue to it, the chipped paint of the trim around the windows more a deep chocolate. The little brick walkway leading around the side of the double garage ended at a rickety, faded brown porch. The door on the porch sported an island of metallic grey in the middle of it, where a huge patch of paint had peeled off.

O'Meara let the engine idle for moment, her eyes scanning first the various windows of the house and then the woods that encircled the lot. The house sat in the middle of said lot, on the very tippy top of the hill, and seemed content to be glumly silent as we sat in the driveway. I started to sit up from my hiding place, but O'Meara urged me to stay where I was, despite my protesting muscles.

"Stay here until I call for you," she thought at me as she popped open her car door.

"You should at least let me look for spells." I bit back a grumble about how uncomfortable my position felt. No point to it—had she cared to know how it felt she could

feel it. Although her concentration centered on the house, I kept my mind open to hers. I watched her walk up to the front door through her eyes. She glanced at the unkempt flowerbeds along the side of house, weeds starting to choke out the original occupants.

With some trepidation she walked onto the porch and rang the doorbell, resulting in an audible chime from inside the house. O'Meara counted the seconds, and after precisely thirty, a grinning face appeared in the long narrow window beside the door. A chill ran down our spines as O'Meara reached for her anchor, the warmth of her flames filling her. Dark memories bubbled, stirred to wakefulness by a glimpse of the face that dominated so many of them. I had recognized it too; the hair had greyed, but the face had the same strong jaw and cold grey eyes I had seen within O'Meara's nightmare back at the Archmagus's place. O'Meara had not been forthcoming on the nature of this guy on the way over.

The door swung open, revealing a man so massive that my mind immediately slapped him into a Zangief cosplay. A bit of dye to cover the grey and a beard and he wouldn't be far off. He wore jeans, and a loose flannel shirt hung off his broad shoulders. His wide grin seemed friendly as he held out his hands to O'Meara, not quite wide enough to request a hug but certainly ready to receive one. "Sammy girl! So good to see you!"

O'Meara visibly recoiled and stepped back out of range of his arms. "Good to see me?"

The arms fell away and he shrugged. "It's always good to see one's apprentice. Even one who is ungrateful such as yourself. But! We are doing something that will make even you happy today."

O'Meara did not even try to hide the dubious look. "You

were never someone who cared who you made happy or not, Whittaker. Certainly not me."

"You learned, did you not?"

"I learned far more from Cedrick than I ever did from you."

His massive hands rose up in a placating gesture. "You came here for a fight. Makes sense. It's all you do well now. My fault. I bet the council's got your back against the wall. Calling for a head publicly while privately they're all glad the ol' bastard's dead. And if you can't produce a head, well, plenty of folk will settle for yours."

O'Meara nearly staggered back. "Since when do you follow politics?! Who the hell even talks to you?"

"I don't—that's all as plain as day. It's not complicated, darlin'. Just like how you came here to pin it all on me. Get me angry. Maybe you even win. I die and you've got a body that can't testify back. If you lose, well, I'm sure somebody on the council might take exception to that."

My stomach flipped as I saw this scenario as described surface in O'Meara's mind, already prefabricated. I couldn't quite grasp how hard she had considered it, but at least a little corner of her head regarded it as an acceptable outcome. I mentally growled at her.

"Witches ashes, Thomas, if I did half the things I thought about there'd be nothing but charred ground for miles around," she thought back.

"I have no death wish, Whittaker," O'Meara said stiffly. Whittaker's eyes had gone cold, calculating, flitting up and down O'Meara's body, looking for something. Whatever he sought, he found and smiled, warmth flowing back into his eyes.

"Nor do I." He stepped away from the door, revealing a solarium stacked with cardboard boxes. He gestured inward with a sweep of his hand. "Won't you come in, Inquisitor?"

O'Meara's wary eyes roamed the scene for threats, and I felt her debate sending for me, but she dismissed the idea. She walked forward into the house.

My tail had begun to tingle with pins and needles; the base of it ground against the door of the car. As soon as the door closed I sat up and took a breath. This drew a sharp rebuke from O'Meara as she inspected the piles of boxes beyond the door to the house. I politely told her to shove it. If there were eyes on me, I didn't feel them, and no way was I going let myself suffocate while she had tea with this star-crossed lumberjack of a magus.

She grumbled but didn't push the issue as I filled my lungs with air that hadn't been conditioned by decades-old carpets and car funk. The air around the house had a bit of a different taste to it than the office; certainly less car exhaust helped. There was plenty familiar about it too. That strange scent I had noted at the office licked at my nose, a bitter musk that set my brain tingling. Had Whittaker been lurking around the office?

Inside, Whittaker led O'Meara through a corridor of boxes to a worn set of wicker furniture. In the corner a huge mound of reddish brown fur watched her with red eyes under a furrowed brow. "Hello, Loki." O'Meara nodded at the bear and tried not to look at the large patch of furless hide that marred his shoulder—a burn scar.

Loki did not respond and continued to regard her—not quite a stare as he did blink, but the vibe wasn't at all friendly.

Whittaker gestured to a seat. "I'd offer you coffee but it's"—he waved a hand at the boxes—"somewhere."

Various images of that same gentle-looking face, red and screaming, demanding coffee, rose in O'Meara's mind, causing the ghost of Rex to play a brief game of whack-a-mole.

O'Meara bit back a sarcastic remark before saying, "So you are leaving. Not waiting for the estate sale?"

"I think it's best. We have nothing to bid that isn't already owed to the council. Nothing here without old Archibald. I'm guessin' that most of us will follow after that." He smiled faintly. "Unless you happen to find a will, and even then I doubt it will make much difference. The council is drooling over the thought of getting their hands on whatever Archibald used to harvest all the tass he had access to."

"And you don't know what it is?"

His eyes flicked to the boxes. "No idea."

"If you want me to let you go, I need to scry both you and Loki's whereabouts within an hour of Archibald's murder."

The bear issued a deep growl. Whittaker's face twitched. "O'Meara—"

"No, you clearly want out of here for some reason, and I cannot take your word. If it later turns out you're lying, then I will be pilloried."

"Who's going to be the scryer? Ixey can't scry through a piece of glass," Whitaker replied.

Suddenly, gravity disappeared. My senses slammed back from O'Meara's perspective to find the world tumbling around me. My vision spun with shapes and colors without context. I hit something soft that wrapped around me and then felt the teeth of the gravel driveway. It didn't hurt. It was too sudden to hurt. Dazedly I chirped in surprise as something clapped down over my muzzle.

"*Thomas!*" O'Meara's voice exploded in my head, but I all I could respond back was a rising sense of panic.

"Got him! Thread the pole!" a gruff voice shouted.

"Go, go, go!" another voice growled, and the ground fell away. My limbs scrabbled to find purchase, ground or flesh it didn't matter, but my claws met only netting slipping between several toes. That bitter musk flared in my nostrils as the gravel raced under me. All of the dark mutterings of the others bubbled through my mind as it finally pieced together what was happening to me. Catnapped. I was getting catnapped! The fucking bastards were catnapping me!

The anger slammed into gear and with it adrenaline. A sound of hellish intensity tore out of me as I thrashed in earnest. Looking up from the ground I finally saw one of my captors. A huge beast ran somewhat awkwardly on two legs, thick black fur with russet red patches around his long muzzle. One thick hand wrapped around a pole that had been threaded through the webbing of the net surrounding my body. His other hand/paw strayed to the ground as he bore me down the hill towards a rusted pickup. Another huge hulk of a beast squatted in its bed. This beast grinned at me with the flattened face of not a wolf but a bulldog, with two yellow tusks jutting up past the bridge of his wide nose.

O'Meara behind burned with panic and impotent rage. An explosion echoed the sound of my impact on the flat bed. My legs finding purchase, I bounded up into the air, only be slammed back onto the truck by the huge beast, his hand swallowing my entire head. The truck rocked with heavy thumps as I heard the spraying of gravel before the wheels caught and the truck jerked forward. Howling erupted around me as I struggled against the vice grip on my head.

"Shut up, ya lot! Get the goddamn collar off!" A guttural voice ripped through my captors' victory howl, prompting several thick hands to grope at my neck. Claws snared the chains hidden there. Several more pressed into my spine, pinning me down. Somewhere behind us O'Meara threw her car into reverse. The chain around my neck tightened, two lines contracting around my throat. I stopped breathing as one of them groaned with effort.

"No, no, no! You're doing it wrong! You're strangling him."

"It's no good, Pa!" The chain went slack, and I drank a lungful of air as fast as I could pull it through my nostrils.

"You're too weak! Switch with me!" The pair counted to three. Two hands quickly replaced Pa's one.

"O'Meara! They're trying to break the bond!" I thought desperately through our link.

"Hang on, Thomas! I'm coming—"

Pa gave a grunt and the link went dead. The space in my mind where O'Meara had resided became a vacuum. It quickly filled with a crushing sort of pain. No specific wound to hurt, but rather a heavy thing that laid down on my head and lungs. I whimpered as it threaded through my limbs. I tried to scream, but it came out as nothing more than a depressed chirp.

24

"Heh, I doubt he'll have much fight in him now." A voice rumbled above me as I heard the chain crumple to the floor. "Hog-tie him—we've got a long drive."

"Sure, Pa."

I heard a distinctive ripping sound that could only be one thing and confirmed that the beasts on my back were true sadists. "Duct tape? Oh, come on. Can't you guys use rope or something?" I pleaded as a feeling of utter defeat overwhelmed me. My limbs felt like lead.

A laugh went up behind me. "Ropes are for boy scouts," one growled.

The group hog-tied me good. It clearly wasn't their first time at this rodeo. They slipped my head in a foul-smelling bag and then wrapped my legs together so tightly that my paws went numb within several minutes. I hissed at them, but couldn't be arsed to do much else and even that earned me a slap in the ribs with a growled warning to behave from the one they called Pa. The truck briefly stopped after about five minutes, and the metal frame groaned as one or two of the wolves departed. Definitely Pa was one of them.

The trip seemed to last a very long time. The wolves in the back with me didn't speak to each other. Perhaps they were too busy hanging their heads over the side and letting their tongues flap in the breeze. The pain of the broken bond ebbed, some of the weight easing, so I could lift my head with effort. But there was little point in exertion, taped up as I was. With time it wouldn't be impossible to work free, but the tape would ensure it would be a very painful experience.

The road got rougher as we went. I could smell the earthen dust of the road, and the increased vibration started giving my side a good pummeling. Worse, it made me aware of another problem.

"Hey, uh, wolf guys? Are we almost there? 'Cuz your truck's tap-dancing on my bladder."

"Heh, fat chance, cat. This ain't no movie, and I'm not falling for that. Hold it or don't. Not gunna do you any good."

"How long we gonna keep him wrapped up like that, Eagle?"

"Always the softy, ain't ya, Noise. Living with that humie is dullin' those teeth."

"Oh, like what I do is very different from the way you and Tallow spend your naked days in that cabin. I saw that satellite dish on the roof."

"Way different! We don't got humies for miles around!" It was an old argument. I could hear the deep ruts it was passing through. Something about Noise itched at my brain. I had an overwhelming desire to try to get a sniff at her.

"Shut up! Not in front of the 'guest,'" a second, new voice said, this one with a feminine growl. Perhaps this was Tallow?

The pressure in my loins gave me a sense of urgency

beyond the black hole where O'Meara had been in my head. "Hey, the guest is curious about Noise's question."

"Shut up, cat." A fist popped me in the ribs, a sharp stick of pain that barely registered compared to the black hole of agony in my head. Nor did it compare with my certainty that the wolves were planning to sell me off to some wizard on the black market for familiars. The flip side of that was they probably wouldn't want to hurt me badly.

"I have a name, you know," my inner snark replied. I couldn't bother with containing it.

Eagle grabbed the scruff of my neck and lifted my front half from the truck bed; the skin around my windpipe tightened. I could smell his hot death-filled breath through the bag. "Right now your name is Meat. Keep talking and it will be Dinner," he growled at me.

"Okay! Anything you say! You're the boss!"

He snorted and started to lower me down. "That's better."

"Just don't breathe on me again." The quip earned me an accelerated trip the rest of the way down, and the bag filled with stars for a moment as the other werewolves snickered. The defiance earned me more pleasure than pain on the balance.

Eagle growled dangerous and low.

"Eagle, you heard Pa. Don't hurt him," Tallow said. A series of growls happened between her and Eagle, ending with him stepping off me and I assumed the weight of Tallow taking his place. She sounded much larger than him.

"You should keep that tongue to yourself, cat. It will be less trouble for you in the long run."

A thought occurred to me, one of many swirling around the black hole in my head. This one made me laugh. "Trouble? I'm not in any more trouble than I was before. You, on the other paw, just stole away a magus's last chance for redemption. I hope you've got both fire and life insurance," I said in a whisper.

She cuffed me. "Quiet cat." The other wolf-dogs snorted.

A few more minutes of silence passed, and the truck rolled to a stop. I heard the doors pop open and the suspension give a sigh of relief. Tallow whispered in a neutral tone, "Bite me and I will return the favor." Then she scooped me up with a slight grunt. Nice to know that I was large enough to require some effort, at least.

"Is he behaving?" asked the gruff voice of Pa.

"He needed some learning, Pa," Eagle said with a snicker.

"Cats usually do. Let's see him." I was handed off. Pa held me under my armpits, heavy mitts pressing on very sore ribs. I grimaced but didn't protest, figuring telling him I hurt would cause the sadistic bastard to press on them harder. So far I had learned that male werewolves were sadistic bastards and the females less so. Despite the small sample size the conclusions seemed sound.

He found a developing bruise on the side of my head, which forced a hiss of pain.

"Nothing's broken, just bruised," Tallow piped up.

"Good." He handled me with the ease of a vet handling a house cat. He was nearly daring me to bite him, and I very sorely wanted to. But there would be no point. Not like I could run away. For now I had to wait. Hopefully O'Meara could track these fools.

Inspection done, he encircled my torso with his arm, which felt nearly as thick as O'Meara's waist. He started walking, and I could hear the snap of twigs and the crunch of gravel as the rest of the pack followed him. "Merlot, get the cage ready," Pa ordered. I heard someone scamper ahead. Was Merlot the omega? Or was it Noise? How closely did werewolves emulate their animal cousins, I wondered as I tried not to move.

I heard the scrape of metal on metal somewhere in front of us, sending a chill up my spine. I didn't have to imagine the origin of the sound for long. Soon I was pitched forward, landing on a surface far harder than the ground I was expecting.

I heard the cage door shut, and the floor creaked as something came closer. "Don't move, cat. I might slip," one of the wolves growled. A hand roughly seized my legs. There was a harsh tug on my fur, and my legs could suddenly move again, the compression of the duct tape gone. "Stop moving, not done," hissed the werewolf. Three more cuts and my legs separated from each other. It was an effort not to sigh in utter relief. Then the bag was ripped off, and my vision went from black to pure white. There was a blur of movement, and the sound of the door opening and then closing. I blinked several times as blurred lines resolved into iron bars, beyond which the alpha and his pack stared down at me. I slowly got to my feet, wincing a little as pins and needles flooded into my extremities. I glared back at them. All twelve of their yellow eyes were on me as if they were waiting for a show.

"What you want? Some kind of congratulations?" I huffed and pretended to study the duct tape on my foreleg, idly calculating how much fur I was about to lose.

"He's not breathing fire," the smallest said disappointedly. He was definitely the wolf that had cut me free. He was tiny compared to the others. About five feet tall with jet black fur, he barely stood much taller than the alpha's waist. His muzzle was blunted compared to the others, who all sported the long muzzles of wolves, except for the alpha, who looked more like a bulldog than anything else.

Eagle, I imagined, was the one standing next to the alpha. He had a prominent underbite, but looked more like a deformity than fearsome like his Pa. Almost as big as the alpha and standing on the other side was a female who I guessed was the alpha's mate. Jet-black fur with a patch of russet red on her cheekbones. Her stance was almost apelike, with her arms nearly as long as her legs. Her muzzle was long and narrow, like a shaggy Doberman. Behind her was probably Tallow, as she looked unrelated to the rest of the pack, with a more wolfish cast to her face and light grey fur with a mottling of darker spots. Her belly was swollen below two titanic human breasts. Judging from her size, I'd guess werewolves must have full litters—yikes!

Of the entire pack, only Noise's eyes squinted in suspicion. Seeing her next to the alpha's mate, I could see the family resemblance: the fur was the same quality of her mother's and the slight build reminded me even more of a Doberman's. A different father, maybe?

I didn't bother responding to the small werewolf; instead I let my eyes settle on the big one, Pa. His eyes were cool, and bespoke far more intelligence than the cartoon bulldog he resembled through an artist's eye. "He'd be stupid to breathe fire in a cage that's mostly wood," he said after a long silence.

"Almost as stupid as stealing a familiar from a lady who can." The words slipped out before I could stop them.

The alpha smiled, which was a horrible thing both in terms of the number of teeth and the terrible state they were in. Any dentist would have screamed for mercy. "We have something far better than mere fire. We have a god! And you're gunna meet her soon, cat."

His utter conviction gave me a cold and prickly feeling

that ran down my spine and pooled into my stomach. I didn't see a hint of doubt in any of their eyes. Great, I thought to myself, kidnapped by a bunch of fuzzy fanatics.

An unspoken decision swept the group as I failed to do anything interesting. Big Alpha pointed at their most slender member. "Noise, you watch him."

Noise's eyes flashed, and she rounded on the big creature. "What? No! I'm still tracking that nymph! Get Merlot to do it."

Pa's eyes narrowed. "You got your ears jammed with wax, girl? I ain't gonna repeat myself."

"Besides," the older female cut in, "your brother isn't in our guest's weight class." She placed a steadying hand on Noise's shoulder.

The lead weight in the middle my brain squeezed an embryonic joke about my weight before it reached my lips. Probably wise, that lead weight. Merlot, the little wolf, now bared his teeth at his mum's condescension while Noise's tail drooped. Huffing like a put-upon teenager, she said, "Fine, but I'm getting my phone first."

Pa's counter-objections to that were cut off with a soft nudge from the grizzled female. Merlot stewed with skill and practice as he and the rest of his family wandered towards the edges of the clearing and Noise rooted around in the cab of the truck. Only once she had exited it with a small rectangular object clutched in her paw and a solar charger clamped in her armpit did Pa take his eyes off me and head into the forest.

Tallow, the one who might pop if you poked her, had slinked off in a different direction, somewhere I couldn't see beyond the viewpoint of my cage.

I watched Noise as I licked at the tape. *Yeerrach!* Duct tape adhesive was not a flavoring I'd be using as a spice any time soon. She didn't look at me. She sat cross-legged, her back to me, the solar panel next to her and the fading light of the sun shining off its surface. She hunched over the tiny screen as if her and it were the only things within the world. Despite her towering form and rippling muscles of her back, she looked vulnerable and small.

25

"Hey," I said.

She hunched over her screen a bit tighter. I cocked my head and attempted to figure out this strange reaction. Was she afraid of me? The cat in the cage. The way she held her shoulders, the duck of her head, I had seen that before. But where?

"Hey, fuzzy girl," I tried again. "You know I'm not joking about my magus. She's gonna be real pissed about all this."

Noise put down her phone and hugged herself with both arms, giving a slight rock. "Shut up, Thomas—please shut up," she whispered.

Something in the way she said my name, the intimate way it rolled off her tongue, not as if it were new but one of long practice, stilled me. The words of rationality faded as a sense of panic began to burble in my stomach and crawl its way up my throat. I flehmed, pressed my muzzle to bars and drank in the scents on the breeze. I sorted out all the pollen and decaying scents of the forest living and dying around us and grabbed hold of her canine musk. I flehmed again, singling her out, and she winced as her scent unwound in my mind. The scent of barbecuing meat in the back yard, Angelica sweeping into my arms and nailing me to the wall with a savage kiss, the glee of her laughter as we tussled with each other, trying to distract the other in a game of Smash Brothers. It was the scent that entered my lungs as I drifted off to sleep happy.

My legs gave out, all four of them, and I thumped to the bottom of the cage. My brain feebly tried to work through the logistics and ignore the fact that she could let me out. Two weeks on, two weeks gone, corresponding to the lunar cycle, I'd bet. But why was she so . . . wolf now? The full moon was only three days long. Why two weeks?

"Angelica, why?" I asked.

Her giant head flung back, pointing her long muzzle at the sky. I expected her to howl, but instead she choked and drew in a ragged breath before plunging her face into her massive paws. After a moment, her voice drifted back to me, muffled. "My name is Noise, Thomas. This is what I really am. You never noticed that I come back to your place with a short tail." She straightened but didn't turn around. "No matter how I joked about you making me howl or you'd comment on how cold my nose was when I poked you with it. You couldn't see the monster in your bed." She spoke so softly and into the wind. Had my ears still been naked and round I doubted I could have caught a single word. The sniffle was far louder.

"N—" I tried to use her real name but it caught in my craw like a piece of dry straw. "Angelica, I see you now okay. We can talk about this."

She whirled up onto all fours and snarled, displaying savagely sharp teeth, her golden eyes clouded with anger. "Stop calling me that here! She was my escape from this! You wanted to know where I went? I come here with my family, my pack. Now you know! Happy? Because now it's over."

"It's only over because I'm in a cage you put me in."

She stared at me, puzzled for moment, and then a look of disgust passed over her features. "Ewww! You're a cat!"

I thrust out my chest. "I fail to see the problem with that. They tell me I'm a very handsome cat. O'Meara practically had to get the crowbar to pry off Jowls."

She snorted. It might have been the birth of a laugh, but she swallowed it down and glared at me. I caught a sparkle of something deep in her eyes. "Shut up, Thomas, and wait. You'll at least get to leave this town."

"I ain't leaving, Angelica. I've gone through way too much trouble in order to stick around."

One of her ears drooped in an adorable manner as puzzlement stole over her face. "Why the hell would you do that?"

"Because you live in this town and I love you."

Her jaw opened and then shut. Before we had always danced around the L word, but it would slip out of us both on occasion. She spun away from me and sat down hard on the ground, clutching her head as if trying to squeeze something out of it.

"Come on, Angelica—let me out of here," I pleaded.

"I can't do that. Please don't ask me to do that, Thomas." She looked down and stared shamefacedly into the dirt.

I looked at the cage, an old circus cart. The sort they used to transport the lions in between tents back in the day. Just enough room to pace in, a very solid wooden frame and ceiling with an iron grate at one end and bars along one side for the adoring public. I noted that there was no padlock on the grate, just a heavy latch. "I'm pretty sure you can, Angelica. It's not locked, just latched. It is simple. Hell, I could do it from outside these luxurious accommodations, and I'm sorely lacking in the dexterous digits department. You could say it was an accident."

Angelica made a guttural sound of canine despair and clutched her ears, as if that would make this go away. "Don't do this to me. I'm sorry. But I can't let you out." She looked up, the fur around the wild golden orbs now damp with tears, her back hunched as if in pain. "Please be good. The princess won't hurt you. You'll understand when you meet her. Please just be a little bit patient, for me, please." And deep behind the black of those eyes I caught that sparkle of something, a reflection of something deep in her head. Yet, her eyes fell back to the ground before I could see it clearly.

"All things considered, I'm pretty damn done with being good, Angelica. Clearly we have some, uh, revelations we need to sort out, and meeting the family is going poorly. I'm not kidding about the vengeful fire magus who's now without her Jiminy Cricket. Your family's not fireproof." I stared at her, looking for some trace of the Angelica I knew in the whimpering monster before me.

"The princess wants you, Thomas. I can't, I won't defy her. I love her too much." She curled into a fetal position as if under great strain.

"Love her? What about me?" When she didn't respond, I turned away from her, growling with my own frustration. My eyes fell on anything else. While I stared at the bare wooden walls, my headache reemerged. Were all werewolves scary loyal to their gods? Angelica had never struck me as a religious type. Seeing nothing but solid wood, my gaze shifted back to the latch mechanism as I pondered the sheer wrongness. If I could figure out some way to reach through the bars with a stick or something, I might be able to open the cage. Angelica couldn't let me out, but maybe she was too conflicted to stop me if I got myself out. However, the cage's supply of long sticks was fresh out. In fact there was nothing in the cage at all, which invalidated the fleeting hypothesis that I was trapped in an inventory-based video game. I wondered if a magus could install bottomless pockets in my fur coat.

I imagined this princess as a horrible amalgamation of teeth and claws. She had to be something pretty scary to get these characters to fear her punishments. I had a feeling that their god was a bit more hands-on than the one I learned about in Sunday school as a child. Either way this was exactly what Oric and Cyndi had warned me about with much waggling of their nonexistent brows.

I looked at the gate, the rusty iron frame bolted to the wooden planks surrounding it. It all looked fairly solid, but I had to wonder how much force it had been built to sustain. After all, trained lions really weren't the brightest of bulbs, right? That did lead to the thought of how many circus animals had been TAU material, but I shook the question off. Worry about TAU after I assured I wouldn't be mincemeat.

I lay down to study the grate. Rust covered every surface of the metal, but the damage looked more decorative than structural. Flehming in frustration, I drank in the metallic scent and found something far more promising. A dark, wet scent, like that of a swamp in the afternoon sun, the scent of decaying wood. I followed the scent, flehming repeatedly, to the bottom edge of the wall. In the corner, closest to the bars but where sunlight would have a very difficult time reaching, the distinct scent of decay became stronger. My claws sunk into the softened wood easily and pulled out small bundles of splinters. The scent became hope. I turned and gave the wall a two-pawed donkey kick. The sound of my head hitting the opposite side of the cage car sounded far louder than the impact of my feet.

"Thomas! What the hell?" I heard Angelica say. Her face popped up to stare inside my cage.

I didn't respond, too busy figuring out how to brace myself to prevent a repeat flight. Clearly the wood had not rotted all the way through and would need more convincing to open. My second kick produced a solid *whump!* That made the entire cage shudder.

"Stop it! You're going to hurt yourself."

I snarled at her and readied for another kick, my pulse already pounding in my ears. My back paws stung from the force of the last impact, and an almost palpable feeling of reluctance pushed up against me. A tremor of panic fluttered through me, similar to when I first leapt on top of a house to escape the cops. But I did not yield to the sensation or release myself to the whims of instinct. It did not understand what I was doing, why I was inflicting pain on us. I forced them back as I peered over my shoulder at the targeted section of the wall. The wood above it above it bore twin smudges. I had to go a little lower.

Wham! The entire cage shuddered around me, but the wall held as pain shot through my legs. I checked the wall; the impact marks were still a smidge too high.

"Thomas! *Think!* You're in the middle of my pack's territory. Even if you get out, you won't get far! Pa will break your legs!"

"He doesn't have to know." I set up for another kick, ignoring the pain in my pads.

Crack! Now that was a sound that was music to my ears. The rotten board exploded from its moorings.

The wolf sputtered as a grin spread across my muzzle. "I prefer boxes that are open." I turned to inspect my handiwork. My hind paws had punched out a section of board about a foot across. Too narrow to squeeze through, but judging from the holes in the board below it, pulling it out wouldn't be hard.

Angelica sprang up into view through the hole as I put my paw into the gap. "Stay the hell away from that!" she screamed at me, spittle spraying from her muzzle, eyes blazing with that unhealthy blue light. Her sheer ferocity drove me back into the cage.

I snarled back, "Listen to me, Angelica! Or Noise. Something is wrong with your head! I can see it! You need to let me go. I'll get you help."

"*Lies!* I'm fine! You'll be fine too once you see the glory!" That light in her eyes didn't die away completely; a blue sheen stayed in the deep black of her eyes. Unyielding, uncomprehending and utterly beyond reason. The entire reason I had been fighting so hard to stay in Grantsville now planned to sell me into slavery, thanks to some magus's spell in her head.

No, just no.

I screamed with pure frustration, turned and kicked out with all my rage. The wet wood shattered under my paws, and I found Noise staring through a nearly cougar-sized hole three boards high, the glow gone. I hesitated an instant too long and only leapt after she dived out of view. A metal wall slammed into my nose just as I passed into freedom and forced me back with a yowl of pain. Angelica had pressed a large metal garbage can lid over the hole. I raged against it, kicking and clawing. "Let me out!" My words bled into an animal screech. Kick. *Clang!* I rolled onto my back, beat my paws against her shield and hollered, "Let me out!" *Clang!* "You hear me! Angelica! Snap out of it!" I battered her shield like Animal from the

Muppets attacks his cymbals. *Clang, clang, clang!* "I won't let you do this to me! *Let me out!*" I gave the lid a last kick and then collapsed to the floor, my chest heaving, and my head feeling on the edge of an explosion. So much for the power of righteous anger.

"Noise!" A deep voice cut through my head. I opened my eyes to see the very pregnant Tallow glaring down from a nearby hill. "What the hell is this ruckus?"

"He went crazy and broke the cage!"

"Well, fix it then!" She knuckle-walked towards us with more ease than I would have liked. My mind ran through multiple scenarios of escape. All involved getting up at that moment, but I barely had the energy to watch Tallow's approach.

A scent in the air caught my nose—smoke, with the faintest trace of cinnamon. I breathed it in like a fresh breeze. The big wolf mother paused and lifted her nose to the air, nostrils flaring. Her eyes flicked to the right. I wondered if there was a plume of smoke blooming over the tree line. Perhaps that had been Eagle and Tallow's wooden bungalow? It was a lot to hope for. I couldn't see any horizon from the front of my cage, just the hill Tallow had walked down and tree after tree to the right of it.

Tallow's yellow eyes stared at me, looking through me. Calculating, perhaps. "Noise!" she barked. "Call the princess's servant. Tell him that we need her here."

Noise whimpered. "What? But only Pa is allowed to . . ."

She took the lid from Angelica. "Go find some reception! I'll take this." Tallow growled, and Angelica scampered up the hill. A few moments after she left, the lid of the trashcan lifted away from the hole I had made. Tallow peered into my boxy prison. "Don't hesitate. We did." I blinked at her, wondering what the hell she meant at that when she tossed a length of silver chain at me. I stared at it, shocked as she slammed the lid back over the hole, and let loose a long, almost mournful howl.

The chain animated as soon as I prodded it with a tentative paw, snaking up my foreleg and settling in around my neck. A tendril of it settled onto that gaping hole in my thoughts, and the lingering pain of the break relaxed. I had not realized how much it still hurt until it disappeared, a weight lifting from my mind. Yet the connection through the chain to O'Meara remained dark. Had her end of the chain also been removed? Or had she just taken it off? Drat. So much for summoning up the fire starter cavalry.

Distant howls echoed back from the forest, long sounds that seemed to end with a questioning note. Tallow answered with a fierce, dominant bellow that seemed to shake the walls of my cage. I didn't hear any howls answer her, so it had to translate to something either fierce or the equivalent to a dinner bell.

I considered telling Tallow that the chain wasn't going to be much help in whatever was coming, but she wasn't being very forthcoming with what she expected me to do. Angelica came back looking downcast. She confirmed that their "princess" was on her way and wasn't happy about being summoned. They secured the garbage lid over the hole via a few nails that Tallow pushed through the metal lid and into the wood as if they were thumbtacks. I resolved never to allow a werewolf to put their hands on me again.

There was nothing to do but wait for something to happen. I sat and licked at my aching hind feet. They hurt, and most of my claws were bent or shattered from the impact, but beyond that my paws were intact, the bones unbroken.

As I waited I peered at the skulls of my captors, trying to see more of that blue light, but unlike the man at the station, no spell shined through their heads. As the day started to fade, my stomach ached.

26

Slowly the werewolves crept into the clearing. All were panting slightly and shooting cross looks at Tallow, who had settled against my cage, resting her hands on her belly protectively. There was an unspoken tension in the air. Pa bared his teeth at her, but she just patted her belly and Eagle stepped between her and the alpha, staring his father down. Pa turned away with a dismissive grunt.

Angelica had retreated from my cage, putting a stout tree between her and it. She flinched whenever another of her pack glanced at her. The scent of misery radiated from her like an open bottle of bleach. Her mother, the only wolf I yet had a name for, made to go to her child, a worried expression on her muzzle, but a shake of Tallow's head warded her off too.

A few minutes later, everyone's ears perked up when the sound of an engine drifted into the clearing. All the werewolves stood up, except for Tallow, who glanced at the others with narrowed eyes. Only when headlights were visible through the foliage did she reluctantly stand up at Eagle's urging.

My lips peeled back from my teeth as an ancient Cadillac bounced its way up the rocky road. As it came to a stop, warm blue radiated from the vehicle like a fine mist, pulsing around the werewolves. They all stood straighter. I recognized the color and my lips pulled back to sneer. A man wearing round spectacles and a t-shirt sporting a logo for the animal welfare society stepped out of the driver-side door. He scanned the assembled werewolves, as if counting them. "This is highly irregular! The princess is disappointed that you have forced an alteration to her royal schedule." All the wolves' muzzles dipped lower. "She wishes to remind you that you exist on her land and at her sufferance." They all shrank at the man's words; the alpha's jaw was actually trembling. Tallow covered her stomach protectively. "However, the Lady is merciful, provided you indeed have accomplished your task."

"We have!" Pa exclaimed and jabbed a finger in my direction. "The cat sits in that cage!" His voice nearly cracked with desperation.

The man looked in my direction. I hissed.

Pa turned to me, his eyes blazing. "You will show respect," he barked at me as he took a step in my direction.

The human held up a hand. "Hold, Walter—the princess will deal with him."

Pa grunted and returned to his place in the front of the pack, quickly sinking to his knees as the human circled around to the back door of the Cadillac. As he opened it the clearing was absolutely flooded with the blue light. The wolves bowed and pressed their muzzles into the dirt as a cat, white as snow, hopped onto the ground. I recognized Cyndi instantly. Her unearthly beauty radiated blue light like a saintly halo.

Thoughts stirred around the edges of my mind,

promising me that this was nothing less than an undefeatable goddess. That conjured an image of Oric wiping the floor with her not twenty-four hours ago. *Undefeatable, my ass.* I growled at the voices.

She surveyed the wolves. "My noble hunters, let me see what you have brought me here to see." I squinted at her, and I could see shapes moving within her halo, thin weaves of something flowing between her and each wolf, each thread knotting around their heads and through their ears and eyes. The human had it far worse, however. He was nearly encased in the strands.

"I can see you well enough from here, Cyndi," I hissed.

She turned her head to look at me for the first time. "Oh, I see you did get the right kitten. Just as grumpy and confused as ever, I see, Thomas."

"See, Thomas? Do you see that it will be all right now?" I heard Noise whisper.

I couldn't afford to think about Noise right now. I could feel Cyndi pouring her magic over me, cooling my anger. "I think I have you pretty well figured out, Cyndi."

"Oh, do you now? I'm just trying to make sure you go to a family that is appropriate for your talents. And save your miserable life," she huffed prettily and cast a glance at the human, who produced a red velvet pillow from the car and offered it to Cyndi, who carefully climbed upon it.

I grinned. "What's the matter? Get beaten up by a little birdy?"

Her serenity wavered for a moment, and I saw her ears twitch in annoyance. "You rejected the TAU. That makes you fair game for other clients, kitten."

"Fair game, nothing. O'Meara's my bond. Call off your dogs."

"Oh, but I don't see O'Meara here to defend her claim.

Do you?" Her posture bordered on triumphant. "That's the trouble with fey chains—they're quite fragile.

"You think she'll forget, you think she'll forgive, until you're burned to an extra crispy cat on a stick."

She gave a pretty little sigh and fluttered her eyes. "I heard differently. I heard she drove you half mad after bonding with her, and you escaped into the forest." After a nod with her head, the man carrying her began to step forward and the pressure on my mind grew. Her beauty blossomed with each step.

"Stop it! Stay back!" I growled, backing into the corner with the hole.

She put on a dazzling smile. "Why would I do that? All my subjects benefit from up-close attention." Her voice was a rolling purr as her beauty transfigured from physical to divine.

My muscles screamed in protest as I wrenched my gaze away from her and catapulted my body into the garbage lid. It swung up like a doggie door and I felt a nail's stinging burn all along my spine as I pushed through the opening. The pain reawakened my anger. How dare she do this to me! How dare this world presume that it could harvest me like a lump of coal you pull out of the ground! I turned towards the source of the blue light, my teeth bared, with every intention of violence.

And looked into the eyes of divine beauty. She was the purest of beings, her flawless fur whiter than any that could be captured by mere light. Her sapphire eyes glowed with a soft blue light that bathed my entire being in warmth.

My anger evaporated like droplets tossed onto a hot stove. Only a thread of fear survived, for I had displeased this goddess, and I was so ashamed that I bolted away towards the forest.

"Thomas. *Stop!*" Her voice hit me like a leaden pillow, and I careened into the ground.

I looked back to see the goddess within a pyre of her blue fire, her body trembling with her divinity. I could barely see the human that held her little pillow through the flame. A flash of white teeth showed for a moment, and I saw the dark shadow of a universe without this goddess within it. The pyre resumed. "*Come here,*" she commanded, and I obeyed, knowing I had done something truly horrible for the goddess to stoop to issuing a command. Truly, all she had to do was ask. I would do anything for her. I'd even let her enslave me. But she'd never do a thing like that. The goddess embodied goodness.

I settled five feet from her and her pillow as the pyre calmed to a radiant glow. Then with an indignant squawk, her beauty faded to a dull dirty white as she fell from her perch. Cyndi yelped as she hit the ground.

Blinking as if I had been staring into a pair of headlights, the rest of the world came into focus. The man who had been carrying the pillow lay on the ground behind Cyndi, a froth of spittle leaking from his mouth as he convulsed. The man had been at the epicenter of all that divine energy. Cyndi watched the man for a moment and sighed before turning back to me. Her eyes were rimmed with red, and the white of her third eyelids were visible in the corners of her eyes. Independent thought had begun to stir, but the return of the blue light of the goddess stomped them back into my lizard brain.

The goddess somehow looked down her nose at me despite the tininess of her body. The weight of her disapproval pushed me back several inches. She turned from me, her gaze falling first on the fallen man behind her and moving onto Noise, who stood glassy-eyed a few paces away from the car. "You there, dear, fetch me the tranquilizer gun behind the seat."

"Yes, m'lady!" Noise hurried to comply. First she tried the door handle, and when it failed to open the door, she pulled back her fist to smash the window in.

"*Stop!*" my goddess screeched, and my heart nearly complied. The divinity before me wavered as her ears folded back. "Before you break the window of my chariot, do you know how to use a tranquilizer gun?"

Noise shrank back from the Caddy, hands clasping together in a way that tickled my brain, reminding me of something. "It's a gun! You pull the trigger, right?"

"Have you ever loaded one? Do you know the dosage?" The goddess pawed at the ground in frustration. "Forget it!" Noise grabbed both sides of her jaw in utter mortification at the rebuke, but the goddess had already moved on. Tallow stood the closest to us, leaning against a thick oak tree that dominated the clearing. "Tallow, right? Choke him out and put him in the trunk."

Slaver. The word stole across my mind along with the scent of the princess.

"Yes, princess." Tallow's voice sounded as far away as her glassy eyes, but she moved to obey all the same. She lumbered forward, using that particular knuckle walk of hers. She drew up and reached out her huge hand for my neck, and the mere image of the pain it would cause me drove me backwards.

"Thomas, be still!"

"She's going to hurt me!" I whined at the slaver—no, the goddess. "I'll be good, I swear!" I once again dodged a huge mitt, drawing a sawing growl from the she-wolf. I circled around to hide behind the goddess, to plead my case. Tallow followed, resulting a in a slow chase around the goddess.

"Stop moving!" the goddess pleaded. We both froze. "No!" she hissed in utter frustration, and her divinity fell away. There was no hesitation in what came next; my awareness burst forth, along with a red haze of hate and fear. My teeth clamped down on her fragile neck. I felt her neck and shoulders shatter under my teeth. Her blood was hot and bitter. I recoiled, but my teeth had hooked on her skin and she came up with my mouth. With a twist of my neck, I flung her away. She sailed away from me, all the wolves' eyes tracking her arc like automated turrets. She landed soundlessly on the ground, slumping bonelessly.

The werewolves just stared at Cyndi's body for a moment. So did I, before two shaggy arms wrapped around my torso and lifted me. I chirped in surprise as Tallow growled, "Trust me," in my ear. She charged around the gathered wolves and tossed me through the open window of the truck cab. I landed in the passenger's seat as she yanked open the door and squeezed herself into the driver's side. The rest of the pack stood there, blinking stupidly as she started the engine and threw the truck into reverse. We backed out of the clearing and onto the road before she slammed it into first, flooring the engine. The wheels spun in place for a brief moment before we shot forward. A long mournful howl rang out behind us. First just Pa's baritone sang, and then the entire pack joined in.

Tallow cursed.

"What the hell is going on?" I cried, watching as Pa dashed onto the road behind us, the rest of the pack right on his heels.

"You hang on. If I can get us on a paved road . . ." She trailed off, eyes on the road. I clung to the seat with all four sets of claws to avoid getting bucked into the ceiling. All I could do was watch Pa's muzzle, twisted into sorrow and rage, loom closer and closer to the bed of the truck. A brown blur bounded past him, and Noise/Angelica leapt into the truck bed, snarling with a maw of very sharp-looking teeth.

"Sorry, hon," Tallow muttered, and she twisted the wheel. The truck hit something that kicked the left side into the air. I have never in my life wished for a seatbelt more. At least I had a chair—Noise had nothing, and the truck bucked her into the air. Her hands and feet pinwheeled in the air, but to no avail as her momentum carried her over the side of the truck. I winced in sympathy as I saw her hit the road, striking her leg on the road first, her knee bending sideways.

Tallow put us around a corner and onto a much smoother road. Pa, still right on our tail, started to fall behind, the other wolves lagging behind him. Then he suddenly darted off into the forest to the left. "He's taking a shortcut," Tallow growled. "The road circles back up ahead."

"What do we do?"

She grinned. "We play a little chicken." She said it with a sort of sinister delight that left me with the impression that Tallow had very little love for her alpha. "We get to find out what's stronger, his rage at you or his love for his grand-pups."

"Maybe you should let me out?"

Sure enough the road began to curve. "We're forty miles from town. Out there you're meat."

I couldn't disagree. So I watched as we rounded the bend to see Pa standing in the middle of the road. His eyes shone like evil orbs in the headlights.

Tallow poured on the speed, the engine roared and the truck started to shake so badly that it felt as if the frame would shatter. Pa hunched down, putting one foot in back of the other as he stretched his hands out towards us as if the truck were a ball to be caught.

"Is he going to catch the truck?" I asked.

"No." Tallow jerked the stick back into fourth gear, and the truck continued to accelerate. "Jump, damn you, Walter." His mouth opened, and I frantically looked around trying to figure out how to brace myself for impact, but the truck had no seat belts. All I could do was dig my claws into the dashboard and hope.

The glare of the headlights parted on him as the trunk screamed towards him. Thirty feet, twenty feet and then, just as the beams of the headlights parted on his grey fur, he sprang into the air and to the side. A sharp crack echoed through the truck as the headlight kissed his foot. We heard the howl of pain cut through the roar of the engine like a scythe.

"Stupid hoary old beast," I heard Tallow mutter as I slumped down into my seat, shaking from the adrenaline.

Minutes later we were sailing along on paved roads, streaking back towards town. Only then did I find my voice again. "How long was she doing that?"

Tallow was silent for a long moment. "She came to the pack about a year ago, offering the usual trades that magus types offer us. Kill or hunt this or that nuisance—it started subtle. Within six months we thought she was our god, and we did what she said, even when she wasn't there." Her words were pure loathing. "We didn't even realize what had happened to us."

"But you did?"

"She made a crack last month about how much my babies could be worth." Her teeth appeared at the thought. "It stuck in my head like a piece of gristle between the teeth. But only after she left and only if she stayed away for more than a week. I couldn't tell the rest of the pack. Pa wouldn't tolerate even mentioning her. She was the pack's secret, our special truth."

"What happens now?"

Tallow's eyes flicked to the rearview mirror. "They'll be nothing but grief and revenge till mid-moon. After that maybe Walter will listen to reason."

"What's mid-moon?"

"The gibbous moon, that's when we are human enough for the Veil. The pack splits up, and we all go our separate ways to play at being human."

In my mind's eye I saw Angelica limping back to the house on crutches with that unthinking rage in her eyes. A shiver passed down my spine.

Silence reigned for several miles. Worry gnawed at my stomach.

Tallow broke the silence first. "Where do you need to go?"

"Do you know where O'Meara's office is?"

"You're going to rebond with her?"

"Yeah." A deal was a deal.

"Good, because from what I know of the woman, your threats were not far off the mark. Call her off."

"Then we better hope that Ixey is at the office."

27

A door hanging off its hinges is never a good sign. The scorch marks around the holes burned through the metal were even worse. The way Tallow had started to pant and clutch at her stomach the last few miles of the drive had also become worrisome.

Hopping out of the truck brought a variety of Cajun-style flavors to my nose. Plastic, metal, wood and a cocktail of chemicals. My heart dropped from my chest and started rolling around in my stomach. What the hell had happened? I'd been captured for less than a day! I poked my head through the doorway and saw the devastation of what had been O'Meara and Ixey's office. Charred cubicles lay scattered about. Huge holes had been torn up through the carpet floor, looking like something had erupted from the ground. Ixey's double-wide looked to have been smashed with a giant hammer. The carnage tracked back into the room and to a door that had previously been boarded up. It looked to have been "unboarded" via lightsaber. That lifted my mood a little. Hopefully O'Meara was still out there somewhere.

I turned around to see Tallow just inside the doorway, eyes closed as she sniffed at the air. "No blood, no scent of barbecued flesh. A lot of damage for nobody to actually land a blow," she said.

I looked at the scene. The doorframe was ringed with a layer of ash and char, but inside the ring was untouched. Similar marks appeared in several spots along what had been the central walkway of the cubicle farm. Ricochets from O'Meara's magic? Ixey's cubicle walls were marked with smaller scorches. Ashy bullet holes. The carnage widened halfway down the hallway. A little part of me noted with some alarm that the office was bone-dry, despite the ceiling being studded with sprinkler nozzles. I didn't smell any blood or cooked flesh either, but mostly because Tallow's scent had flooded the room like a sweaty foot being pulled from a shoe, except this musk reached up into my skull and screamed *pregnant!* behind my ear drums. Disturbingly, it set my hackles on edge and then had the gall to make my stomach rumble. Both the ritual cube and O'Meara's office seemed intact. They each sported orange-gold runes that had a threatening brightness to them.

"You look lost," Tallow rumbled.

I let my head thump against the hastily opened doorway, closed my eyes and let loose a very heavy sigh. "I don't know either of their cell phone numbers. I don't know where they are." Exhaustion lapped at me with the insistence of an incoming tide. A squeal of metal stopped me from passing out where I stood. Tallow had lifted up the wreckage of Ixey's cubicle and peered into contents.

"Magi and cell phones. Not something I'd have put together." Tallow reached a long arm into the debris and withdrew the handset of Ixey's cheap office phone. With a tug, half of the handset came with it, dangling like a squished spider. She tossed it aside with a grunt, and then swayed before sinking back to all fours. I took a few steps towards her, but she heaved herself back onto two feet and turned away. "Find another phone!"

"We've got to find the number first. It might be some-where in that desk." I looked at the office. The ward glow-ered threateningly at me. There had been an old Rolodex on O'Meara's desk. It might not have O'Meara's number in it, but it could have Ixey's. Hopefully they were together. That would make things simpler. Tallow followed my gaze and started to knuckle-walk over to it. "Stop!"

She threw me a glance of pure annoyance.

"It's warded. That office and that cube." I jerked my head towards the intact ritual cube. "They won't let us open them."

"Or what?"

"Knowing O'Meara? Fiery doom."

Tallow let loose a growl and bent low so her eyes were level with mine. "We are running out of time, cat. You need to call off your magus be—yip!" A shock rippled through her, and she collapsed to her knees and elbows. A beat later and a keening whine filled the air. "Oh, damn it, come on—you can't wait one more day?" Growling, she rose up to all fours, grabbed a cubicle wall and tore the lining from it, her motions so violent that I found myself backing away, my ears flattened.

"Tallow?" I asked timidly. My nose screamed at me what was happening. "Uh, should I get a doctor?"

She didn't even glance in my direction as she continued to pull any reasonably semi-soft substance in reach out of its container. First the fabric of the cube wall, and then the foam from Ixey's office chair. "I've done this before. Go find a way to contact your magus. I'll be human enough to need my house in a few days. I'd rather not go home to a cinder, if I go home at all." Her voice was steeped in bitterness.

I nodded, wheels turning in my head. Sabrina was out, and Whittaker probably wasn't a good idea. That left Jowls and Jules as my best hope for help, which meant going out and hoping the store was still open. Visions of the cops who had chased me there with their guns swam through my mind. Had I been a proper familiar, with training, I might have known how to operate the equipment that Ixey used to correspond to the magical world. I pushed that regret far away and padded towards the damaged door.

I turned back to look at Tallow as she methodically pulled apart the office furniture, her face a grimace of pain. "Uh, I know a place that might be better than here for this. It's got a lock on the door and a bed."

She shook her head. "Unless it's no more than fifty paces away or you can drive that truck I'm not going anywhere. If O'Meara's hunting my pack, I'll be done by the time she gets back. Whoever did this won't come back here."

There were holes in that logic, but if Tallow couldn't drive, then telling her that if they failed to get O'Meara they might return for the files in the warded office wouldn't help her. I had cursed my lack of thumbs so many times in the last few days, but never more than that moment. "Okay," I said as I found an old, slightly charred coffee cup and shoved my muzzle into it.

When I was halfway out the door, Tallow spoke again. "Thomas?"

"Yeah?" My voice echoed through the cup.

A pause. "Please hurry back. I'd . . ." She trailed off. I peeked behind me and caught the turn of her head, hiding her eyes from my gaze. Her shoulders heaved. "Just if I'm here and O'Meara comes back."

I imagined myself in her position. When she had scooped my shell-shocked self up to save me from her pack, the wrath she risked was directed not just at her own life but also at those of her children. She could have just let them eviscerate me, and then they could have dealt with O'Meara as a pack. Now, in answer to that, all I could offer her was a charred office and vague promises of calling off O'Meara's vengeance. "I'll be back as soon as I can," was all I could offer her as I trotted into the bright, moonlit night.

28

I had learned that a fast trot was about the max speed I could go without having to lie down for a bit as my breath caught back up with me. I hadn't been in peak physical condition as a human, but I hadn't sported an entire spare car tire, only a few bicycle ones. Still, I could feel the different ways my new body had been tuned by evolution. I had copious amounts of strength in my coiled muscles, but the reservoir simply wasn't as deep as my human self's had been. That said, my four-legged trot was hardly slow.

It took longer than I would have liked to walk to the plaza, but even if the cops saw me as a dog I doubt they'd just let me pass by. So I kept to the bushes along the road and threaded between the darkened buildings where I could. A familiar scent hit my nostrils as I vaulted over the fence and dove into the bushes that segmented the barrenness of the grocery store parking lot and the more Mr. Rogers' Neighborhood stylings of the plaza. I couldn't quite put a face to the smell for a moment, so I sat there, mentally combing through my head for it. A dusky musk. *Cornealius.* Why would he be here? Was Sabrina here too? *Yes.* The air answered the question without an additional sniff. It had all been there in that breath.

Carefully as I could, I crept up to the side of the building that housed Jules and Jowls' shop and peered around the corner. The door of the shop glowed with orange light and chimed as it swung open, pushed by a bejeweled hand. I pulled back behind the wall as Sabrina's voice reached my ears. "Don't worry, Jules, it will be better for all of us this way. It's perfectly legal. I should have done it a long time ago."

A muffled reply I couldn't catch made her laugh. "Oh, don't flatter me. I just did what everyone else dreamed of. Goodnight." The door chimed as the hinges squeaked shut. Unable to help myself, I peeked around the corner and prayed that the half-moon light would not strike my eyes and give me away. Sabrina had floated several steps off the curb and into the nearly empty parking lot. She wore a brilliant white dress draped with countless silver bangles that pulsed with colors, some of which my brain struggled to assign a name to. A canvas bag hung from her hand, which she carried with some effort but it did not weigh her down. One did not need to see her face to tell that the woman had a grin from ear to ear. Cornealius scampered down from her shoulders. I had not even seen him nestled among the energies that pulsed around Sabrina's neck.

Cornealius, in contrast to his mistress, did not look happy. Sabrina laughed at him, and I mentally cursed the bonded mind speech. If I ever got to the point I mastered one of these familiar superpowers, listening in on magus-familiar conversations would be damned handy. Of course, what Cornealius did next was pretty damn impressive too.

The weasel seemed to grab hold of the ground with all four paws for a moment as his head bowed in concentration.

With a rush of air that I felt on my whiskers, his body expanded until he filled the length of the parking spot, his fur shifted and a saddle rose from his back. Sabrina sat down, sidesaddle style. Once she grabbed the saddle's pommel for stability, Cornealius exploded into motion. They departed the plaza in less than two eye blinks, leaving me with a tingling sense of deja vu.

My memory rewound back to the word that had glared at me from the grey trunk of a sedan. Lacking a hand to smack myself with, I drove my head into the nearby wall several times as the word *sable* stared back through my memory. *Stupid! Stupid! Stupid!* Archibald had been hit by a Mercury Sable! It had been staring me in the face the entire time. Archibald hadn't been mauled by a bear! He'd been mauled by a giant weasel! Cornealius's words, "I hope you live to regret this decision, Thomas," echoed back to me.

It took an effort of supreme will not to shout obscenities into the night air. In my mind's eye I could already see Sabrina assaulting O'Meara's office. Flicking away O'Meara gouts of flames as she imperiously advanced into its heart. Now she had just stopped into Gossip Central to brag!

Question was, would they help me or would they be the latest contestants on the "Box up the Cougar!" game? I pondered my options.

The only other people, and I use the term loosely, I knew were Rudy, Scrags and Oric. Nobody liked O'Meara. Scrags might chuckle and slam a door in my face. Rudy might help, but his payday rested on Sabrina selling me to Oric, which would produce a major conflict of interest that might not work out in my favor. Oric might help, but the bird could be in a different time zone. No good options.

I put community outreach on a mental list of things for O'Meara to work on should she keep her job.

Hugging the building, and trying not to think about how long it had been since the walls had been cleaned, I slunk up to the door. The large metal pull handle was actually something I could operate, which was a bit of a thrill. It would have been far cooler had I gotten a stronger grip. My attempt to fling the door open resulted in just a few inches before the "fingers" of my paw slipped off the metal. I shoved my "dog nose" into the gap to stop the door from closing, and then clumsily pawed the door open. So much for a dramatic entrance. Only after I had my paw in the crack did I notice the handicapped-labeled button that would have made this endeavor much easier.

I hadn't really known what sort of reception to expect from Jules and Jowls, but looking into the shop to find Jules pointing a pistol at my head went on the list of less desired outcomes. I chirped in surprise as sudden fear crawled across my skin. "I guess this means you're closed. Can I come back later?"

"What the hell is this? A joke?" Jules said. His eyes had narrowed to a point I could not see his eyes.

Jowls stood in his previous spot on the counter, back arched and tail puffed. His eyes were wide with fear. "Sabrina just said O'Meara killed you!"

"Uh, no. I got jumped by a pack of werewolves who broke my bond with O'Meara, stuffed me a box and then tried to sell me to the highest bidder." I decide against informing them that I had personally killed Cyndi, and I licked my chops self-consciously, the taste of the cat's blood suddenly rising on my tongue. I grinned in what I hoped was a friendly manner while staying absolutely still. "Now if you care to stop pointing the gun at me, please."

Jules and Jowls looked at each other in silent communion, and then Jules lowered the weapon to the counter but did not let it go. "So O'Meara didn't erupt in a fit of rage, and blow up Whittaker's house, leaving him and Boris for dead?" His shoulders had relaxed a fraction, but he continued to watch me with a wariness that told me not to make any sudden moves.

"I got kidnapped from Whittaker's driveway. She might have gotten upset with him if she thought he had been part of it." I shook my head, hoping O'Meara hadn't burned the—well, according to the memories I had seen, *innocent* was the wrong word to attach to Whittaker, but the wrong guy in this case. Not relevant to me now anyway. "Listen, the werewolves broke my collar. I was hoping that either of you might know her phone number?"

"*Wait!*" Jowls exploded from the counter and landed on the ground more like a mass of Jell-O than a quadruped. "How exactly did you escape from a pack of werewolves?" He advanced on me, jabbing his small nose at me as if it were a pointed instrument of pain.

"Look, can we not get into that now? I just want to tell O'Meara that I'm okay," I explained as Jowls thrust his face into mine, flehming repeatedly. I wished I had thought to jump in a puddle.

"A pregnant werewolf? What the hell were you doing around a pregnant werewolf! Do you know how dangerous they are!?"

"I didn't have a choice in the matter!" I jerked my head away from Jowls and pushed past him, desperately hoping he'd miss the scent of Cyndi's blood. I looked to Jules as a savior, but found only his hard glare. His lips pressed into a thin line. "I'll tell you the whole story after I've got ahold of O'Meara. Come on, Jules—call her now."

He shook his head. "No, I can't do that. You need to leave." Jowls froze, and Jules' eyes flicked over to him and then back to me. "It's for your own go—"

I cut him off with a snarl, the anger coming back with the speed of a reflex. "Don't patronize me! I will make my own goddamn decisions." His grip tightened on the gun, but he didn't raise it. My own legs were tensed to spring. I could see the same question in his eyes as in my mind—what was faster? A leaping cougar or a man raising a gun and firing?

"Aw, come on now! Let's not be all *rawr* and stuffs! Relax, both of ya. Jules wants to help ya, Thomas, he does." Jules shot Jowls an angry glare. "He's just terrified of Sabrina."

The air seemed to go out of Jules. "Damn it, Jowls."

"You do not get to shoot a cub to preserve your yellow stripe from view! Totally unfabulous!" Jowls' voice dropped low, into a mock whisper. "And I don't think he would have won that fight anyway. He ain't much of a fighter."

"I am not getting involved in a war, political or otherwise, between Sabrina and O'Meara. Especially not on O'Meara's side!"

"Why the hell not? She's honest! That's a lot better than Sabrina, who's been trying to box me up and send me to Abu Dhabi since I woke up sporting a tail."

"And what a tail it is!" Jowls sang, and I realized I was lashing. I stilled it, to Jowls' visible disappointment, and looked back up to Jules.

"And you would be better off if she had succeeded in convincing you to join up with the TAU," Jules replied.

I growled in frustration. "Stop saying that. It did not end well for the last person who tried to force me down a path I didn't want to go. If you won't call her, then give me the number and I will find someone else to do the dialing."

"You don't even know what you're asking." Jules pulled

a cell phone from behind the counter and started to page through numbers. "She'll know it's me because I'll have to talk to her. And then after she manages to rebond with you, she will go on to still lose this fight with Sabrina. Then you will be either dead or exiled, and Sabrina will be pissed at me for making her goals that much harder."

"Does it help at all that I'm pretty sure that Sabrina killed the Archmagus?"

"No. I would not be surprised in the least, and it only illustrates why helping you is a bad idea."

"So I owe you a favor."

"No, you owe Jowls a favor, as he is making a convincing moral argument on your behalf as well as promising to lose weight, which I have been trying to get him to do for half a decade."

Jowls pushed up against my flank with a purr that was mixed with chortle. "I take payment in chicken livers, catnip and long walks on the beach."

"And making me uncomfortable?"

"Oh, heavens no, you get that for free anytime."

"You realize you are a stereotype on four legs, right?"

"I am not! I've never been in a drama club!"

"Ahem." Jules held out the phone towards me. It read, "Dialing The Flaming Pain in the Ass," which made me think more of Jowls than O'Meara, but I kept my chuckle to myself as I trotted up to the outstretched phone.

"Jules? What the hell do you want?" O'Meara's voice rushed out of the phone in an angry wave and struck that place in my head where the link had been with the force of a gunshot. My head rang with pain and longing.

"O'Meara! It's me!" I said, suppressing a wince at O'Meara's phone etiquette, memories of working at a call center stirring in my mind.

"Hello?"

"Your voice won't work over the phone, Thomas—just make a noise," Jules said.

Disappointed, I gave a dejected chirp.

"Thomas?!" Disbelief and hope surged out of the tiny speaker. I responded with a much more enthusiastic chirp. The link started to thrash and probe.

Jules lifted the phone away and spoke to it. "He just walked in about five minutes ago. Said he got kidnapped by werewolves."

"I know! The bastards. The fur bags are impossible to find! We found two of their haunts, and we're sending them a message!"

Oh, crap. So much for Tallow's house. "Tell her to put out the fire!"

Jules shot me a confused look. "He says put out the fire."

"What? Why? They kidnapped him. They moved against a magus! By law they knew to expect vengeance."

"They were being controlled! It's not their fault. Just . . ." My teeth chattered in frustration, my eyes moving from Jules to Jowls, who had retaken his usual perch on the counter. How much could I say? What had these two thought of Cyndi? "Come back to town. Sabrina's telling people you killed me." Jules repeated my words.

A pause on the other end. Jowls cocked his head and looked at me with an impenetrable expression. Jules's brow furrowed before the speaker came back to life. "All right, we're three hours from town," O'Meara said. "Stay low." The call winked out.

Jules put the phone back behind the counter. His movements were precise; a tension had filled the room between us. "Thomas," he began, and then took a breath. "Jowls says you have blood on your breath. Feline blood. Whose blood is it?"

I took a step back and looked to Jowls for help, but while there was no sternness there, a wide-eyed sadness confronted me. Guilt, which I had no time for, welled up inside me like a molten lead balloon. I could have lied to Jules but not to Jowls' hurt expression. My teeth clenched. I would have ground them together, but my teeth locked together too tightly. "Cyndi had the entire pack utterly dominated with that blue aura of hers. She tried the same trick on me. I didn't have much choice."

"She's dead?" Jowls' voice choked.

I started to hedge, to think maybe I had been mistaken. But the sound, the sharp crackle of her vertebra shattering between my jaws, came back to me. I had killed her. Quickly, hopefully painlessly, but it had been what I had done. "Yeah."

Jowls' lower lip trembled, and I thought I was about to see a cat cry for the first time in my life. "You *mad idiot!*" He roared at me so loud that I took steps backwards until my rump hit a display and cell phone cases rained down on top of me. "*I liked you and now you're dead, dead, dead!*" He flopped over on his back and paddled at the air. "Oh, why do I always like the murderers! Oh, why, cruel world!"

I looked to Jules, who was trying to look stern while giving into the urge to eye-roll at Jowls' melodrama. "You need to leave now. If you happen to survive whatever Sabrina is cooking, then you best find yourself a powerful patron. When that detail gets out, the TAU will come down on you like a ton of murderous bricks."

Jowls sniffed. "It's bit more like a mob than a union sometimes. Good-bye! Enjoy life while you can!" Jowls waved with his paw.

Eyeing them both, I backed up through the door and skedaddled.

I was halfway back to O'Meara's office when a howl pierced the soft sounds of the town at night. Long and low, not as deep as Pa's but still familiar. Two more shot up after it.

The pack had come to the city.

29

I tried to run all of the way back to the office and almost made it before a cramp hit me like a punch to the stomach, and I had to limp the last block. The muzzle extender had been lost in order to breathe. The door to the building still hung loosely off the hinges, and the door to the office was still splintered at the edges.

I heard Tallow's heavy groans and labored breathing before I left the stairway. The air was thick with a pregnant musk and the sweet tang of blood.

I poked my head through the office door and got a very good view of Tallow's teeth. And then a *far* too close encounter with her tongue.

"Thank Luna it's you!" Tallow exclaimed as I snorted and sneezed, trying to get the werewolf spittle out of my nose. She had been crouched right near the door, ready to take a chunk out of anyone who came through it. I made a mental note that I had to get back in the habit of knocking on doors, even nonexistent ones, before opening them. "I heard the pack just a few minutes ago." Her voice changed to a deep groan as one paw went to her belly.

In the corner, she had built a large nest composed of every remotely soft thing that had been in the office. The dividers were stripped bare of their fabric to make the skin of the nest, and the couch and chairs had been liberated of their cushions. Ixey's teddy bear sat in the middle of the nest, its stuffing poked through rows of holes and soggy fur. Its glassy eyes seemed to plead for mercy.

Tallow turned and limped back to her nest, collapsing into it with a relieved groan. "It won't be long now."

I paced over and gave her a nuzzle. "What can I do for you?"

A series of howls drifted through the room. I shuddered, and she grimaced through a painful contraction.

"That's Eagle, Kia and Merlot. They'll find us here eventually. They'll be able to smell the birth for miles." By process of elimination Kia had to be the alpha's mate.

"What happens when they do?"

"We'll see. Gah!" She seized me by the shoulders and pulled me into a crushing hug. "In the meantime, you'll do much better than the teddy bear."

I swear that teddy bear looked relieved.

The next thirty minutes were both painful and rewarding. Tallow's contractions started coming more and more, causing me to be hugged, squeezed and, in one particularly harrowing moment, bitten. I found her a broomstick to bite after that one. As the birth approached, she seemed to know what to do, which was good because I hadn't a clue. She stopped trying to crack my ribs and settled on her back, just using one hand-paw to squeeze a massive handful of my loose skin while bracing the other on the wall behind her head.

She was panting and groaning constantly, her tongue hanging sideways out of her mouth. Her teeth started to chatter, and the pressure on my poor scruff became a death grip. I asked her what's wrong.

"I-I-I c-can't hold it!" No sooner had the *t* sound passed through her lips did she throw back her head and let loose a howl so loud I swear the windows rattled. Three more howls answered it. "Damn." Tallow groaned but it was too late. It had begun.

The scent of it all was so heady that it almost made me dizzy and, more disturbingly, hungry. Still, once the births started it happened quickly. First a small nose appeared, then as Tallow's entire body seized with the force of the contraction the entire head appeared, and with another the rest of the silver-furred body slipped out. The little cub was adorable, even slick with juices. With his mother groaning and heaving, another soon joined its sibling, this one black with white speckles, and finally a third was ruddy brown, the only one that I could say looked like the wolf I presumed to be their father. They were all far smaller than I had imagined them being in Tallow's huge belly but bigger than mere puppies, about the size of small terriers with huge paws and eyes.

"How many?" Tallow whispered.

"Three."

"Shit. It's going to be weeks before I have enough tits." I chuckled as she gave a final groan and the mass of afterbirth slid out of her. The scent of the gore redoubled as the pups started to cry for their mother. "Give them to me," Tallow asked in a tired whisper. I looked at her, suddenly nervous, a bit afraid of both her and the fact the cubs smelled delicious. But there was nothing in her amber eyes but trust. As carefully as I could I took the scruff of each one in my mouth and delivered them to their mama. She took each one and began to clean them as only a canine mother could. Three howls split the night air. They were getting closer.

"Nothing to do but wait now." Tallow's ears were bent with worry.

I looked at the pile of viscera that sat in the middle of the nest. The entire room shouted *pregnant* right up into my nostrils, a scent so potent that even the faintest trace of it would lead the wolves right to the drafty office. An idea occurred to me. "They'll come by scent, right?"

"Yes."

"Then let's spread the love around." I tugged the topmost layer of fabric free from the nest and folded it over the afterbirth, first one way then the other. I grabbed the top corner and wa-bang—instant afterbirth in a bag.

"Thomas, we'll be safer facing them together. They might listen to reason if they're faced with a fair fight." She sounded as convinced as I was about the idea.

"Well, if I do this right, they won't find you at all."

I took my bag of guts and ran out the door.

It occurred to me I had no idea what I was doing, but I figured that wouldn't be any different from the last two days. I ran down the street in the direction I hoped the pack's howls were coming from. I didn't know this part of town particularly well. I never had cause to go down to the police station. But there was a motel somewhere around here. That might be a good place to stash the first bit of viscera. If I could find a vet clinic or hospital, that would work too.

The streets were absolutely deserted, so I loped unimpeded down the sidewalk, dodging around the pools of light cast by the occasional streetlight. I found the motel just as the wolves let loose another howl. Nice of them to let me know that they were so close by.

30

The motel itself was one of those basic discount hotels. A cheap wall of concrete blocks surrounded the parking lot and was topped with steel spikes painted white. The motel itself was a long narrow building, three stories high and just wide enough so you could hold two rows of rooms and the hallway. It was my hope that the wolves would be reluctant to rampage through a populated hotel. If not, this was probably an incredibly stupid idea. I had to admit it might be stupid regardless.

Still, keeping Tallow and her pups alive seemed worth the effort. Trouble was, how to get a cougar the size of a Saint Bernard and carrying a sack of dripping meat to boot inside. The front door was out.

I skulked through the car entry gate and hugged the wall as I prowled the perimeter of the building. The parking lot wasn't exactly full as I slunk in between the cars. I didn't see any cameras, but that didn't mean they weren't there. All the doors were closed, but somebody had left a second-story window wide open. It looked like my only way in that didn't require a key or thumbs.

I wondered if I could jump that high. If a house cat could jump to the top of a refrigerator, then I should be able to get up to that window. I actually wanted to put about half the viscera in there, so no need to jump with the whole bag in my mouth. I dropped the bag and unfolded it, getting a fresh whiff of the stuff, which set my stomach growling. How long had it been since I had eaten those sausages? It felt like a decade ago. I gulped down a mouthful of afterbirth before I realized what I was doing. The fats were so sweet and tender that I couldn't even manage a little bit of disgust at myself. My human dignity was going to be completely gone by tomorrow at this rate.

Of course, living to tomorrow was an open question.

I tore off a chunk of the bloody mass off using a paw and my teeth. Careful not to swallow, I charged towards the wall and leapt. To my surprise I sailed up to the window almost effortlessly. I just needed a little push with my back feet to get all the way in. I was pretty proud of myself. Too bad the room's occupant didn't share my joy. To be fair, I probably would be upset too if somebody jumped through my window with their mouth full of dripping meat.

Still, there was no cause to scream that loudly. It hit me like a physical blow as soon as my paws touched the carpet. Humans are so loud. I barely got a look at the figure that leapt from the bed and sprinted out of the room. The door opened to a blindingly lit hallway, and I caught a glimpse of tanned buttocks.

The stealth gig that cats are known for? We'll file that under a learned skill and not a standard feature. I worked as fast as I could, listening to the woman screaming, "*Tiger! There's a tiger in my room!*" as I smeared the afterbirth all over the room. I wiped it on the walls, smeared it on the mirror and tossed it on the bed before I leapt out the window. The whole business had taken me maybe a minute.

I landed to sound of somebody shouting, "Holy crap!" I checked over my shoulder to see a guy staring at me through a first-floor window, his eyes round as hubcaps. A snarl sent him scrambling deeper into his room. Not waiting for him to come back with a gun or anything, I grabbed my bag of leftovers and booked it for the wall. After the second-story window, an eight-foot-high wall felt like a baby hurdle. Unfortunately I landed right in the path of square headlights. The car rocketed past me, brake lights on and tires squealing. I saw a silhouette with a long muzzle hanging out of the driver-side window and heard excited exclamations to turn around.

I popped back over that wall without a thought and broke into a sprint, dropping my bag of guts. The sound of squealing tires chased my pounding paws. Crap—I'd only spread the scent at one location so far. Would they be able to follow the scent back to Tallow? I dashed from car to car, working around the parking lot to the back. Inside I could still hear the woman screaming hysterically while the guy I had startled came out of the building through a side exit, a rifle in his hand. His head scanned the parking lot as I crept from car to car. He had both hands on his gun but wasn't aiming with it. The wolves screeched into the parking lot as I rounded the corner of the building. I paused to watch what might happen.

"Holy crap!" The guy didn't seem to have much of a vocabulary. He aimed hastily and fired as police sirens began to roar in the distance. The wolves exploded out of the car, each running for cover. I wondered if you needed silver bullets to down a werewolf. Judging by the fact that Pa and Noise weren't in this posse, I guessed that werewolves healed slower than the movies implied.

A howl went up among the group, and Mr. Holy Crap wisely ducked back inside the motel. I had to wonder what the Veil had shown him at that point. Were the wolves all tigers? Were they rabid dogs driving a car? The sirens were approaching with speed. I hoped the prospect of tangling with more humans with guns would convince the pack to leave the hunt for another day.

Either way, I'd wasted too much time. Trying to be as quiet as possible, I slipped around the back of the building. Oddly, the fence here was a little higher and topped with razor wire. Coiling the muscles in my legs, I leapt over it.

An acrid stench hit my nose before my paws hit the ground. Piles of old cars were stacked four high in front of me, along with piles of junk that looked sharp and scary in the moonlight. Not the best of places to wind up, but I was reasonably sure the place was deserted until the growling started.

A dog stood in the shadows of a junk pile. A big one too, although I couldn't really make out details, other than he was large with broad shoulders and had a lot of shiny teeth in his wide mouth. His growl sounded like a saw working through a log, up and down in pitch. Probably related to Pa. I hissed at him, making sure he got a good look at my own fangs, hoping he'd think twice about taking me on. Fighting him was the absolutely last thing I wanted to do at the moment.

The question really was, how fast was he? Could I streak through the scrapyard and jump the gate before those teeth clamped down on my leg or did I have to bounce back over the wall? Either way the bastard would probably bark. I made to sidestep him, and the tension snapped like a chain.

He came at me barking like a rapid-fire cannon. *Ruff! Ruff!*
With my own yowling growl I slammed a paw into the side
of the dog's head, spinning him in midair.

I was running away before he landed, legs bounding for
the gate as the pack's howls erupted behind me. The mutt
was right on my tail, literally. Several times I felt his jaws
close around it only to slip through his teeth as I zigzagged
across the junkyard, doing my best Rudy imitation. A quick
vault and the tin roof of the junk shack banged beneath my
feet, nearly buckling under my weight. From there a quick
hop over the circular razor wire deposited me onto a dark
street lined with fences.

I recognized the place, Broad Street, the place in Grantsville where secrets were stored. Now I hoped it would
provide a decent place to hide. My chest heaved as I trotted
down the road, looking for a likely spot. I would have run,
but my ears felt like they might explode from the blood
pressure.

It wasn't looking good; the street was lined by high fences
topped by barbed wire too high for me to jump. The gates
weren't much better. The damn dog was still barking his
head off. I hoped that meant the wolves hadn't followed me
over the fence. Can wolves jump? I knew they could run.

A pickup truck rolled through the intersection ahead, but
I saw it for what it really was—my salvation. A final sprint
landed me and my bursting lungs in the back of its bed, my
paw narrowly avoiding getting skewered by a fierce-looking
rake. The driver didn't seem to have noticed me as I hunkered down next to a tarp-covered lawnmower. I pressed
myself against the cool metal of the truck bed and listened
to the thundering of my heart, which worked its way into
my ears. Frantically I thought over my options. O'Meara
was still an hour away. I had to keep the wolves busy and

away from the office until then. Two options occurred to me. The trouble was the truck, wherever it was going, was going away from both of those options.

I peered around the lawnmower to look at the man in the cab of the vehicle. He had wide shoulders with a balding head connected via very little neck.

I thought about jumping out and doubling back towards the burbs, but the appearance of square headlights in the distance behind me made that feel like a very bad plan. The pack was barreling through the lights to catch up. At this rate they were going to catch me still a mile from my house. This wasn't going to do at all. I looked around the truck bed in desperation. There, wedged between two cans of paint, lay the brim of a ball cap.

Not wasting any time I ripped the ball cap from the cans with my teeth and carefully hooked my claws through the fabric. Then I sat it on my head, using my paw to hold it there. Carefully, I crept up to the window to look at my oblivious driver. He seemed to be in his own little world, mumbling lyrics to some pop song that didn't jibe very well with his middle-aged body. Slowly I reached a paw inside the cab and extended my claws, carefully hovering them an inch from the back of his hairy neck.

"Hey," I growled.

He startled, and I press my claws against the base of his neck. The big man squeaked.

"Ever wanted to be in an action flick?"

"What?" His eyes went to the rearview mirror and widened.

"*Don't look at me!*" I snapped. He tore his eyes from the mirror, back to the road ahead of us. "Do you know where Maurice Road is?"

"Yeah . . ."

"Good—you are going to take me there as fast as you can, and then I won't slit your throat. Understand?" I hissed.

He nodded.

"*Now drive!*" I roared in his ear. His foot stomped on the gas, and we bolted through the intersection to the scream of angry horn. The truck's engine roared as we sped down the throughway. Behind us I heard a howl as the pack's sedan swerved around traffic. Over the hill behind them the scenery flashed with red and blue.

Up ahead a yellow light loomed, but the street was empty. "Keep going!" I urged as my hat flapped once and lifted from my head. Needing one paw on the driver's neck and one to brace against the acceleration, there was nothing I could do to stop it. I felt the air around me shift; had that been the Veil shifting around me? No way to know. The driver's eyes strayed back to the rearview mirror. I showed him my teeth and pricked him a little harder with my claws. His eyes went back to the road. We sped through town, the Caddy's square headlights glared at me from less than two hundred feet away as we approached the turnoff. The driver seemed to dig that the Caddy would hit him if he slowed down, so he jerked back into the left lane and hit the brakes hard before the turn. The turn was so fast that it took all my strength not fall out of my perch as the other vehicle streaked by us, its tires squealing as the scent of burned rubber met my nose.

We were nearly a quarter mile away from the intersection before those square headlights reappeared behind us, the engine roaring like a mechanical lion. Luckily, I didn't have much farther to go. The truck turned the corner onto Maurice Road, my street. My territory. The truck began to slow, and I removed my paw from the driver's neck. Feeling an impish impulse, I stuck my head into the cab and gave him a cheek lick. He tasted awful, but the look of utter bewilderment was worth it. I bounded out of the cab before he came to a complete stop, just as those headlights rounded the corner.

I waited until the little werewolf, Merlot, jumped out of the window before breaking into a sprint. I knew this neighborhood like the back of my human hand. I'd say paw, but it was a much newer acquaintance. Some of these houses had dogs in them; most of them were small, but not all of them. Dodging through the hedges, I raced into Mrs. Hildy's yard and around back, where I knew Grayson, the family's Great Dane, was probably napping in his deluxe dog house shaped like one of Paris Hilton's mansions. I jumped on top of it, purposely smashing my front paws down hard, then launched myself into the Daltons' yard as the air filled with a confused *wuff-wuff*.

I grinned as Grayson began to growl. I hoped the werewolf would at least be slowed by the territorial Great Dane as I sprinted around the Daltons' garden and snaked myself through their maze of prize-winning rose bushes. Several growls opposed Grayson's. Guilt pulled at my chest as I tore across the street, but the wolves were probably too focused on me to injure Grayson too badly. I hoped.

Breaching the next garden, I sprinted through a backyard filled with sprinkler mist and scraped myself along the corner of the house before bolting back across the street. The wards across the Archmagus' house shone with threatening energy even before I approached it and brightened with every pounding step. Interlocking plates of runes blocked off even the walkway. I tossed my thoughts against them. *Hey, dragon! You want out?*

No response—I did not have time to get into a staring contest with the wards. I veered off towards plan B as a howl shattered the night behind me, vaulted over my own fence and tore into my front yard. I could already hear my neighbors complaining about the length of the grass as I circled around to the back of the house, praying that the bathroom window had not been closed. Half of me desperately hoped that some other brilliant plan would manifest itself if it was.

The bathroom window stood open for all the world to see, and I leapt through. Cat's grace and tile flooring led to some unfortunate skidding, resulting in my head hitting the cabinet below the sink with a crushing thud. A small grey head popped around the corner of the door, pointing the barrel of a bottle rocket in my general direction as I shook off the blow. "Thomas? Flying fur balls—what the hell!"

31

"Werewolves trying to eat me. Explain later!" I shouted at Rudy. I got up, walked past the bewildered squirrel and stopped dead when I saw the sheer amount of fireworks piled in my bedroom. The squirrel had transformed my bedroom into a miniature munitions factory for a very small but well-armed artillery. Three large firework variety packs stood against my bed, their contents sorted into like piles on the floor. On a blue minitarp about two by two feet lay fireworks in various stages of deconstruction and reassembly. My laptop lay on the edge of it, its screen open to a site entitled Pyro Club.

Rudy grinned up at me, chest puffed out, pride shining in his eyes. "So nice to have a dry space!"

Two grey shadows shot into the backyard, and suddenly there was no more time for quips. Cursing myself for not turning off the lights, I dove out the door to the bedroom, kicking it closed behind me. The kitchen would the best place to spring an ambush. The fridge stood right by the entrance, and I jumped on top of it as I heard the sharp crack of glass.

"Hey, isn't this—" the mother's wolf's voice growled.

"Doesn't matter." Eagle cut her off. "I'm getting me a new rug tonight."

My eyes caught a shadow over the window beside the front door. Thin curtains blocked me from seeing Merlot directly and he from seeing me on my perch, but I knew he was there. The big bay window across from me in the dining nook had no such curtain, and the moonlight streamed in through it. Of course, they would pick this moment, when I really needed them to be stupid, to be smart enough to get me in a pincher Merlot was the weak link—the only werewolf I outweighed, but I didn't like my odds in the experience dimension.

"What the hell is all this? Gunpowder?" The voice of the wolf mama—Tallow had said her name was Kia—came from the other room.

"Who cares . . ." A long sniff. "He's here," Eagle replied, his voice a pure animal growl. I hoped none of Tallow's pups would inherit their father's brainpower as I jumped from the fridge to crouch behind the kitchen island. My new location was far from ideal for ambushing monsters coming from the hallway, but at least Captain Runt wouldn't be able to see me.

The bedroom door slammed open, and I winced at the thought of the crack the door knob probably made in the sheetrock wall. My lips peeled from my fangs as I hunkered down, panic fluttering up into my stomach. This wasn't working. Damn wolves were being far too cautious. I had hoped to be able to fight them on my own turf, but now I was just trapped. "Here, kitty, kitty, kitty," Eagle taunted.

I was as good as treed. A sharp pop came from my right as Merlot punched through the glass next to the door. No good options. I ran through the least bad options, and they all came back to the runt. The omega had no backup. If I got through him, then . . . Well, at least I'd have a bit more room to maneuver. I heard the deadbolt slide open on the front door. No more time for planning. I threw myself over the counter, my body launching towards the door like a rocket. I'm sure Merlot felt an explosion of pain as my teeth punctured his hand. He gave a sharp yip of pain before I tugged downwards, impaling his arm on the breaking glass. The little were-mutt filled my ears with a blood-curdling scream. The ground below me pulsed. Instinctively I turned, only to see white teeth streak past my vision before Eagle slammed into me, jaws clamping down on my neck. A sliding sensation and my neck popped free, thanks to loose skin. A twist and my mouth found something meaty, a leg or arm—either way it had hot blood in it.

Gravity left me, the world whirled as something white zoomed large and I slapped into it, paws first. The fridge. Gravity found me and slammed me, back first, into the floor. A mass of black fur hurled herself on top of me, teeth snapping in my face, her breath stinking of rotten meat. My hind claw found her belly flesh and dug in, but it didn't deter her. She bore down on me with all her weight, and it took all my strength to keep her monstrous muzzle off my face. I felt my claws catch as her hands closed around my throat. Something tore beneath my claws, and my foot found soft wetness, but pain didn't even flicker into those murderous eyes.

Just as my vision began to darken, something ripped her off my claws. Those narrowed eyes widened in shock as she flew backward into my living room and crashed onto the back edge of my sofa. A loop of intestines streamed after her like a bloody streamer. Eagle stepped in front of her, his muzzle a grin with far too many teeth. I stayed on my back and made sure that he saw the gauntlet of claws he'd have to go through to get to my throat. Dogs rolling on their backs might be submission, but for us cats, it's more a statement of "I will fuck you up." Kia hadn't counted on the damage they could do.

Eagle did not look like he was about to make the same mistake. He pulled Angelica's meat cleaver from the rack by the door. Once again I realized that I had miscalculated Eagle's intelligence. He'd just saved his mum's life and wasn't about to make her mistake. He stood there, growling loudly, but I could still hear the click of claws on the other side of the island. Merlot was coming around the other side. Still pinchered.

"Oh, by the way, there were three pups." The words came out more of a hiss than the casual tone I had intended. It's tough to talk while baring your fangs at the same time.

Eagle flinched and then his growl deepened; the handle on the knife made a cracking sound as it snapped in his fist. "Where is she? Tell me!" he barked.

"Heeeeyaa moonbag!!" a high-pitched voice screamed from down the hallway. Eagle's eyes flicked to the side and did a double take as a battery of bottle rockets whistled out of the bedroom towards his head. He almost ducked them but was a fraction of a second too late. One of the rockets caught on his pointed ear and buried itself in the ear canal, fire spurting from the shaft, making the tip of the ear sizzle. Eagle's hand had wrapped around the stick jutting from his ear when the firework exploded into a flash of brilliant green.

Moments later, my third eyelids flicked back from my vision and revealed the aftermath. Eagle stood there, but all outward signs of his ear had disappeared. The other had been chopped down to half-mast. His hand opened, and the fur crackled as he touched the gory hole that had been his ear. Pain, shock, fear, panic, anger and finally rage flash through his eyes, focused not on me, I assumed, but on the tiny grey figure I imagined standing in the middle of the hallway, holding a bottle-like bazooka. A small "Oh, crap," drifted from the hallway as Eagle lowered himself into a linebacker's charge stance, growling dangerously.

A shadow stole over me, and I found Merlot standing not a foot from me, peeking out from around the corner of the kitchen island, his mouth hanging open. He was completely focused on his pack brother, not looking at me at all. I couldn't see his eyes through the angle of his muzzle. A BBQ fork hung limply in his left hand, the other arm dangled useless as blood dripped down his fingertips.

Eagle charged into a cacophony of snapping cracks before the entire house exploded with ear-deafening pops. A swarm of bottle rockets screamed out of the hallway in his wake. I upgraded my mental assumption of what Eagle had seen of Rudy. Not a lone shoulder-mounted bottle rocket, but an entire battery of homemade fireworks. Twin howls of pain and panic went up as multicolored flames filled the air within my home. I found myself on my feet without remembering getting up as a grey blur streaked out of the doorway and towards me.

"*GO, GO, GO, GO!*" Rudy screamed at me as he impacted my side. Dumbly, I obeyed, trotting out the front door and into the now very awake neighborhood.

Every light on the street was on. People's silhouettes stood in the windows facing my house. I could feel the pressure of those eyes on us, a physical force. My ears were beyond ringing. They were screaming so loud that I felt rather than heard the rapid series of dull thuds that indicated even more fireworks igniting behind me. In *my* house! The house I had been fighting so hard to keep, that I had deliberately gone to, knowing that Rudy had rigged it to blow.

Something shifted on my neck. *"Run! They're not dead yet! Get those legs of yours moving!"* Rudy's voice rang through my head, clear as crystal. *"Can't you hear them?"*

"No," I thought back, my brain starting to whir back to life. How Rudy was talking through the broken collar gnawed but other thoughts pressed it out. I was still in danger, and the battle wasn't over yet. I still had part two to accomplish. The werewolves' car idled at the end of the street, about five houses distant. Actually I realized it hadn't been their car at all, but Cyndi's. I started towards it at a trot. Then slowed to a staggering shuffle as the seeds of injuries blossomed into pain. The fight replayed in my head, identifying the source of each individual pain as I hobbled to the car. The ribs had a fridge handle–shaped pain, Rudy's foot claws dug into scruff and my skin had been ravaged by Kia's teeth. My forelegs hurt up and down their length, along with my spine from the sheer impact with refrigerator and then the ground. A growing headache, triggered by the ringing in my ears, threatened to blot everything out. Yet it was all nothing compared to the initial agony of my broken bond.

"Uh, Thomas, you might want to move a little faster, wherever you're going. That guy really doesn't look all that happy with us."

I should not have looked back, but I did. Eagle stood in my front yard, fur smoldering and red ichor dripping from the wound in his head, as he clutched the white picket fence in my front yard for support. One of his eyes had swollen shut, but his other was clear, and it broadcast pure hate. Unlike the animal hate that I had seen in Kia, there was plenty of intelligence behind this look. Regardless of the circumstances, whether or not he ever realized how he and his pack had been manipulated, this wolf would never forgive me. That was all right.

Behind him, smoke poured from the windows of my house and an orange glow pulsed from the bedroom. Because of him and his instinctual need for vengeance, everything I had been fighting to preserve, to hold onto, would be nothing more than a smoldering ruin by morning. It turned out that I had been willing to pay that price to survive and keep his children alive.

His mouth was moving, but I couldn't hear it over the ringing. Maybe it was some oath of vengeance or praise for fighting him to a standstill. I didn't care. Behind him Kia, leaning heavily on Merlot for support, limped out of the house. Kia clutched at her stomach. She'd survive— that was good. At least this bunch wouldn't be going after Tallow tonight.

I looked back to Eagle; his eye seemed to be searching me for something. "Go home," I said, barely hearing my own voice. "Go home and stay there. This town is mine." His eye still searched, giving no indication that he had heard me, but behind him, Merlot nodded. Then I looked up sharply when Rudy vibrated on the back of my neck.

"Rudy, shut up," I sent via the collar, and he did.

"Hey, I kicked his ass and saved yours. You owe me!"

"You've also burned down my house."

"You're welcome! Buildings are so much prettier when they're on fire."

Our thoughts were like bits of electricity leaping over a gap. As long as he touched the collar, we could exchange mental text messages. I growled somewhat halfheartedly. I wondered where Rudy learned that trick as I took one last look at my burning house and the wolves before walking back towards the wolves' car. It probably wasn't the wisest plan to take the wounded wolves' transportation but . . . I laughed at the thought. No, the entire plan couldn't be classified as wise. What I had planned probably bordered on insane.

"*What's so funny, Tommy?*" Rudy asked we reached the car. Cops and maybe animal control would be here soon. Not much time left.

"*Just thinking about an old cartoon show where a family of raccoons drive a car.*"

"*Oh, it ain't that bad. I've gnome-styled cars plenty of times before. Don't worry about it. Wide one's the brake, tall one is the gas.*" With that he leapt from my head into through the window.

Gnome style? I both wondered what the name referred to and worried that a bunch of animals drove cars often enough that the magical world had a name for it. I followed after him much more clumsily, jarring more than a few developing bruises as I pulled myself through the window.

32

Rudy proved to be far better at the pedals than I was at steering. The ringing of my ears had dulled from the obliteration of everything to the point where I could dimly hear the sirens of the cop cars that raced by us on their way to my house. I still couldn't hear Rudy at all, but he did a pretty good job at translating my barked "Stop!" and "Go, go" into movement of the car. By the time we arrived at the park that contained Archie's dragon, I could hear faint sounds of Rudy's confused chittering. We stopped in the parking lot next to the park's playground, and while I looked for the best spot to drive the car down onto the grassy field, Rudy climbed up from the pedal well.

I had been here before with Angelica when she had been on a fitness kick. The landscaping here gently sloped down towards a river that lay beyond a thick band of secondary growth forest. Due to the incline, the park had been constructed on several terraces. The parking lot raised up about three feet from a grass field that contained a well-weathered baseball diamond and two small soccer goals. The playground had been raised higher and sported a small stairway to reach. Beyond the playground, the hill crested with a covered panic area on the top. Down on the field, a stone general rode a horse in his eternal charge into the soccer field from the baseball diamond's backstop. It was a very odd place for a civil war memorial. Now we just had to get this hammer of a car down there.

There was a gap in the low wooden fence that surrounded the parking lot, but a thick chain was strung across it. The heavy Caddy could probably bust through the chain, but I had to hit the chain at some speed and the posts were a stout three-by-three inches thick. I needed to get the Caddy in operational condition down the hill and then point it at the statue if this was going to work.

Rudy leapt on my neck and made the connection. *"Why the hell are we here? I thought we'd be driving to O'Meara's."*

"Nope. I want to get this done before she can stop me." I hadn't meant to tell him, but clearly I wanted to tell somebody.

"Stop you?"

"There's a dragon in this park, and I aim to let it out." With that I hooked my paw under the shifter and moved the needle on the dash to R. The Caddy started inching back without any gas. My body was large enough to reach the pedals, but I couldn't hit the gas, steer and get my head high enough see the road in front of me. A nine-foot tall statue, however, would be very different.

"A dragon? You're serious?"

"You are serious! There is a dragon here?"

"Archibald caught it about a hundred years ago. He's been pulling pieces off it and using it to fuel his magic. If we don't let it out, then some other magus is going to do the same for another hundred."

A silence followed as I carefully lined the car up with

the chain across the gap in the fence. Not having Rudy in the pedal well made this a bit tricky.

"Okay. Got it. How do we get it out?"

I froze for a split second, momentarily forgetting that the car was still rolling. I shifted the car into park and winced at the crunch of the gears. *"You're cool with this?"* I had a very strong urge to look the squirrel in the eye but couldn't get the right angle with him clinging to my neck.

"Dude, I get it. I've seen what magi do with somebody's who's made of tass." I felt the squirrel shiver.

"Floor it then, but get ready to break." I shifted the car to D.

A moment. *"Wha— Oh! On it!"* Rudy raced down to the pedals and threw his entire body into the gas. The sedan jerked forward like a startled rabbit, nearly knocking my paws off the steering wheel. We roared across the parking lot, the ancient automatic shifting through two gears before we hit the chain. It popped from the posts, ripping the timbers open as the anchor bolts were torn free. Then the seat below me bucked, catapulting me into the padded ceiling with a bone-echoing *whump!*

I fell but didn't seem to hit the seat as the car launched into the air beyond the fence. I finally slammed into the seat as the car hit the bottom of the hill. "Brake! Brake!" I yelled as the force drove me into the foot well.

"I'm trying!" I heard Rudy's chitter and felt his claws rake at my leg. "Git off my tail!"

I shifted and heard the engine rev, as my foot snagged the gas. The car accelerated, only to slam my already tenderized noggin into the steering wheel as Rudy threw himself on the brake. Our heads muddled from the force of the impact, it took several stop and start cycles before I managed to disentangle my feet from the pedals and crawl out of the well. We probably looked like a teenager's first time with a stick shift.

After much cursing and registering that my hearing had recovered enough to hear Rudy if he shouted at me, we lined the car up with the granite statue, backing it all the way across the soccer field. Under the headlights of the car, I saw no glimmer of magic on the statue itself, but there was clearly a ring of something around it. Dark and greenish, it certainly wasn't a ward like I had seen before. This was subtle. Had I not been looking for magic, I would have missed it entirely. It flickered in the corner of my eye as I stared at the statue.

Rudy looked a bit worse for wear, sitting on the dashboard and wincing as he ran his paws up and down his tail. A single beady eye watched me. "So it's in the statue?" I heard him say over the firework-induced dial tone that had taken up residence inside my head.

"Yeah, that's what it said." I leapt out the window.

"*Hey!* Where you going?"

"I'm going to ask it not to kill us when we let it out. And to find something to weigh down the gas pedal with." My bruises were getting bruised. Being inside of a car crashing into a stone statue was not on my bucket list filed under survival.

"Oh! Good plan!" He gave me a victory sign with his paw. "A brick will be best!" Again I wondered just how long the squirrel had been around.

I shook the thought away as I walked up to the shadow ring around the statue. I sat down and stared at the monument. It did not look magical. The only glimmer of light was the pale moonlight bouncing off the general's pitted mustache. He had not been well maintained. Moss and lichen had invaded the cracks that the assault of many winters had worked into the stone. Of course, if you were trying to hide something like a dragon, you probably wanted to make the prison as subtle as possible. If the statue had been a geyser of magic, then the secret wouldn't keep long. I stared at the statue a while longer, but no layer of complexity peeled away before my eyes like the wards. There simply was nothing to dig into.

Except the ring at my feet. It was doing a bad job at being subtle now. I looked at that. It wasn't Archibald's spell. That much was clear. Like all spells placed on objects, it was built in layers, each one stretching farther and farther into a direction that was neither up nor down but a new angle entirely.

This as Sabrina and Cornealius's. The Archmagus' runes all ran in straight lines; these were more waving, running in a sort sinusoidal curve. They were much simpler than the wards on either magus' house, and I did not get the sensation of sheer danger from it. An alarm perhaps. But what would set it off? Surely just moving across it wouldn't do it; during the day there had to be a good two hundred people in this park. Two hundred normal people, which I was no longer one of.

I didn't dare cross that line, not until we were ready. Instead I looked at the face of the statue. "Dragon, I don't know if you can hear me, but if you can, give me some sort of sign."

Nothing happened. The statue stared impassively in the direction of the car. I wondered how far O'Meara was now. Three hours had to be nearly up, between the birth and the wolves and the drive over to the park. When this was all over, I wanted a watch.

"Well, if you can't give me a sign, then just listen. We're going to try to free you. I don't know if knocking down the statue will be enough, but that's all I got. If it does work, well, it would be nice if you didn't hurt anybody on the other side of the Veil. They're not a part of this. Maybe I'm naive and I'm just opening up a Pandora's box here, but you've got to start somewhere."

A purple flash flared above the statue and the shape of Cornealius materialized on the statue's head. "That you are a dangerous fool will surprise no one, Thomas," he hissed.

33

I started and glared up at Cornealius on the statue. "Hey, I didn't cross the damn circle! That's cheating!"

Cornealius just shook his head. "You know absolutely nothing about magic. It's your damn stubbornness that's gotten you killed. I tried so many ways to avoid this. If you'd just gone along with the TAU or Cyndi or bonded anybody other than O'Meara, it would have been fine."

I started to back away from the statue and Cornealius, who was wrapped around the statue's neck like a scarf. He appeared relaxed and unhurried and still managed to be threatening. Where the hell was Sabrina? I tried to scan the area with my peripheral vision, but nothing moved other than the leaves in the breeze. I tried to put on a brave face, trying not to remember just how large Cornealius could be if he wanted to. It didn't work. My brain started cataloging places to run to. "Kill me here and everyone will find out about your treasure."

He laughed. "It's way past time for secrets, cub—tonight is all about possession. But even your precocious O'Meara will thank us for stopping you. Every magus in the region is dependent on this spot for tass in one way or another."

"You two know what's best for everyone, don't you?"

"So—" The roar of an engine cut him off, and his eyes widened as they flicked between me and the car. Whenever he had started listening in, he had missed Rudy's presence entirely. The car's wheels spun on the grass and in a second they caught, shooting forward across the field. Cornealius's face contorted into a mask of panic as he leapt from his perch, his skin aflame with a green glow. He hit the ground with enough mass that I felt the impact under my feet, landing just to the left of the car's path.

"*Banzai!*" Rudy flung himself out the driver-side window as the car roared into the space between Cornealius and me. I got a face full of squirrel and heard the sickening crunch of bone followed by the sharp crack of metal and stone. Rudy quickly used my ears to scramble onto the back of my head before I could give voice to my protest.

The car lay on its roof twenty feet beyond the statue, wheels still spinning as the engine choked and sputtered. Cornealius, now the size of a stretched-out draft horse, leaned against the statue, his face a grimace of pain. His left foreleg seemed to sport several new joints as it hung from his shoulder. Blood bubbled from his nose. In the distance I could hear two engines screaming as they approached. At first glance, I thought the statue had escaped unharmed, but then I realized the general's outstretched sword had disappeared, and indeed the statue's left arm had been snapped off from the elbow. An angry orange ichor from the stump of the arm was slowly beading up on the stone.

"Well, that's poetic karma for ya, Scrags," I muttered to myself.

Cornealius spat blood onto the ground. "Bloody idiots."

His ears twitched, and one zeroed in on the leaking stump, his eyes widening. "You had better hope Sabrina is strong enough to patch this, or you've just killed the entire town. Not that you care for anything but your own hide."

I growled back, "Says the guy who killed someone over a power source."

"Archibald was a senile idiot, deadlocking the council while the council should be preparing for war!"

"Still murder," I growled. The engines were getting closer, one far louder than the other, less like an engine and more like a rocket. A light grew on the horizon. Below my feet I felt the ground stir. Doubt flared in my mind. Had I been duped? Nervous, I started to pace around the oversize weasel, circling towards his injured side.

Cornealius's eyes narrowed as they followed me, but he made no effort to move; he only breathed.

The light was almost on us now, reflected on the windows of the nearby houses. *"Is he right, Rudy?"* I thought at the squirrel as I felt his mind brush my chain.

"Maybe. The Veil should protect the Munds. It's a flaming dragon, Thomas. Everybody dies."

The source of the light tore around a corner down the street, and O'Meara's Porsche burst into view, sporting a ten-foot cone of flame out of its rear. I heard the high-pitched scream of a woman as the car screeched into the parking lot, its flame dying away. O'Meara burst from the car almost before it stopped moving. Ixey followed from the passenger side, wobbling unsteadily and looking green.

"Thomas!" O'Meara vaulted the fence and ran down the hill into the field, directly towards me. With a heavy lunge, Cornealius threw himself between O'Meara and me.

"Stay back, O'Meara!" he snapped. O'Meara skidded to a stop, her hands filling with fire.

"Out of the way!" she snarled. A flash of light and heat hit my eyeballs. A blink and the grass all around Cornealius was gone, replaced with black charred dirt. Cornealius stood unmoved. This only infuriated O'Meara further. "Damn you!" Her eyes burst into individual suns as she drew forth so much power that her outline was lost within the pulsing light of her energy.

Ixey looked down from the fence of the parking lot reaching towards O'Meara. "Mistress, *no!*"

A purple spot bloomed behind Ixey, and before I could shout a warning, tendrils of yellow force burst from it, seizing her from behind. They wrapped themselves around Ixey's head and forcibly twisted it to look away from O'Meara. Another plucked the lizard from her shoulder and flung the poor thing off into the playground. A green puff of energy burst out of Ixey and dissipated. The purple resolved into Sabrina, her teeth gritted in concentration, the yellow tendrils extending from her left hand. In her other she held a staff of pure shadow. "*O'Meara, stop!*"

O'Meara spun, sending a focused jet of intense heat and hatred at Sabrina. A black beam from the staff met it not two feet from her head. The blackness engulfed the heat jet, eating it like a black hole. Flame spewed off in random directions. "Thomas! Run!"

"O'Meara! *This is not the time to fight!*" Sabrina screeched, her arm starting to shake under the sustained assault. "There's a dragon to deal with!"

O'Meara did not halt her assault as she pulled the sword from her belt, runes glowing along the length of the blade. "Then yield!" The blade twirled, sending projectiles arcing from the tip of the sword and hailing down onto Sabrina.

Sabrina spun, dropping Ixey and sending tendrils of power slicing up at the oncoming bolts, batting them from the air. One got through, slicing through Sabrina's grand-motherly bun. She hissed invective that I didn't catch as I searched for a way to use the time O'Meara had given me.

I padded closer to the statue, searching mentally for any hint of the dragon's presence. It had contacted me at the house. Surely it could do it here, where it had been imprisoned. Then again, magic seemed to have its own bizarre rules about space. Rules I didn't know. Knocking off the arm had done something. But had it done enough?

Cornealius turned. "Dear cat, you best get away from that." He threw himself upwards, growing even larger as he reared up on his back legs. His long snaky body tow-ered unstably over me and the squirrel, face contorted in a grimace of both pain and determination. I hurried over the rest of the distance to the statue, hoping for some opportunity to appear.

"Damn, this thing is high-pitched! I hate stale magic!" Rudy commented as we raced around the statue, putting it between us and Cornealius.

"It's not that bright to me," I thought back.

"Dude, we are not trying to hash out the hearing versus sight thing now! What do we gotta do?"

"I need to talk to the dragon."

"How'd you do it last time?"

"I scryed through the wards at the Archmagus's place."

"Okay, so he's powering the wards, right?"

"I guess. The first time it just sort of manifested in the house."

"The house is different. If there are any wards on this statue, they'd be Archibald's. Otherwise the dragon would be impris-oning himself, and I bet that wouldn't hold."

"What can you tell me about the magic leaking out of the statue?" I thought at Rudy.

Cornealius stomped towards us unsteadily, while behind

him the magi hammered at each other with multicolor magics.

"I dunno—it's just wrong. I've heard it before. If you go into a shop that sells elementals, and if all the elementals are sickly, it can sound like that. Just not this loud."

The sound of mistreatment and sickness. Perhaps the orange stuff was the magical equivalent of blood or pus. Maybe the prison was less of a cage and more like driving a stake through its foot. Had the Archmagus then harvested the pus dripping from the open wounds? Who knows. Still, I needed a connection to it. The decaying wards in the house had perceived the occupants of house—they were designed to. The dragon had no such eyes here.

"Step away from the statue, cat!" Cornealius looked down at me over the statue. "I'm done asking."

"Rudy, can you find the end of the chain?" The chain had moved on its own before, but it had been totally inanimate since Tallow had given it to me.

"Yeah, I see it."

"Grab it and stick it into the stump of the statue's arm. I'll deal with Cornealius."

I felt the chain shift on my neck, and I tried to will it thinner, longer. It obeyed sluggishly. Rudy grunted. *"I love bad plans."*

I looked up at Cornealius as Rudy climbed up to the back of the statue. I grinned at him and his mangled arm. "Now you know something about how the Archmagus felt after you ripped him in two."

The giant weasel huffed. "A service to society, I assure you. At this point, you have convinced me that killing you has a similar value." The chain had begun to rotate around my neck, letting out more chain length as Rudy clambered up the statue as if it were a mountain. The chain's weight in his teeth prevented his usual vertical scamper.

"So how long did it take you two to switch from watching an old criminal to coveting his power?" I crouched low, preparing to spring.

"You have—no!" Cornealius's eyes tracked upwards as Rudy climbed up to the shoulder of the statue. With the grace of a falling tree, Cornealius fell towards us, his massive talons aiming to bisect the squirrel. I leapt at his face, and my claws missed, but blood splashed down the back of my throat as my teeth sunk through his flesh. My world became a flurry of violent motion mixed with Cornealius's roar of pain. With a mighty jerk of his head, I sailed away from the weasel, Rudy's screaming in my head as the chain jerked him off the statue.

I hit the ground on all fours. The chain around my neck thickened, reeling in Rudy, and he thudded into the middle of my back. In the back of my mind I felt a sliver of the chain's own awareness, waiting, eager for a new connection. Cornealius had toppled like a tree, hitting the ground on his bad shoulder and screaming in pain with a new hole in his cheek. I spat his torn flesh onto the ground.

O'Meara lay on the ground in a smoldering circle. Sabrina stood on the hill above. Ixey was nowhere to be seen. Sabrina raised a hand at us, blue light gathering in it. "One more time!" I shouted and burst into a run back towards the statue. Blue light erupted in front of me, and I dodged to the side as lightening arced into the grass. I zigzagged my way towards the statue, running around spots of gathering energy. Sabrina shifted from trying to hit me to driving me backwards, away from the statue. I ran around the statue in a wide circle, trying to work my way closer.

"*Just die!*" Sabrina screamed at me, and the entire field beneath my feet turned blue.

"*Jump for it!*" Rudy cried.

Pivoting hard, I leapt for the statue, but I knew as soon as I left the ground that the statue still stood forty feet away. Tiny claws pounded up my back. Rudy ran forward and jumped, using my face for a springboard. The chain, a thin fiber, trailed behind him like a spider's line. His arms and legs stretched out like wings as he sailed in front of me. He hit the general's stump, and the world blossomed first into green, and then pain.

34

Pain beyond anything I had ever known, and magnitudes beyond what I had ever wanted to know, struck through my entire body. Ripping, tearing, burning all at once. Nowhere and everywhere. Was this what electrocution felt like? No, it couldn't be this bad. I screamed. I screamed despite having lost my mouth. I screamed not with flesh, but with my very soul. The scream resonated and echoed, and then was answered, by another scream, another voice. A long, agonized moan that rumbled through the very fabric of myself. I pushed towards it, calling up every foul word my mind could recall and hurling them against the pain. It wasn't my pain at all, but the dragon's. That color, that sickly orange that surrounded me, it wasn't infection or pus. Far worse, it was a distillation of pain, and I was swimming in it.

Push. I had to push. No matter the pain. Like a pregnant woman in the final hours of her labor, like Tallow as she struggled not to howl in pain. I had to find that damn dragon. Deep in the pain, deep in the ground, it howled. It didn't matter anymore why. I had to find it. I screamed for it.

It howled back. The ether shifted, spinning blades in

my flesh became rending hooks. Moments, tiny eternities of agony and then I touched it, brushed against it with my mind and screamed anew.

I had been a fool. They called it a dragon, and I had fit it into a form of a large reptile chained in a cave. It was so utterly beyond that. Even if the dragon in the cave within my mind had been as long as the Empire State Building was tall, this dwarfed it. It stretched into brain-shattering dimensions. Sabrina had been terrified of this, and she was right to be afraid.

A mouth that opened in four different directions reached through the ether of pain, and hundreds of garnet-like eyes stared at me from the roof of its open mouths. *"Ah, well. At least I saved a couple of werewolf cubs from getting sold,"* I thought to myself. I was glad to leave this fucked-up world a little better than I found it. I waited for the end, welcoming the ceasing of the pain.

The jaws closed over me and the pain stopped. It took a few more beats for me to realize that I had not died.

"You came." The dragon's voice exploded in my head, shattering that brief respite from pain. *"Yet you fear. Why?"*

I started to respond, but the thing just lifted my explanation right out of me. I can't really explain precisely what it did with words, but I can try. It took the thought and held it up to a light, like one might inspect a jewel for flaws. Then just as casually, it popped it back from where it had plucked it. The experience was extremely disconcerting.

"I do not understand."

Still disoriented, I readied a more detailed explanation, but instead of taking the single offered thought, it plunged into my mind like a child into an untended candy bowl. Memories I had not thought of in years flashed through me, along with recent events. Then the memories were gone, leaving me feeling strangely empty.

It spread the memories out in front of me, examined them with its strange eyes and huffed with frustration. This close, I could watch its thought process. The random bits of me had only confused it further. It decided that a more thorough investigation would be required. Watching its thoughts were oddly hypnotizing, and I could barely manage a note of protest as it took me apart piece by piece. Memory by memory, urge by urge, it pulled me apart and sorted everything I was into piles. Somehow it kept me vaguely aware or perhaps its memory of me kept me sane. It replayed memories, made copies of various pieces, altered them and replayed the memories again. Dozens of me's operating through the same scene in parallel but each scenario a little different.

It went through my entire life, from beginning to end, and replayed every single memory. It learned everything about me.

Yet, I learned about the dragon too. While it pondered me and explored my world and my existence through me, pieces of me circulated through it. I flowed through eddies of its memories as bits of flotsam in its circulatory system. Perhaps it chose to show me how little it knew of the world that had captured it. Or each thought it had was simply physically reenacted within it. A hundred years ago it had been recovering from a competition with another of its kind. Wounded, it had sought shelter to nurse its wounds, feeding on tangles of dimensions as its kind is wont to do. Apparently one of those tangles had been some sort of lure because it hooked and dragged him into our single plane. This pure world of agony it existed in now might have lasted an eternity for all it knew. It had hoped for death, for the pain to stop, and indeed was slowly starving from the strain of its injuries. Archibald used to feed it but had stopped decades before. Like us, time only marched in a single direction for it, although it could surf the edges.

Satisfied, the creature began to put me back together. Fear came back, and I trembled before it. Piece by piece Thomas Khatt, the cougar, came back into existence. The sheer realization of what had happened hit me as I was completed. Terror and awe and a deep raw sensation of violation flooded through me. Anger surged. *How dare it!* After all I had done to help. This is how it repaid me! I lashed out at the flesh-like stuff that held me, but my imagined claws found no purchase. I raged and gnashed my teeth, but it was no more effective than a week-old kitten's attempt to murder his mother's tail. My efforts stymied and futile, I sagged under the weight of pure despair. I was just an insect, a machine as simple as a 1970s car before the might of this great and terrible thing. And I had just released it on our world.

"I understand," it said. The voice was now calibrated to a more comfortable timber but still one that brimmed with power. *"Your temporary dissolution was necessary. I am not sorry. Grasping the contradictions of your thoughts is difficult. Some of your most considered courses of actions are ones you will not act on. Your world is strange and limited, but surprisingly difficult to predict. It would have been easier had you gathered more experience with this situation."*

"If I had more experience I would not be in here," I sneered at my host. Had its pain just been an illusion to take me in?

"The pain is real. I have stilled time so the way forward is best considered. I am distracting myself from it with you. Yet this stillness is also an effort. The way forward must be decided soon."

"What's stopping you? We broke the statue."

"The statue is nothing but a marker to hide my prison; the anchor within me must be removed."

"You expect me to help you after, after you did t–that to me?"

"Yes. Unless you wish to die. You still have a very angry magus waiting for you."

I picked a nearby eye and gave it a baleful glare. The monster had me dead to rights. Goddamn it. Despite it all, I still wanted to walk away from this stupid train wreck of a rescue mission. But what was the point of living through this if I just wound up in chains again? Had Cyndi been a bit smarter or less obvious, she could have had me and I would be hopelessly in love.

The creature spoke again. *"I understand that a bargain is required. Your independence will never be threatened again. That will be my gift. You will never fear the magi's bond nor their mental manipulation. It is already done."*

"But it won't help me against a lightning bolt," I replied. The dragon did not answer. It did not need to. It knew what to give me to earn my cooperation. It had probably run me through a dozen different scenarios to determine what I required to forgive it for its violation. I only needed the answer to one more question.

"I shall use restraint. Six is all that I require." It spoke before I had voiced the question.

"Six? Why six? Archibald is dead."

"Six."

Six lives. I could see each of their faces in the dragon's mind. I knew three. I would be trading their lives for mine. Cornealius, Sabrina and Scrags. Then a wizened man, an ancient woman and a tiger. The reasons were written there as well. All were involved in the dragon's capture and torment in some way, and Sabrina and Cornealius for plotting to extend it. The list could be far larger. The entire magical world seemed to be a place that acted with no consideration for those outside it. They considered the less powerful mere resources to be traded. What had been done to this terrifying creature would never even be considered wrong. Even O'Meara had barely blinked an eye.

What could I do? A parade of men stood up in my mind and declared they would never trade the lives of others for their own, no matter what their crimes. But all those men were fictional. In this world, there was only power. And I didn't even have thumbs to call my own.

"How do I destroy the anchor?" I asked.

"Take this." And I felt something fold into my mind, fitting neatly into a space that had not been there before. *"Now go."*

The mouth opened, and a deluge of pain swept me away before I could ask another question. I shot through it like a ball tied to the end of a bungee cord, the miasma turning into a sea of hooks and needles.

35

I slammed into my body with a scream, only to choke on black smoke that invaded my lungs whenever I took a breath. My eyes saw only shiny green before a fit of coughing drove them closed.

"Thomas!" Rudy cried as I felt him impact between my shoulder blades. "Did it work? Did the dragon get out?"

I could only cough in reply as something inside my chest started to rip free. "How long?" I managed to croak out after a brief respite between coughs.

"Thirty seconds. Somebody summoned up a cage around us and grounded the lightening. O'Meara might have come to—I heard an explosion." I could feel Rudy vibrate with energy on my back. "We gotta go."

I heard a wet ripping sound deep in my chest, and with a final *hurk* felt something the size of a baseball force its way up my throat and onto the ground.

"What the hell?"

I looked down. The thing appeared to be a frog's egg, roughly the size of a softball, except its yolk looked to be a fusion reaction. It didn't take a genius to figure out how the dragon planned to destroy the anchor. "Now we run!" I declared and booked it.

The green metallic plant stuff around us parted like any other shrubbery, and I dashed back into the moonlit field. I glanced at Sabrina, her black staff raised as if it were a javelin towards the top of the hill. Ixey had fallen against the fence like a fighter on the ropes, her hands gripping the top of the posts on either side of her. The little metal gecko was perched on her head and its little body sheathed in green magic.

Sabrina's head snapped towards me, and our eyes met for a moment. I don't know what she saw in my face, but she didn't like it. With a twist of her hips she leveled the black hole rod directly at me. I zigged but needn't have bothered as the world blew up before she got the chance to blast or skewer me, or worse.

Not for the first time that night, gravity fled the scene, and I was tumbling through an undefined space, the white intensity of magic burning straight through my skull and baking my brain. The ground found me before gravity, and my feet completely failed to land first. I bounced and rolled like a sausage fallen out of a speeding hot dog cart. The white light blinked out as soon I came to a bruising stop. A sort of dull roar met my ears, and they quickly found the source of the sound.

A tree sprouted directly from the place I horked up the dragon's egg. It was growing at over a foot a second, its bark twisting around the trunk like waves. Eye-breaking runes appeared and then sunk back into the tree over and over. The roar I heard deepened into a heavy groan as the tree continued to grow. The top of the tree sprouted thick branches with only a few token leaves.

"Where do I get one of those?" Rudy asked. I glanced

over to find Rudy, apparently none the worse for wear, looking at the tree with wide eyes. "Oh, Sabrina is pissed!" He
pointed and my gaze followed. Sabrina was charging down
the hill, her black staff held over her head like a claymore
sword. Her target was clear. Cornealius, now normal-sized,
desperately struggled to free himself from a snarl of roots
that had wrapped around him like a pack of pythons. The
roots rose to meet Sabrina, rearing up like cobras, and she
sliced through them with her black staff like a light saber
through human flesh, trying to hack a path to Cornealius.

"Hang on, baby! Hang on, Cornealius!" Sabrina shouted
as she cut her way through, but it would be far too late.
Cornealius uttered a high-pitched wail that hit me right in
the gut. I couldn't look away. I didn't know how the dragon
would claim the lives it desired, but I hadn't imagined the
sudden pop and crunch of Cornealius's spine, nor the spray
of blood from his mouth.

With Cornealius's death, the light went out in Sabrina's
eyes. There was no explosion of rage, no death curse; she
simply fell to her knees. When a rearing root drove itself
through her chest and out her back, she gave no recognition
of the wound. She merely shuddered and went limp.

Yet the tree had not finished with them.

I had assumed that Cornealius and Sabrina had more
to do with Archibald and the dragon than I knew, but their
inclusion on the list apparently had a more practical purpose.
As they had sought to use the dragon for fuel, the tree used
them. Their auras had not dimmed with their deaths, and
I watched the roots pull the energy from their still bodies,
the cool light flowing along the roots like a child drinking
juice through a straw. My stomach churned with guilt.

On the hill, Ixey watched with open-mouthed horror as
the two were drained. The tree seemed content to enjoy its

meal for the moment and had stopped its roaring growth. I cautiously pushed up to a standing position. The now distant ringing in my ears hinted at perhaps a minor degradation of my hearing.

"What's going on?" Rudy stood on his hind legs like a meerkat, his ears twitching. "What is it doing to them?"

I wondered how Rudy perceived the sound of what I saw. Ixey's gecko must be a visual familiar, although she could have just been reacting to what the roots had done physically. "Nothing good," I told Rudy as I began to trot back into the field. The weight of him impacting my back was beginning to become a familiar sensation.

"Why didn't it go after O'Meara?" His question was whispered.

I didn't answer it as I slowly wound my way towards O'Meara, giving the now still roots a wide berth. She lay facedown on a patch of blackened earth. Ixey stood at the fence on the hill above, chewing her lip as her green eyes flicked between her mentor and the bed of roots.

For a moment I feared that O'Meara had been killed too, but I saw the faintest shimmer of her aura as I got closer. There was a twitch of movement as my paw crunched onto the seared earth, not from her but a slither of silver from around her neck. The chain, thin and delicate, unwound itself from her neck and S-lined towards me. I felt my own chain shift, and Rudy gave a bark of surprise before scrabbling backwards along my spine.

"Holy crap! Snake!"

I chuckled, watching the chain make its way towards us. "Rudy, it's okay—it's just my ch—" Something flashed into my vision from below my muzzle, striking the "head" of the chain.

Instinct reared and I jumped back. But the silver thing

came with me, dragging the chain along. It turned to give me a cool glare with crystal eyes. I recognized the folded hood of a cobra behind the head of a snake, composed of tiny interlocking chain links. O'Meara's half of the original fey chain hung limply from its jaws.

"The hell are you?" I asked it.

With an air of casual distain it slurped up the fey chain like a long noodle and then sunk from sight. I felt it curled against my neck, exactly where my own chain had been. The dragon's words came into my mind like an echo. *"Your independence will never be threatened again."*

Good gravy. Now that I thought about it, I could feel the entire length of snake around my neck. There was even a mind there, a small mind to be sure, but a mind nonetheless. Other things nestled near that mind, things that radiated a dangerous sort of warmth. The mind clearly wasn't the conversational type, but I could see its few thoughts readily enough and they made me shiver.

I felt the pinpricks of Rudy's claws on my rump. "It's just my fey chain, Rudy. I don't think it will hurt you."

"The hell! It's a snake!" His claws dug in deeper.

"Ow! Get off my ass, Rudy—I don't have time to explain." I shook my butt a bit, but it failed to dislodge the squirrel.

Growling, I stalked towards O'Meara, and I felt the snake wriggle. "O'Meara!" I barked, "Come on! Get up, we've got to go." She didn't stir. "Rudy, wake her up!"

"What? Why me?"

"Cause I don't want to get any closer with a cobra thing around my neck!" I did not add that the snake really thought O'Meara looked nearly cooked to perfection. It seemed willing to listen to my instructions, but I didn't trust something that hungry.

"Well, of course, I can protect her from your freaky friend there by waking up someone who could make crispy squirrel fritters with her mind." Despite the grumbling, he sprang from my rump, scurried over to O'Meara, grabbed her ear and shouted at the top of his deceptively powerful lungs, "Hey, O'Meara! *Wakey, wakey!*" She didn't stir. Rudy looked at me and held up his paws. "Gee, that was supereffective!"

"That won't work!" Ixey shouted. With a worried glance at the roots, she picked her way down the hill. "She burned herself out." I looked up at her; she was still watching us with that same horrified expression on her face.

"Come on, then! Help get her back to the car." I cursed myself and my own optimism. I had figured O'Meara had just worn herself out. The way Ixey had said it, this would take a bit more than a good nap to fix.

"What is that thing going to do, Thomas?"

I opened my mouth to answer when a sharp crackling reached my ears. A glance back revealed the roots starting to twitch and squirm around the white desiccated corpses of Sabrina and Cornealius. There was no more time. O'Meara hadn't been part of the deal, but I didn't want to take any chances. Regardless of the viper around my neck, I went to O'Meara. I pushed my nose to her cheek and found it cool, a coldness that reached up and clutched my heart. She wasn't burned. God, she was dying!

I looked up to Ixey, who stared down at me uselessly; now closer, I could see the shine of wetness in her eyes. "Don't just stand there! *Help me!*"

"I can't help her! Nobody can help her. She's burned herself out. You don't come back from that without the council, and they're not coming."

"Did you tell them that a dragon's about to break loose?"

"W-What? You mean that's—?" Realization struck her

with physical force. "That's what Sabrina had been—" She crumpled to the ground. "Oh, gods, you didn't!" The lizard on her head glared daggers at me as Ixey fell to her knees.

"I did. Tell you why later." I looked down at O'Meara and thought at the snake. *"My contract is still valid."*

It gave a flicker of irritation but did as I requested. The snake's head unwound itself into a continuous metal chain and slipped around O'Meara's neck. I felt it thread through the seeping wounds on the surface of her mind and find the smallest stump of a link, which it curled around. The world turned sideways as the dead space in my head thrummed into a sudden life.

Yet, there was barely a stir on the other side. O'Meara's mind rippled as if made of molasses. *"Thomas?"* The thought moaned into my head. Then a spark within the mind flared. *"Missed you."*

"Come on, O'Meara—we've got to get moving. I released the dragon."

"Good. Glad I bought you the time. I hope it burns the magi world to ash."

My mental processes piled up behind the thought. I had expected her to express surprise or at least a tsking, but not that she had knowingly bought me time.

"Listen, take care of Ixey for me."

That also threw me. *"O'Meara, you are not going to die!"*

"Thomas, I'm holding together by a thread. I'm borrowing a part of your brain to think. I'm done. After you got ambushed, I freaked. I might have killed Whittaker. Sabrina had every right to demand I step down. When the inquisitors come, you tell them it was my plan. Play dumb. Join the TAU. *Blame me for leading you astray."*

"Not going to do that. Sabrina and Cornealius are dead. I let the dragon eat them. If you need my brain for a bit,

then that's fine, but don't blame me if you start licking your privates."

That brought a tired chuckle, and her flickering mind steadied.

I looked up to see the tree come back life, writhing and roaring as if in pain. Five thick limbs were forcing their way from the top of the tree, looking almost like the fingers of a giant. How long had I just been standing there, wasting time?

"Rudy! Call 911! Get an ambulance here!" I grabbed the shoulder of O'Meara's dress with my teeth, but it tore before I moved O'Meara an inch.

"You want me to call the Munds?!" Rudy chittered.

"Just do it, Rudy!" I hissed back. Switching tactics, I searched for something strong enough to bite and drag. Cougar pulled prey up into trees, right? Sure, O'Meara had a hundred pounds on me, but I was a super apex predator. The tree's fingers were starting to twist into brain-hurting directions. Why hadn't I realized that O'Meara was so hurt? I could have bargained with the dragon for healing, maybe—something. I should have rushed past Cornealius and reconnected with O'Meara as soon as she had arrived! But I had been too afraid she'd try to stop me. I grabbed onto her belt and pulled. Ixey grabbed the other side.

"What is that thing going to do, Thomas?" Ixey's voice nearly wailed.

"Shussh up and pull!" I shouted around O'Meara's belt.

Together we dragged O'Meara up the slope and onto the blacktop of the parking lot. She had slipped into a sort of sleep or unconsciousness.

I glanced back at the tree and nearly vomited again. The limbs of the tree were bending around the statue in ways that hammered sharp nails into my mind. But far worse was that I could see the dragon, its claws straining against the very fabric of reality, its furious hiss the scream of tortured machinery. Ugly red runes had appeared on the general's skin, bleeding with molten granite.

Turning, I found Ixey watching beside me, the skin of her lips pale. Beyond her sat the barest outline of a gangly figure—a figure that I would not have recognized if not for the tiny cat perched on his shoulder. The tiny cat turned his head towards me and nodded slightly before the pair faded out.

Swallowing hard, I looked back to the tree just in time to watch reality pop like an overripe pimple. Orange magic gushed from a tear in the world. A giant maggot composed of eyes and tentacles wormed its way through, inch by terrible inch. Ixey buried her face into my neck and shook, reeking of terror and revulsion. Longer than the field itself, the dragon coiled onto itself like a snake, coated in the orange ichor, and watching me through thousands of eyes. Its exhaustion weighed down everything around it; the trees of the forest bent under its weight. Unseen coils slipped over my own shoulders, and O'Meara groaned in her sleep as Ixey shuddered.

It smiled. A single mouth ran along its entire length, exposing its jagged teeth, each a warped mirror of our surroundings. The sight sent my mind scrabbling for cover. I shut my eyes, but still the terrible smile waited in the blackness of my eyelids.

A massive sound, vibrating not through the air but swelling up from the ground and back down my vertebra, reached us as those teeth parted, and the dragon's great mouth yawned open. I closed my eyes and waited for the end.

The end did not come.

36

"Ashes to ashes, dust to dust," I muttered irritably as I batted a charred piece of drywall aside. It splintered and kicked a cloud of ash into the air.

The squirrel clinging to my neck sneezed. "Hey, careful! I got allergies, ya know, and they ain't to nuts!"

Rudy's cheerfulness among the ruins of my now, admittedly, former life grated like a rusty band saw on my nerves. "Just keep looking!" I growled at him.

"You're not going to find it, big guy." Rudy hopped down from my neck and scanned the room, sniffing on two legs. "This has to be one of my better burns!"

We stood in the wreckage of my bedroom, the half-moon peering down at us curiously through the gaping hole in the roof. The furniture, mostly cheap IKEA chic, stood in mockery of its former durability, its surfaces blackened and wearing scales of char. Everything looked so brittle that I feared if I touched anything it would collapse into dust. My laptop still sat on the desk, the metal halves twisted away from each other as if in agony. The external hard drives next to it were singed rectangular metal boxes lying in pools of plastic.

I had to agree with the squirrel—the chances of a photo album surviving this would be slim to nil. Grimacing, I hoped for a miracle as I pawed at the drawers of my desk. The brittle wood splintered and gave way after a few tries. I felt O'Meara stir through the link. She crested into consciousness as a whale breaches the surface of the ocean.

"Thomas? Where are you? Your bed is empty." A mental image of the dog bed in the hospital flittered across my mind, along with a trace of fear, of vulnerability.

I had a flutter of hope in my heart; she had to turn her head to see that—definite improvement. They had just taken her off the respirator the day before. *"I'm out looking for a picture of myself, my human self to remember."* I couldn't help but show her the purpose of it. When she had recovered, I'd learn to walk on my hind legs and she'd pin an illusion of my human self to a hat. It would in no way be perfect, but a stroll down a street without a coffee cup over my muzzle and a leash around my neck would be worth the hip pain. Also I had given myself a panic attack that morning when it took me too long to remember what the color of my eyes had been. Brown, I think. *"Don't worry—Tallow and Ixey are on guard. They know where I am."*

O'Meara didn't relax much with the image of the hulking mama wolf guarding her hospital room; it summoned a recollection of Tallow's home to the top of O'Meara's mind on a very large pool of guilt. Injured and exhausted, O'Meara's mindscape stood open to me, but stayed colorless and barren compared to the whirling chaos it had been before. Everything, including her demons, was slow and sluggish, rising and sinking in the murk of her painkiller-addled mind. A worry about the Council of Merlins surfaced.

As I had the last time she'd asked, I mentally shook my

head. The council had its own difficulties to deal with. Two of the seven Archmagi had disappeared four nights ago. With three seats now open, the magical world had been thrown into chaos as decade-old schemes and alliances came untethered. Our little town had fallen off the radar, and if anyone thought it odd that Archibald's house had literally disappeared from the lot before the estate sale, nobody with power had made it their business to care. Yet.

O'Meara was not reassured, but sleep claimed her anyway. Her mind sunk away from mine into a haze of disordered dreams.

A reckoning with the rest of the world hung over all our heads like an evil sword suspended from a burning rope. It could be days, months or even years. Not just the council either—Cyndi's death was still rippling through the ranks of the TAU. She had been viewed by many as a loveable rogue. Death threats from her fans were literally piling up inside the door of O'Meara's still decimated office. Oric's demands that I join the TAU were getting less polite by the day.

"Hey, Thomas! Heellllooo!" A fuzzy object waved in front of my muzzle, and I sneezed.

"Sorry—O'Meara woke up."

The squirrel tsked. "You gotta learn to multitask. Walk and talk."

I did not want to explain the state of O'Meara's brain to Rudy, so I simply peered at the contents of the drawers. All that remained of the photo album was flaky ash clinging to the metal spine of a three-ring binder.

Rudy chittered with amusement. "See, you've been *deleted*. The Veil's been erasing all traces of awakenings for centuries."

I pawed through the ash with a growl of disgust. "You set the fire, Rudy. Not the Veil."

Rudy sat up on his hind legs, ears twitching. "Don't matter now! Come on, let's get you back to the hospital. Can't let O'Meara pop another vessel, right?"

I tried to shoot the friendly arsonist a suspicious look, but he leapt up onto my neck, so the glare struck an innocent pile of ash.

"Come on. You're getting your fur all sooty. Seriously, you look like a black panther. Ain't nothing here anyway."

Instantly every follicle on my body tensed as an itchy sensation spread up from my paws and then along my spine. I swallowed, desperately trying to keep my tongue in my mouth and not on my paws. A primal part of my brain shouted *dirty!* at the top of its lungs, while my stomach coiled at the idea of eating all the ash, probably laced with all sorts of toxic chemicals. I needed a bath and a brushing stat. At least the bath.

I had already tensed my legs to leap through the back window of the house and disappear back through the woods when I heard the pop of a car door. My left ear rounded on the sound. Quickly two muffled clacks that elongated into quiet metallic creaking followed it. The door shut.

Tiny claws pricked at my neck. "Come on, let's go!" Rudy's voice had pitched up another octave. "Forget about it!"

Curiosity warred with caution. I spun in a tight circle to relieve the tension as the unhurried scuff-clacking drew closer to the house. "What is that?" I asked.

"Nothing good. Let's get out of here!"

A scent caught my nose as a breeze whistled through the house, and I stilled. Angelica. Rudy chittered at me to get moving even as I slowly padded towards the front of the house. The fire had not damaged the kitchen nearly as much as the bedroom. Blackened certainly, but not charred. The front door still stood, sans glass.

"Oh boy." Rudy sighed.

I peeked through the left window to see Angelica with metal crutches tucked under each armpit, advancing up the walkway. Her amber eyes glowed with the light of the overhead moon as she glared directly at me. My stomach twisted so hard I sat down.

A small weight disappeared from the back of my neck. "This is all just gonna be bitter almonds from here on out. I'm outta here." I didn't give the departing squirrel a single glance.

Now that I thought about it, it all came back to her. She wore a Green Day t-shirt and knee-length black shorts, one of the three outfits she usually came home in. I had never noticed the tail hole in the shorts before. Her black fur still remained but had lost its smooth sheen and become a bit shaggy-looking since I had seen her last. Her imposing figure had lost nearly a foot in height, but her clothing still stretched tight over her muscular frame. Nostrils flared at the end of a muzzle that had become so short her face had gained a cat-like quality.

We stared at each other, her face twitching with warring emotions. "You." She stopped her mouth working as if the word tasted foul. "You're not supposed to be here. Haven't you done enough!" Her teeth flashed, white and sharp in the pale light of the waning moon.

My ears wilted in the face of her anger. After all that had happened, she still wanted me to go away? I knew she had been controlled the last time I saw her—did she? Maybe the squirrel had the right idea after all. But I couldn't quite bring myself to turn tail just yet. "Listen, Angelica—"

"I am *not* Angelica! And you are not the Thomas I"—she swallowed—"loved. I'm Noise—that's who I always am."

A tiny bit of hope burbled within my heart. "I'm still

the same guy I was! And you're still who you are!" I took a step out of the doorway and into the moonlight.

She barked with bitter laughter. "You were a marsh-mallow. Not a violent bone in your body. Four days ago you hurt my mother so badly we had to take her to a *vet*!"

I winced, remembering the feel of her intestines hooked on my claws. "I'd say I'm sorry, but she was trying very hard to kill me."

Noise crossed her arms. "And she will again, Thomas."

"But didn't I save—"

"You disfigured her son, stole her grandpups and O'Meara burned down her cabin." A growl rose into Noise's voice. "You're meat to my family."

I blinked, frustration and amusement dancing in my head at how none of those three things were directly my fault, but all those events had probably saved my life in one way or another. I searched for something diplomatic to say as the silence grew between us. Nothing of the sort came to mind. "So what type of meat, then? I think I've proven to be fairly inedible. Somewhere between shoe leather and rusty iron?"

Noise guffawed and quickly covered it up with a saw-tooth growl. "Damn it, Thomas. Don't make light of this— my family wants you dead and we heal fast. They'll hunt you down the next moon!"

Another small flicker of hope there, and I took a small step forward. "But you won't, right?"

Her eyes closed as she squeezed out a sigh. "No, I won't. But that doesn't mean I can protect you."

I crept down the stairs towards her. "Meh, I apparently have more practice being a chew toy than I knew. You always come home with those chompers?" I looked up at her bare-toothed grimace and past the teeth I saw the same expression that appeared on Angelica's face when I made a terrible joke. Concern about her family fell away. Angelica was here in front of me—no mind control, no cage.

"Thomas . . ." she warned.

I sauntered forward and pressed the top of my head into her stomach. "Go ahead and hurt me if you want—I'm right here."

Her hand briefly caressed my ears before she jerked away, the big bad werewolf girl emitting something like a squeak. I tried to follow her, but she warded me off with the end of her crutch.

"Thomas, think—I'm a werewolf! You're a familiar! We're over."

"We'll invest in a really good vacuum cleaner." I gave her a little purring growl. She snorted, and I caught the flicker of a tail wag between her legs.

"Argh! Will you be serious for once!" She swung at me halfheartedly with her crutch, but I dodged and circled around to nip at her stubby tail.

The werewolf gave a yip of surprise, her arms splaying out, grasping at the air as she toppled backwards. I tried to catch her, interposing myself between her and ground. She fell on top of me. One of her crutches clonked me on the head as her body bowled me over.

She snarled and rolled before I could react, and sharp teeth clamped down on the back of my neck. I froze as panic spiked through me, and her arms grabbed me into a steely embrace. Growling, she savaged my scruff hard, shaking it from side to side with enough force that the world went blurry as my third eyelids flicked up.

The attack stopped, and something warm lapped at my ears before Noise buried her face into my neck, the steel around me becoming a warm embrace.

"You're such an ass, Thomas," she muttered into my neck. "It will never work."

A purr rolled up my throat as I pushed myself into her. "I'm getting really good at breaking rules."

Continue the adventure in...

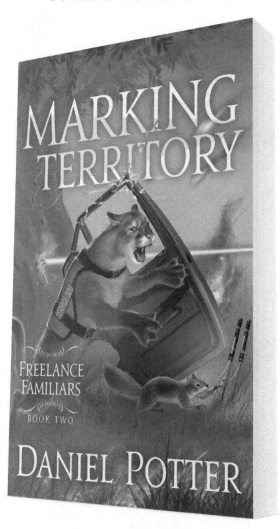

MARKING TERRITORY

FREELANCE FAMILIARS

BOOK TWO

DANIEL POTTER

Buy it Today
Exclusively on Amazon

CPSIA information can be obtained
at www.ICGtesting.com
Printed in the USA
LVHW080838310521
688928LV00013B/1306